Guiding Emily takes readers through the heartbreak, the fear, and the triumph that so many of our visually impaired adult clients face. At the Foundation for Blind Children, we believe vision loss is a diagnosis, not a disability. Read this book—Emily Main personifies that belief, as she digs deep to find the confidence and strength she never knew she had.

–Marc Ashton, CEO, Foundation for Blind Children

Guiding Emily

Also by BARBARA HINSKE

The Rosemont Series

Coming to Rosemont

Weaving the Strands

Uncovering Secrets

Drawing Close

Bringing Them Home

Shelving Doubts

Recovering What Was Lost

No Matter How Far: A Rosemont Christmas Novella

Novellas

The Night Train

The Christmas Club (adapted for The Hallmark Channel, 2019)

Paws & Pastries

The Emily Series

Guiding Emily

The Unexpected Path

Novels in the "Who's There?!" Collection

DEADLY PARCEL

FINAL CIRCUIT

Connect with BARBARA HINSKE Online

Visit **barbarahinske.com** to sign up for her newsletter to receive
a Free Gift, plus Inside Scoops and Bedtime Stories.

Search for **Barbara Hinske on YouTube** to tour inside her
historic home, plus learn tips and tricks for busy women!

Find photos of fictional Rosemont and things related to her books:

Pinterest.com/BarbaraHinske.

Facebook.com/BHinske

Twitter.com/BarbaraHinske

Instagram.com/barbarahinskeauthor

bhinske@gmail.com

Guiding Emily

A Tale of Love, Loss, and Courage

BARBARA HINSKE

Casa Del Northern Publishing
Phoenix, Arizona

Copyright © 2020 Barbara Hinske.
Cover by Keri Knutson and Elizabeth Mackey, Copyright © 2020.
All rights reserved.

ISBN: 978-1-7349249-0-9
Library of Congress Control Number: 2020906862

Casa del Northern Publishing
Phoenix, Arizona

Dedication

To everyone connected to the Foundation for Blind Children (Phoenix, Arizona)—both human and canine—for the remarkable work you do and the light and life you bring into our world. You've illuminated a pathway to a happy, independent life for thousands of people. I'm honored to support your work with a donation of proceeds from this book.

Prologue

Emily. The woman who would become everything to me. The person I would eat every meal with and lie down next to every night—for the rest of my days.

She was just ahead; behind that door at the far end of the long hall. I glanced over my shoulder. Mark kept pace, slightly behind me. I could feel his excitement. It matched my own.

Everyone said Emily and I would be perfect for each other. I'd overheard them talking when they thought I was asleep. I spend a lot of time with my eyes closed, but I don't sleep much. They didn't know that.

"A magical match," they'd all agreed.

I lifted my eyes to Mark, and he nodded his encouragement. I gave a brief shake of my head. Only four more doorways between Emily and me.

I picked up my pace. A cylindrical orange object on the carpet in the third doorway from the end caught my eye. *Is that a Cheeto? A Crunchy Cheeto? I love Crunchy Cheetos.*

I tore my eyes away.

This was no time to get distracted.

We sped across the remaining distance to the doorway at the end of the hall. The door that separated me from my destiny.

I froze and waited while Mark knocked.

I heard Emily's voice—the sound I would come to love above all others—say, "Come in."

What was that in her voice? Eagerness—anxiety—maybe even a touch of fear? I'd take care of all of that right away.

The door swung open and Mark stepped back. He pointed to Emily.

I'd seen her before. Emily Main was a beautiful young woman in her late twenties. Auburn hair cascaded around her shoulders and shone like a new penny. With my jet-black coloring, we'd make a striking couple.

"Go on," Mark said.

I abandoned all my training—all sense of decorum—and raced to her.

Emily reached for me and flung her arms around my neck.

I placed my nose against her throat, and she tumbled out of her chair onto her knees.

I swept my tongue over her cheek, tasting the saltiness of her tears.

"Oh … Garth." My name on her lips came out in a hoarse whisper.

I wagged my tail so hard that we both lay back on the floor.

"Good boy, Garth!"

She rubbed the ridge of my skull behind my ears in a way that would become one of my favorite things in the whole wide world.

Next to food.

Especially Crunchy Cheetos.

Mark and the other trainers were right—we were made for each other. I was the perfect guide dog for Emily Main.

Chapter 1

"Weren't you supposed to leave for the airport half an hour ago?" Michael Ward asked his boss, whose fingers were typing furiously on her keyboard. "You're still planning to get married, aren't you?"

Emily Main's head bobbed behind the computer, her eyes fixed to the screen.

"I can't believe you put off a departure to Fiji to help us launch this new program. Your wedding's in two days."

"We've been working on this for almost a year. I wasn't about to leave when we're this close. I just need to finish this last email." She hunched forward and peered at the computer screen.

"There," she said, pushing her office chair back as the email *whooshed* from her inbox. "Done."

She looked up at Michael, blinking. It was probably the first time she had looked at anything besides a computer screen in hours. "I brought my suitcase so I could go to the airport straight from the office. I don't have to stop at home."

Michael raised his eyebrows at her. "That's all you've got? A carry-on and a satchel for a week—a week that includes your wedding? My wife packs more than that for a three-day weekend."

"My wedding dress is a classic sheath and the rest is bathing suits and shorts."

"I would have thought Connor Harrington the third would have wanted an elaborate wedding—one fit for the society pages."

"Our wedding is going to be very elegant—think JFK Junior and Carolyn," Emily said, flinging her purse over her shoulder and reaching for the retractable handle of her suitcase.

Michael stepped in front of her. "I've got this," he said. "I'll walk you to the street. I'd like to congratulate Connor on snagging our office hero."

Emily hesitated.

"He is picking you up, isn't he? You're flying there together?"

"He went out over the weekend. He wanted to do some diving with his best man … sort of a bachelor party reprise. I was traveling with my mom and maid of honor, but they flew out yesterday as planned. The company paid to change my ticket, but it would have cost almost five hundred dollars for Mom and Gina to change theirs. It wasn't worth it."

"But you don't like to fly." He peered into Emily's face. "Did you talk to Connor about that before you decided to stay an extra day? You have told him about your fear of flying, haven't you?"

Emily shrugged. "I've mentioned it, sure, but I haven't made a big deal out of it."

"So what did he say?"

"He suggested that I get a prescription for Xanax and sleep the whole way out there."

"Really? That's what he said?"

"He's a Brit, for heaven's sake. 'Stiff upper lip' and all that. He's not the sort of guy to coddle anyone—and I'm not a needy type of gal. You know that."

Michael cocked his head to one side. "Do you have to change planes?"

Emily nodded.

"You don't want to be knocked out for that."

"I'll be fine." Emily threw her shoulders back. "You don't need to worry about me."

"I know—I'm sorry. It's just that I wouldn't let my wife make the trip alone if she felt like you do about flying."

"I fly alone all the time, and nothing's ever happened to me. There's no reason this time should be any different."

Michael lifted his hands, palms facing her, and shrugged. "Okay, but I think he could have at least offered to pay to change your mom's flight or something."

"I'll be perfectly fine." Emily walked past him into the hallway. "I promised Dhruv that I'd say goodbye before I leave."

"He's going to miss you. You're the one person here that really connects with him."

Michael watched her shoulders sag slightly.

"Hey," he said, rolling the carry-on to a halt beside her in the hall. "I'm sorry. I didn't mean to worry you. The whole team is going to step into your shoes while you're gone. We've talked about it."

"Of course you will. I shouldn't worry about him. I've got the best team in San Francisco. Scratch that. On the entire West Coast." Emily gave him a teary smile and punched him playfully on the shoulder. "I know you'll take care of everything while I'm away, Michael—including helping Dhruv stay connected with the team."

"Good!" Michael continued down the hallway. "I don't want you to give this place a second thought while you're gone. If anyone deserves a vacation—and a gorgeous beach wedding—it's you, Em. But don't get too comfortable." Michael turned and smiled at her. "We do need you to come back. We'd be lost without you here."

Emily laughed and pushed him toward the elevator. "Why don't you go push that button, you wonderful suck-up. It'll take ages to get an elevator this time of the morning. I'll stick my head into Dhruv's cubicle and be right back."

R

Emily found Dhruv, as usual, leaning into the bank of computer monitors, intently focused on the complex strings of code in front of him. She cleared her throat. When Dhruv didn't move, she tapped him lightly on the shoulder.

Dhruv sat back quickly and spun around. A smile spread across his face when he saw her.

"I wanted to say goodbye before I go."

Dhruv nodded. "Goodbye."

"I'll see you a week from Monday."

"I know. You're getting married in two days, then you have your honeymoon for a week, then you come back to work," he recited.

"That's right. You remembered."

"I remember things."

"Yes, you do. That's one reason you're so very good at programming," she said.

"I know."

"Okay ... well ... have a good week. You can go to Michael if you have ... if you need anything."

"I know."

Emily regarded the shy, socially awkward middle-aged man who was, by far, the most proficient member of her extremely talented team of programmers. "Bye."

Dhruv nodded.

Emily stepped away.

Dhruv leapt out of his chair and called after her. "Have a happy wedding."

Emily swung around and gave him a thumbs-up then turned back toward the elevators where Michael was waiting.

Chapter 2

The plane settled smoothly onto the runway. Emily released the breath she had been holding. They'd encountered turbulent air on the second leg of the long flight to Fiji. The captain had assured the passengers that everything was fine, but he'd kept the Fasten Seat Belt light on for the last ninety minutes of the flight.

Emily's panic had come in waves, and she'd alternated between meditating and concentrating on the audiobook playing through her headphones. Her stomach rose to her throat with every jarring dip and bounce of the plane. By the time they stopped, she was more than ready to get off the plane and stretch her legs.

She retrieved her suitcase from the overhead bin and made her way to the terminal. Emily approached the exit and her pace slowed as she searched for her tall, dark-haired fiancé. Hadn't she hinted, strongly, that she'd like him to meet her at the airport?

She checked her watch. Her flight had landed twenty minutes early. Wasn't her husband-to-be habitually late—to everything? Maybe she should wait before setting out for the resort. It would be a shame if she was in a cab on the way to their hotel as he was arriving at the airport to meet her.

Emily moved to an out-of-the-way spot along the outside wall and composed a text: "Landed. Early. Are you coming?" She tapped send and gripped the phone in her hand, hoping for an immediate response and keeping her eyes trained on the entrance to the terminal.

Passengers came and went, and yet she waited. A tall, dark-haired man in linen trousers and a shirt that contrasted with his deep tan appeared at the door. Her hand shot up to wave, then dropped quickly to her side when she got a good look at his face.

She checked her text messages for the umpteenth time. Connor had not responded. Irritation at his silence made her cheeks flame. She reached behind her for the retractable handle of her suitcase and felt a large, warm hand close over hers. Her head jerked up, and she found herself staring into the double-espresso eyes of Connor Harrington III.

"Sweetheart," he said, pulling her to him and kissing her intently.

She slipped her arms around his broad shoulders and leaned into his large, solid frame, allowing the tension of the flight to dissipate.

When their lips parted, he stepped back and held her at arm's length. "Was it as bad as all that? You look like you've been through the ringer."

"A bit choppy, actually."

"Oh, honey," Connor replied. "I know how much you hate that. I'm sorry I wasn't with you."

Emily laughed. "I doubt very much that there's anything you could have done. Even you can't control the weather."

"Maybe not, but I could have held your hand. Taken your mind off of things?"

"And miss diving with Scott Dalton? Because your fiancée is too much of a nitwit to fly on her own?" Emily grimaced. "Not a chance." She linked her elbow through Connor's, and they made their way to the taxi stand.

"Did you have fun?" Emily asked. She loved him and wanted him to be happy, but she hoped that he'd missed her at least a little bit. This was their wedding trip, after all.

"Best dive I've ever been on," Connor said. "The water is beyond beautiful here, and I saw the most incredible fish. Maybe one of these days you'll reconsider and come with me?"

"It's not a matter of not wanting to dive, Connor." She stopped and turned to him. "I can't—not with my myopic degeneration. The pressure on my eyeballs could cause my retinas to detach. I won't risk it."

"Of course not," Connor replied hastily. "I—I forgot. I'd never want you to take any risks with your eyesight." He cupped her chin with his hand and kissed her softly. "Don't be cross with me."

Emily brought his palm to her lips. "I'm sorry if I seem short. I resent the things I can't do because of this condition. That's why I was so happy that you and Scott got to come out here early to dive—I'm never going to be able to do that with you."

"That doesn't matter. All I care about is that you're here and we're getting married tomorrow."

As they made their way off the airport property by cab, Connor chattered enthusiastically about their resort and what a perfect venue it was for a destination wedding.

Some couples would have visited the property before booking it, but Emily and Connor weren't that kind of couple. Their careers consumed most of their hours, and they were lucky if they could squeeze in one date night a week. They certainly didn't have the time—or the energy—to race around the globe searching for wedding venues. When Connor had found this place online, she'd scrolled through the website and quickly agreed to book it for their wedding.

Connor was saying something about the tropical fish he'd seen. Emily powered down the rear window, allowing the humid breeze to ruffle her hair. She relaxed against her fiancé and stretched her legs. She was on her way to get married to the man of her dreams. She shouldn't feel irritated about anything.

Her eyelids began to droop as Connor described a golf game he'd played earlier that day.

"Here we are," the driver interrupted, pointing to the elaborate entrance to the hotel, set in lush tropical landscaping.

Emily tucked her unruly mane of hair behind her ears as the cab pulled to a halt and a bellman opened her door.

"Have you seen Mom and Gina?"

"Not yet. I talked to them yesterday after they checked into their suite. Their flight was three hours late, and they were exhausted. They wanted to stay at the hotel for dinner, and I already had plans to try that sushi place we read about in Conde Nast, so we decided I'd see them when you got in this afternoon."

"I can't wait to see Mom," Emily said. "I hope she likes this place. It's her first trip in three years. She hasn't traveled since Dad died. I'm praying that the whole thing isn't too much for her."

"Your mother's more resilient than you give her credit for. She's a tough old bird." He tugged on Emily's hand pulling her back to him. "Are you sure you want to stay with them tonight?"

Emily pushed at his chest playfully. "Of course I am! It's bad luck for us to see each other before the wedding."

"That's just an old wives' tale."

"And I plan on being your old wife someday. You know that we're going to do this old school. We talked about it."

"You can't blame a guy for trying." He pulled her to him and kissed her again.

Emily leaned back in his embrace. "You're trying to make me change my mind, aren't you?"

"I'm nothing if not persistent."

"You are that. But it's not going to work."

They passed potted palm trees ringed with exuberant cyclamen and headed toward the reception desk when Emily heard her mother call her name and turned.

Martha Main rose from a plush lobby sofa and opened her arms to her daughter. She was swathed in a bright coral pantsuit accented with a lime-green and aqua scarf that she'd undoubtedly bought specially for her daughter's island wedding. "How's the happy couple?"

Emily rushed into her embrace. "We're fine, Mom. More importantly, how are you?"

Martha squeezed her daughter's hands and looked up at her with a worried frown. "How do I look?"

"Beautiful, Mom. I don't think I've ever seen you in bright colors. They look great on you."

Connor hung back, looking slightly uncomfortable.

"You think? I went shopping with my neighbor Irene last week. She said I needed to dump all my navy and black—that I needed to 'snazz up my look' as mother-of-the-bride."

Emily put an arm around her mother's shoulders. "I think she was exactly right. Do you like what you're wearing?"

"It's taken some getting used to. I've changed in and out of this pantsuit at least a half-dozen times."

Emily laughed. "I know how that is. I'm glad you stuck with it." She gave her mother an appraising glance. "You look younger. And so pretty."

Martha blushed.

"Don't you think so, Connor?" Emily turned to him and extended her hand to him.

"Absolutely," he said. "If you wore white, nobody would know which one was the bride."

Martha laughed. "That's laying it on way too thick." She reached over and hugged Connor. "You don't need to butter up your future mother-in-law, you know. She already approves of you."

"Phew." Connor made an exaggerated gesture of wiping his brow. "That's a relief."

"Why are you down here—in the lobby? Is something wrong with our room?"

"Our suite is lovely. You should see the view of the beach. *And* the huge bouquets of island flowers that a certain person had waiting for us in our room." She squeezed Connor's hand. "Thank you so much. They're the prettiest flowers I've ever received."

Connor grinned and patted her hand.

"Gina wanted to take a nap, so I decided to clear out and let her have the place to herself. This weekend is about to get very busy so she should rest up while she can. Besides, I was impatient to see you and wanted to be in the lobby when you got here."

Emily looked into her mother's eyes. "Was your flight bumpy?"

"Well ... a bit."

"And you figured I'd be terrified if mine were the same, so you wanted to be here to … what? Comfort me?"

Martha shrugged. "I don't know. It was just mother's intuition, that's all." She looked between Connor and Emily. "Don't be angry with me."

"On the contrary," Connor's voice grew husky. "I think Emily's lucky to have such a concerned mother."

"I'm sure your parents felt the same way about you," Martha said. "That's the way we're made."

Connor turned his head and cleared his throat.

"Why don't you unpack and then we'll go for a swim? All three of us," Martha added quickly.

"That's a great idea, but I'm going to bow out." Connor shifted his gaze from mother to daughter. "You two probably have tons of wedding details to go over. You don't need me for that."

"No," Martha said. "Everything's all set. Too late to change anything now, even if we wanted to."

"We'd love to have you," Emily said.

"I'm beat after the dive this morning. Gina's got the right idea. I think I'll take a nap."

"And catch up on emails from work?" Emily asked.

"Maybe a few."

"We're on our wedding trip. You're not supposed to be working."

"I know, I know. It'll be so much easier when I get back if I'm up to date."

Emily touched his check. "On one condition. No work on this trip—no emails, no texts, no calls—once we say 'I do.'"

"You've got my ironclad guarantee on that," he said.

Emily smiled and turned to her mother. "Then we'll have a girl's dinner tonight, Mom. Order room service and talk our heads off."

"Honestly, sweetheart, I'd rather do that than anything else in the world."

"You mean it?"

"I do." Martha swiped at a tear. "Now let's get you up to our room and settled in. Gina asked me to wake her up when you got here, anyway. The three of us girls can take a dip before dinner."

Emily hugged her mother. "You're the best, you know it? I'm so glad you're here."

"Nothing on earth could have kept me away. I want nothing more than to see my little girl step into her happy future."

Chapter 3

Gina secured the final jeweled hairpin into Emily's veil. "There," she said, stepping back and leaning over Emily to the right and then the left, inspecting her work. "You can't see the ends of any of the pins. How does it feel?"

Emily pushed at the headdress, attempting to nudge it out of place. "Feels secure. I think you've got it."

Gina blew out a big breath. "I can't believe that the hairstylist refused to put your veil on. I had no idea what I was doing."

Emily smiled into the mirror and their eyes met. Gina had been her best friend from the moment they'd first met—both as new kids in school—in the fourth grade. "You couldn't have done a better job. Thank you."

"That's what BFFs are for."

Emily swiveled on the bench in front of the mirror. "We've been through a lot together, haven't we?"

"Always had each other's backs."

"And that's not going to change when I'm married. We're going to keep on just like we have been."

Gina shrugged. "Maybe at first. I know you mean well. Now that you have a husband, all bets will be off. Our lives will be very different, and we'll be focused on other things."

"Nonsense—especially since we don't plan to start a family. There's no reason things should be different between the two of us. Besides, you'll get married one of these days." She lifted her eyes to her friend. "You still want to get married, don't you?"

"Of course I do. It just seems like it's not going to happen for me."

"Don't get discouraged—and don't give up. I felt exactly the same way until Connor came along," Emily said.

"You may have gotten the last good man."

"Don't be ridiculous. Your Mr. Right is out there, waiting, for you. He may even be at the wedding."

Gina turned away sharply.

"We'd better make our way to the lawn," Martha said from the doorway. "It's almost time for the mother-of-the-bride to be seated."

Emily rose and went to her mother, taking her outstretched hands in her own. "You look beautiful, Mom."

"That pale lilac is perfect with your silver hair, Martha," Gina said.

"Thank you," Martha said. "I do feel presentable. But the real stars of the show are the two of you. Let me look at you," she said, positioning Gina next to Emily.

"Whoever would have thought, all those years ago when the two of you were inseparable tomboys—bloodying your knees climbing every tree in the neighborhood—that you'd be standing next to each other as a beautiful bride and gorgeous maid of honor." Martha fished a handkerchief out of her sleeve and dabbed at her eyes. "This may be a small wedding, but there's never been a more elegant pair than the two of you. I couldn't love either of you any more than I do now."

"Don't get us started, Mom," Emily said. "I don't want to ruin my makeup." She turned to Gina who was blinking hard.

"Let's get out of here before we're all blubbering our heads off." Gina stepped around Martha and headed to the door. "I'll lead the way."

Martha crooked her arm, and Emily took her mother's elbow. "You're radiant, my darling. Your father would have been …"

Emily squeezed her mother's arm. "I know. I can feel him here. Can you?"

Martha nodded and sniffed.

"It's time," Gina called to them.

Martha and Emily stepped forward together and began the journey toward a new life.

R

Connor watched as a light breeze caught Emily's veil and tossed it gently behind her, opening it against the cloudless blue sky. She stood, regal and elegant in a slim column of white satin, her auburn hair reflecting the sunlight.

He and Scott were a striking pair in their tailored blue suits, and Gina, the only other member of their wedding party, was lovely in a pale blue chiffon gown that showed off her petite form and complimented her blond hair and eyes.

The small party clustered around the officiant, his long white linen robe adorned only by a large silver cross on a large chain. They stood on the lawn at the edge of the beach. Emily's bouquet—a mass of vibrant tropical flowers—punctuated the scene with a burst of color.

"Dearly beloved, we're gathered here today to join this man and this woman in holy matrimony." The officiant spoke the solemn words of the ceremony that would forge the couple's future.

Emily handed the bouquet to Gina and took the ring that the best man handed her. She repeated the words Connor had just spoken to her and placed the ring on his finger.

The officiant pronounced them husband and wife. "You may now kiss the bride."

Connor stepped toward Emily and took her in his arms. She tilted her mouth to his and they kissed deeply, reveling in the intimate moment, oblivious to the others.

A sound at the water's edge drew everyone's attention. A group of riders thundered past on horseback, the hooves kicking up sprays of water.

"Isn't that picturesque?" Emily murmured.

Connor smiled down at her. "It most certainly is." His beautiful new wife would look spectacular on that tall white horse bringing up the rear.

Emily turned to Gina and took the bouquet from her. "This is only a formality," she whispered to her friend. "I'm going to throw this to you in a few minutes."

Connor took his wife's arm, and the tiny wedding party made their way across the lawn to a table set for their wedding dinner. They enjoyed an elaborate meal of nine expertly prepared local dishes. When they were done and the last crumb of wedding cake had been devoured, Emily rose.

She reached over to Gina and pulled her to her feet. "You'd better catch this. We spent too much time on the school softball team for me to believe that you couldn't catch this bouquet."

"I don't believe in these silly traditions," Gina flushed. "Besides— like I said yesterday—you already got the last good man."

Emily turned her back to Gina and took three long strides away from her. She swung the bouquet up over her head and released it, sending it sailing back in a high arc.

Gina's outfielder instincts kicked in, and she reached up and caught the bouquet.

The small group clapped and whistled.

"You're sure to be the next to marry," Connor announced. "The way you look tonight, I can't understand why some man hasn't snatched you up already." He looked pointedly at Scott. "But then, some of us are just idiots and can't see what's right in front of us."

Chapter 4

I sensed something was wrong. Mother didn't have much time for me anymore. Or interest in my siblings and me. I was only allowed to suckle once a day.

The rest of the time I ate food I could chew, which was fine by me. It was delicious, and I've always liked things I can crunch. But it came to me in a cold metal bowl, not from a soft, furry underbelly. Still, I didn't complain. My stomach was almost always full.

My feelings were hurt by Mother's indifference, until months later at the puppy raisers' house when I learned that mothers of all sorts need something called "me" time. Whether you're two- or four-legged, "me time" is spent doing anything other than being with your children. Which I still don't understand because why wouldn't my mother want to be with me? At any rate, I've learned not to take her disinterest personally.

It helped that I was distracted by a large pack of two-legged mothers who converged on me every morning. They were there when I woke up and fed me the yummy, crunchy food.
Different mothers showed up almost every day, but they all walked on two legs and they didn't have any hair—except for the gray on top of their heads. Their sounds were different from mine, but their eyes telegraphed love and their touch made it tangible.

They played with my brothers and sisters and me. I got so involved in playtime that I didn't notice when we stopped going back to the pen to visit our mother. My siblings and I spent time with a bunch of other puppies, chasing each other—or our own tails if no one else was close by. We wrestled, rolling on the ground and taking turns being on top. We put our mouths on each other but never bit down hard.

The two-legged mothers petted me and talked to me—they said I was a very special black Labrador, or "Lab" for short, and that one day I would become a "guide" to someone called a "handler." I had no idea what they were talking about, but I liked the sound of it. The way they said the words "guide" and "handler"—with such reverence. Count me in.

While they talked to me, they would take my black paws into their hands and rub them, splaying my toes and massaging them. God—I love that. They'd say stuff like "look at these paws!—Garth's going to be *huge* when he's full grown."

That's my name, Garth.

Anyway, we spent our days in a large, fenced enclosure with all sorts of toys and things to explore. But I wasn't the most adventuresome of the thirty or so puppies living there with me. The others tried out the new-fangled gadgets while I sat back and calculated the risks. One in particular confounded me. It had four stairs up and four stairs down. What could be the point of that?

I was pacing at the foot of this stairway to nowhere when a petite golden retriever—a younger female puppy—pushed in front of me and raced up the stairs and down the other side. Easy-peasy.

Was I going to let a *golden* show me up? I took two steps back. If she could do it, I could do it.

I put two front paws on the bottom step and pushed myself up, forcing my hind paws onto the same step. There wasn't enough room for all four paws, and it felt weird to be taller than I was just a minute before. My front paws moved to the next step above. *So that's how this goes*, I thought. I was getting the hang of it.

I continued until I had climbed all four steps and stood at the top. I looked to my right and left. I was at least as high off the ground as the top of my mother's back. I could see the entire enclosure and everyone in it. Now I understood the purpose of these stairs. This was glorious.

One of the mothers approached me. I remembered her—she had a mass of gray curls on top of her head. Since then, I've seen four-legged mothers with that hairstyle—they're called poodles. This two-legged poodle mother reached out a hand and patted the first step below me on the other side. "Come on," she said in a sing-song voice.

I lowered my head and wagged my tail.

"You can do it."

I extended a paw to the step below. I wasn't so sure. I retracted my paw.

She squatted next to me and ran her hand over my back. "You've got this."

I put my head down and forced my front paws onto the step below me.

"Keep going," she said.

I followed with my back paws, teetering on the step. She nodded when I lifted my muzzle to her, and I leaned toward the step below and made my way to the bottom.

"Good boy!" She reached into her pocket and pulled out a tiny treat for me and I gobbled it up. This was a nice development.

One of the other mothers joined us. "I don't know about that one," she said, looking at me. "He may be too timid to be a guide."

My ears perked up at the word "guide." I already knew that if there was one thing I wanted—more than anything else in the world—it was to be a guide.

"He's a thinker, this one is," said the poodle mother. "He's going to be a great problem solver." She turned to the other mother. "I've been volunteering here a long time." She reached for my collar and turned over my tag. "Our Garth, here, is going to be one of the all-time great guides. It's his destiny."

I got to my feet, and raced up one side and down the other, like I'd been doing it all of my life. I wasn't going to let any stairs to nowhere stand in the way of my destiny.

Chapter 5

Emily checked one last time on the sleeping form of her husband, his face ruggedly handsome under his dark hair and five o'clock shadow, his arms wound around an extra pillow. She could imagine what he must have looked like as a small child, clutching his teddy bear. Her heart skipped a beat, as it always did, when she looked at him without his knowing it. She tiptoed to the door and slipped into her shoes.

Connor wouldn't be awake for hours yet. He'd never notice that she'd slipped out to say goodbye to her mother. If he did, she'd left him a note, secured under his phone on his nightstand. She slid her room key into the back pocket of her shorts and let herself out of the room, easing the door shut behind her.

Emily made her way to the lobby and found her mother—as she knew she would—ready and waiting, fifteen minutes early, for her shuttle to the airport. Martha had abandoned her vibrant "island wardrobe," as she called it, for her usual black slacks and T-shirt. The lobby was almost deserted at this early hour, and the two women spotted each other instantly.

"You didn't need to see me off," Martha protested as Emily approached her. "Weren't you up late with that new husband of yours? You should still be asleep."

"I did stay up late, but I can never sleep in, no matter what time I go to bed."

"You get that from me, I'm afraid. Sorry."

"I'm fine," Emily said. "I wanted to thank you, again, for coming all the way out here for our wedding."

"It was a lovely ceremony, dear." Martha cupped her daughter's chin with her hand. "I wouldn't have missed it for the world. You were the most beautiful bride I've ever seen."

"So you've had fun?"

"Absolutely. This place is paradise."

"Then why don't you stay a few more days? Do some sightseeing. Take some of the yoga classes that they offer here."

"Hang around on my daughter's honeymoon? Are you nuts? Of course, I'm not going to do that. I should have flown back the day after the wedding with Gina. I did all the sightseeing I cared to do yesterday." Martha pointed to her overstuffed carry-on bag. "I've got all the souvenirs I can possibly fit into that bag already."

Emily held her mother tight.

"Are you happy, sweetheart? Was your wedding and this honeymoon everything you'd hoped it would be?"

Emily nodded, pulling away from her mother's embrace. "We went sailing yesterday. The water and wind were exhilarating. I never would have done it without Connor."

"He's expanding your horizons, that's for sure." Martha looked into Emily's eyes. "Just be careful. Myopic degeneration is no joke. You don't want to risk blindness."

Emily looked at her feet.

"He knows about your condition—that a sudden jerk could cause a retina to detach?"

"I've told him, but I don't think he understands."

"Then make him understand."

Emily turned to fiddle with the retractable handle on her mother's suitcase.

"There's plenty of activities on this island. You shouldn't do anything that's dangerous."

"I'm not going to," Emily said in a small voice. "Besides, the doctor told me that a long time ago. I was a kid."

"The condition doesn't get better over time," Martha said. "You know that." She grasped Emily's hand. "Promise me you'll explain this to Connor. If he loves you …"

"He does, Mom."

"Then he shouldn't ask you to do anything that puts your eyesight at risk."

Emily pursed her lips.

"Promise me," Martha said as a bellman walked up to them.

"Shuttle's ready to leave," he said.

"Talk to Connor," Martha reiterated, drawing Emily toward her. "Marriage is full of give and take. He'll understand."

Emily hugged her mother, hard. She knew her mother was right. Connor was her husband—surely he wanted the best for her. Sometimes there were good reasons for not taking risks. "I love you, Mom. Text me when you're home, safe. And don't worry. Everything will be fine."

R

Connor stretched and reached an arm out to the other side of the bed. He ran his hand over the sheets and cracked an eye open. Where was Emily?

He raised himself up on one elbow and listened for sounds from the bathroom. The only thing he heard was the distant hum of a lawn mower.

"Emily?"

He rubbed his hand over his face as he swung his legs over the side of the bed. He bumped the glass of water on his nightstand, sending a stream of water toward his phone. He rescued his phone, but the water drenched his key card and the papers strewn across the tabletop. He retrieved a towel from the bathroom, sopped up the water, and threw the soggy papers into the trash.

He checked the time on his phone. Where could Emily be at this hour? He called her phone. The device, left behind on her nightstand, began to vibrate.

His mind filled with repressed memories of waking up—alone—in hotel rooms as a child, while his parents played craps or cards in the casino below. He'd wandered through lobbies, unattended, looking for something to eat until his parents had run out of money and collected him from wherever he was for a hasty departure.

All vestiges of sleep dissipated. He wasn't with his parents—he was with Emily. She'd probably gone to get coffee. He grabbed yesterday's shorts and T-shirt out of the pile of dirty clothes in the corner of the closet, shoved his feet into his Top-Siders, and headed out to find his bride.

He punched the button for the elevator and grew impatient waiting for it to deliver him to the lobby. Other than the front desk staff and the bellmen, the lobby was deserted. Despite the heat of the morning, a cold chill ran down his spine. He knew his growing panic was ridiculous, but he couldn't help himself.

Connor walked through the dining room searching for her, ignoring the hostess when she asked if he'd like a table for one.

No Emily.

He ran out of the building and turned toward the pool. He didn't know why he was headed there. Emily wasn't an enthusiastic swimmer.

He jogged past the swim-up bar, reflected perfectly in the undisturbed turquoise surface of the pool. He rounded a corner and there, stretched out on a lounge chair at the far corner of the pool, was his wife. Her unruly mane of copper hair glowed in the early morning light.

Connor stopped short and stared at her.

Emily raised her hand and swung it in an arc over her head in greeting.

He marched toward her, stiff legged.

"Good morning," she called.

"What the hell are you doing?"

Emily recoiled into her lounge chair. "What do you mean? I'm having coffee." She pointed to the tall cup on the table next to her. "Like I said in my note."

"What note?"

She leaned toward him to take his hand.

He pulled it back. "I didn't find any note."

"I left it on your nightstand, under your phone."

He raked his fingers through his hair.

"I told you that I was going to say goodbye to my mom and then get coffee." She cocked her head to one side. "I didn't want to wake you. Didn't you see it?"

He shook his head slowly and sank down to sit next to her. "I spilled water on my nightstand. I threw all the papers away."

"I'm sorry if I scared you." She ran her hand along his arm. "Want some coffee? I've barely touched it."

He took it from her. "Silly of me. What could happen to you here?"

Emily smiled at him. "I don't think it's silly at all—I think it's sweet that you were worried about me." Connor watched the color rise in her cheeks. "A woman likes to feel that her husband is protective of her."

He drained the coffee and crumpled the paper cup. "We'd better get back to our room. We have to be dressed in long pants and at the stable in thirty minutes."

Emily frowned. "What are you talking about?"

"It's meant to be a surprise. I got the idea when those riders went by along the water's edge during our wedding ceremony." He took her hand and pulled her to her feet. "I kept thinking how gorgeous you'd look on horseback. I booked us an early morning ride on the beach."

Emily stepped back. "I ... I don't want to ride."

"I know you might be afraid." Connor stepped toward her and took her hands in his. "You told me about that horse biting you on your grandfather's farm."

"That horse never could tell a carrot from a finger."

Connor laughed and kissed her hand. "But this looks like a lot of fun. And you won't have to feed them—I promise. Isn't it time for you to reclaim riding?"

"It's not that, Connor ... not entirely. If I fell, one of my retinas could detach."

"You're not going to fall! Besides, you said your doctor told you that years ago. Nothing's happened since then, has it?"

"No … but I still don't think it's worth the risk."

"No. Of course not." Connor dropped his hands to his sides. "I wouldn't want you to do anything you're not comfortable with."

"You can go," Emily said. "It sounds like you're really excited about it. I don't mind in the least."

Connor knitted his brows. "Separate activities—on our honeymoon? No way. That's not how we should start out."

"I'm sorry, sweetheart,"

"Don't worry about it." He turned and she followed him back to their room.

R

While he changed clothes, Connor pattered on about the other activities the resort offered, but Emily could tell by the slump of his shoulders that he was disappointed. She sucked in a deep breath. He had been correct—she was terrified of horses. Was that the real reason she didn't want to ride? Was she using her medical condition—if it even still existed—as an excuse? Was that fair to Connor?

"I suppose that the horses from the resort's stable are very tame and well mannered?"

"I'm sure they are."

"And we'd be going on a trail that they're very familiar with? No downed branches to trip them up or wild animals to spook them?"

"The resort wouldn't send people out on anything dangerous. Too much liability for them."

"You really think this will be an easy ride?"

"I do. That's why I suggested it. It'll be the perfect way to get over your fear of horses."

"Well—if it means that much to you …."

Connor stopped and faced her. "I know this sounds silly; I've been dreaming about seeing you on that horse." He tenderly picked up a strand of hair that hung across her shoulder. "This hair blowing behind you, with the sea and sky as a backdrop. I'll have my camera with me. I'm planning to take a photo and blow it up for my office."

Emily raised her eyes to his.

"Every person who walks in will see my beautiful wife and be jealous of me."

She swallowed hard. He'd never talked about being proud of her. She'd be riding on the beach with her husband—not in a wood full of fallen trees and brambles. The horses at the resort's stables did this every day. There wouldn't be any problem.

Connor brought her hand to his lips and kissed it.

Shouldn't she do this to please her husband? This was their honeymoon. They'd only make these memories once. Didn't she want them to have all the special moments they could pack into this week?

She shut her eyes briefly and made her decision. "All right, I'm in."

"You're sure?"

She nodded.

"Who knows—you may enjoy it so much that you'll be begging to buy a horse."

Emily shook her head. "Let's not get carried away."

"Come on—we've got to hurry, or we'll miss it."

Chapter 6

Connor and Emily walked to the stables in silence, Emily struggling to keep up with Connor's long strides. Her feet felt heavy—like she was walking through quicksand. She raised an arm to glance at her watch, part of her hoping that they hadn't made it in time.

Connor turned back to her, and she quickly dropped her arm, ashamed of the thought.

"I'm going to run ahead to check in," he said. "I don't want us to be late."

Emily watched him jog ahead, then drew a deep breath, pushed her foreboding aside, and pressed forward. She was letting her imagination run away with her. By the time she skirted the side of the stable and came around to the front, Connor was seated on a chestnut mare at the back of a line of six other riders.

A lone white horse, at least seventeen hands high, stood saddled and waiting.

A young groomsman smiled at her broadly and waved her over to where he stood at the horse's head. "Here you are, ma'am. We're all waiting for you."

He moved to the horse's side. "I'll help you up."

The horse switched his enormous tail at a fly but otherwise remained motionless.

Emily drew a sharp breath. "He's so big."

"Your husband," the groomsman gestured to where Connor sat on the chestnut mare, "said to give you this one."

She glanced at Connor who held up the camera that hung around his neck and gave her a thumbs-up.

"He thinks you'll look beautiful on this one," he said. "He's right—it'll make a spectacular picture."

"Is he safe? I'm a beginner."

"Sure is. Coconut's the most placid horse in the stable." The groomsman rubbed the horse's nose affectionately. "He's a gentle

28

giant if there ever was one. Just stay at the back of the pack, and he'll follow the others."

Emily hesitated and swallowed hard.

"You'll be fine. We've never had a problem with him." The groomsman bent over and laced his fingers together. "I'll help you up and lead him to the back. Next to your husband."

Emily sucked in her breath, put her foot in his cupped hands, grabbed the reins, and hoisted herself up. She swung her right leg over the horse's hindquarters and settled herself into the saddle with a thump.

Coconut appeared not to notice.

"You're as striking as I thought you'd be," Connor called to her.

Emily gave him a wan smile.

"You're going to be just fine. Would I let anything happen to you?"

Emily looked away so that her new husband wouldn't see the doubt in her eyes. She was being silly. Weren't her friends always chastising her for her constant worrying? It was time to relax and enjoy herself.

R

At the front of the line, Emily watched as the groomsman raised his hand high over his head, then motioned them forward. The line of horses moved slowly toward the beach. They made their way to the water's edge. The morning sun still hovered on the horizon, casting elongated shadows that rolled over rocks, seaweed, and shells abandoned on the sand by the tide.

Connor coaxed his horse farther up the beach and turned to Emily. The waves teased her horse's hooves. A breeze off the ocean caressed her skin and lifted her hair gently from her shoulders, trailing it behind her.

Emily turned to his camera lens and smiled, relaxing in the serenity of the moment.

Neither saw the jagged outcropping of rocks until it was too late.

Emily's horse swerved suddenly, avoiding the danger but tipping her precariously toward the ocean. She threw her weight in the opposite direction, overcompensating, and slipped from the mount, still holding onto the horse's reins. She managed to land on her feet on the slippery outcropping before the horse side-stepped again, throwing her off balance. Emily dropped hard onto her knees and pitched forward, throwing her hands out to catch herself on the jagged rocks.

Connor ran to her side. "What happened? Are you okay?"

She remained on all fours, breathing heavily, as her riderless horse trotted away from her.

"Emily?" Connor asked, sinking to his knees and putting his arms around her.

The groomsman whistled for everyone to stop and galloped up to her.

"Miss," he said, dismounting and dropping to one knee beside her. "Are you hurt?"

Emily lifted her face to where his voice was coming from.

He took her hands in his and began brushing away sand and small pebbles. "You've gashed your knee on these rocks," he said. "We'll need to get you to the hospital to have you looked at. You may need stitches." He reached for her shoulders. "Can you stand?"

Emily let him help her to her feet. "Can you follow me to my horse? You can ride back with me."

She made a sweeping motion with her right arm, grabbing at his arm.

"I can't ... I can't see," she said in a small voice that was more sob than whisper.

"What do you mean?"

"It's like a curtain's closing ... on both eyes."

"Did you hit your head? I didn't see you fall. Maybe you have a concussion?"

"I ... I don't think so," Emily said. "I don't remember."

"You'll be okay," Connor interjected. "We'll have it looked at when we're at the hospital. The most important thing is to get that knee of yours stitched up. You're bleeding all over the place."

"Help me get her onto the back of my horse," the groomsman said to Connor.

"We'll take care of you," Connor said softly to Emily as he put his arm around her shoulders and walked with her. "Whatever's going on, I'm sure they'll be able to help you."

Emily forced herself to move as Connor lifted her onto the back of the groomsman's horse. She clung to the man's waist as they started back to the stable.

"We're turning back for a medical emergency," the groomsman called to the group of riders. "Fall in behind me."

Emily was oblivious to the others—oblivious to their progress. She closed her eyes and noticed the darkness. She opened them and noticed the same darkness covering most of her field of vision.

Fear pierced her like an ax, and she tasted bile at the back of her throat. Were one—or both—of her retinas detaching? Were these her last moments before she was irretrievably plunged into a world of blindness?

Emily squeezed her eyes shut and prayed that something could be done at the hospital to prevent it. This was supposed to be one of the most joyful days of her life.

R

Connor fumbled in his pocket for his wallet and rifled through it for money.

The groomsman waved his hand in dismissal. "Don't worry about it." He pointed to a taxi that was pulling up to the resort entrance to deliver its passengers. "Let's get you into that cab."

He whistled to the bellman holding the cab's door for the arriving guests. The bellman took one look at Emily and leaned into the cab, speaking to the driver.

Connor helped Emily traverse the driveway.

The bellman helped her into the cab. The cut on her knee began to ooze again.

"You'll be at the hospital in under ten minutes," the bellman said. He patted the roof of the cab and they were on their way.

Emily leaned back into her seat and closed her eyes.

"Here," Connor said, taking the cloth the groomsman had given her at the stable. "You're bleeding again." He applied pressure to her wound, and she winced.

"I'm sorry, sweetheart," he said. "They'll get this cleaned and stitched up in no time. We'll be back here with plenty of time for our dinner cruise tonight."

A tear ran down her cheek.

"Don't cry. This won't hurt once they get it closed up."

Emily kept her eyes closed. "I'm not crying about my knee. I know that'll be fine."

"I got all the photos I need, if that's what you're worried about," Connor replied.

"I'm not worried about your damned photos!" Emily slammed her fist on the seat. "It's my eyesight," she whispered, a tear streaming down her cheek. "I think both my retinas may be detaching."

"You didn't hit your head."

"You don't have to hit it—a sharp jolt will do the trick."

"We can ask them to look at it after they take care of your knee."

"I don't care about my knee. I'm worried about my eyes." She prayed that there would be an ophthalmologist at the hospital.

The cab slowed, made a sharp right-hand turn, and crept up to the emergency room entrance.

Before they had come to a full stop, Connor leapt out of the cab, thrust a wad of bills at the driver, and quickly came around to Emily's side. He tucked her hand into his elbow and helped her into the hospital.

"My eyes." Emily clutched at Connor's shirt. "The most important thing is my eyes. If my retinas are detaching, the doctor has to act fast. My knee can wait."

"Okay." He steered her into a chair and handed her the towel. "I'm going to check you in. I'll tell them about your vision and insist that you see an ophthalmologist."

R

An intake nurse led them to a bed in an alcove and pulled back a privacy curtain. The hooks screeched against a metal rod, sending shivers down Emily's spine. "Tell me what's going on," she said to Emily.

"It looks like a curtain is closing, on both of my eyes. I can only see out of the very bottom portion of my eyes."

"This just came on?"

"Yes. With the fall that damaged my knee," Emily said. "That's a sign of a detached retina, isn't it? Do you have an ophthalmologist on staff?"

The nurse nodded. "We have one on call."

"Then call him," Emily said, clenching her fists in her lap. "Right now. It's important that I get this looked at right away."

"Of course. Wait here," she said, hurrying away.

Connor turned to Emily. "Are you sure you want to have your eyes treated … here?"

"If their ophthalmologist is competent, yes. Time is of the essence."

Connor put his arm around her shoulders. They waited for the nurse, listening to the beeping monitors, rattling gurneys, and serious voices of a busy emergency room.

She finally returned. "The doctor will see you tomorrow afternoon," she said. "You'll have to come back at four o'clock."

"This can't wait twenty-four hours," Emily said. "I have to see him today." Her voice rose. "Did you explain that my retinas are detaching?" She was yelling now. "That I may go blind?"

"I told him," she said. "He's not on the island. He's coming back right away and can't get here any faster than that."

A guttural moan escaped Emily's lips. She groped for Connor's hand. "We have to get off this island tonight and back to the United States."

"Even if I can book us a flight, we probably won't get home earlier than tomorrow morning. Maybe we should go back to our room and get some rest. You've had quite a scrape. Maybe you'll be better by the morning. This is our honeymoon, you know. If not, we'll come see the doctor tomorrow afternoon."

Emily felt hot tears prick the backs of her eyes. "You're not listening to me. This isn't something that a good night's sleep can cure." She sucked in a deep breath. "I'm sorry that we have to cut our honeymoon short, but I need to see an ophthalmologist as soon as humanly possible. If you love me, Connor, you'll do this for me."

"Of course I love you," he said. "If you want to go home, we'll go. I'll call the airline as soon as we get to the hotel."

"That's what we need to do." She didn't want to argue or explain. She needed to preserve her energy to get home. The difference between tomorrow morning and afternoon could be crucial. "I'm sorry, Connor. I really am, but I need to get back to the States."

Chapter 7

The day started much like all the others with a bowl of the delicious kibble that we now ate twice a day. I couldn't imagine anything better than knowing I'd be eating the same thing every day—not once, but twice.

I was heading for the stairs—I'd developed a regular routine of running up and down them four times in succession right after breakfast—when one of the two-legged mothers beckoned to me.

Couldn't it wait? I loved to follow a routine.

She started toward me. When she called my name, I stopped on my way up the steps and turned around.

"Garth," she called again.

I went to her, my tail wagging despite my irritation at the interruption.

"We need to get you all cleaned up," she said, clipping a leash on my collar. "You're going to your puppy raiser this afternoon."

I looked up at her. What was she talking about?

She walked me across the enclosure to a door I hadn't walked through before. The room we entered was fitted with crates along one wall and large basins along another. One of my sisters stood in a basin with water running over her back while the two-legged poodle mother worked a milky substance into her coat.

The mother glanced at us as we approached the basin next to them. "Garth!" she cried. "It's your turn."

I wanted to get close to her, to see if she would tell me what was going on. Instead, I felt myself being lifted into the basin. The woman who had brought me in turned on the water. My feet were getting wet, but I didn't mind. I love a puddle as much as the next dog. I leaned forward and lapped at the water with my tongue.

"That's a good boy," she said. "We're going to get you all buffed and fluffed."

I didn't know why I needed to be buffed and fluffed—and I really couldn't figure out why she was rubbing that smelly stuff into my coat, only to work so hard to rinse it out. Didn't she realize she was covering up my unique Garth-y smell? Why would anyone want to do that?

I'd have to find something to roll in as soon as I got out of there. Still, her hands were on me, kneading and rubbing, which was pleasant enough. I felt my eyelids grow heavy.

I closed my eyes for just a minute and startled when she wrapped me in a giant towel and began to rub.

"Here we go," she said as she carried me to one of the crates along the wall. "Let's put you in here and turn on the dryer."

She set me on the floor and let the towel drop as she reached for the door to the crate.

I shook myself for all I was worth, and she cried out.

The poodle mother laughed. "You should have known that would happen."

"You're right." The woman tossed a treat into the crate, and I hopped in after it.

"I'm going to turn this fan on," she said to me. "You'll be dry in no time."

I was pretty sure I'd dry off if they let me go back to the enclosure, but if this is how they wanted to go about it, I had no objection. I pointed my nose into the fan and my ears blew back. The sensation was glorious. I would later learn that it was very much like traveling in a car, with my head sticking out the window. It didn't get much better than that.

I might have fallen asleep again because the next thing I knew, the poodle mother was opening my cage. She reached in and scooped me out, clutching me to her chest.

Her voice quivered and her eyes were leaking. "It's your time, Garth," she said. She massaged my back, and I felt the love pour out of her fingertips.

I put my nose on her damp cheek and licked.

"You're leaving here to go live with your puppy raisers for the next year or so. You'll learn to be part of a family and how to be a well-mannered dog."

I licked her again.

"But that isn't the most important part. When you leave that family, you'll come back here to be trained as a guide." She leaned back and held my muzzle in her hand. "Do you know what that means?"

I sniffed. I didn't know, but there was that magical word again. Guide.

"You'll be the eyes for a person who has lost their sight. There's nothing more noble that a dog can do."

She hugged me close and whispered in my ear. "You have the intelligence and courage and tenacity to achieve this. It won't be easy, but I know it's in your heart."

I tingled from the tip of my nose to the end of my tail.

"This is your destiny, Garth, and you're about to take the first step. I promise you it will be fine." She kissed the top of my head. "And I'll be praying for you every day until you come back to us."

I began to squirm. Her words excited me. I needed to get down and run.

She put me down, and I took off, circling the enclosure three times at top speed. When I was done, a man I'd seen walking the older dogs approached me and snapped a leash on my collar.

"Ready, Garth?" he asked.

I wagged my tail.

He led me out of the enclosure to a large van. It was filled with crates, and all but one of them were occupied by other puppies from the enclosure. He secured me in the one remaining crate.

"Okay, everybody," he said. "We're off. Your next adventure is about to begin."

Chapter 8

"You'll need to remain in your seat, sir, until we reach cruising altitude and the captain's turned off the Fasten Seat Belt sign," the steward said to Connor. She pointed to his seat belt. "Please fasten that. We're cleared for takeoff."

Connor jammed the buckle into position. "Thank you. I know the drill."

Emily leaned into the armrest between them, laying the side of her face against his shoulder. The solidity of him next to her was comforting. "Where did you go?"

"I wanted to see if there were any open rows where we could stretch out to sleep."

Emily's heart sank. She wanted the comfort of having him near. She didn't think she'd be able to sleep, even if she could stretch out. "Did you find any?"

Connor nodded. "There's one—six rows behind us on the other side. You can slip back there as soon as we take off. I don't want someone else to grab it."

She cleared her throat. "Why don't you take the row? I never sleep on a plane."

"No ..."

Emily swallowed hard. She hated flying under the best of circumstances, and this was far from that. She was terrified of losing her eyesight, and the comfort of having him near helped to ease her mind. But what was the point in both of them being exhausted when they got off the plane?

"You should claim that open row, Connor. Red-eye flights are brutal. If you can get some sleep, you should. I'll be perfectly fine right here." She pointed to her carry-on bag stowed under the seat in front of her. "Maybe you can help me find my earbuds so I can listen to my audiobook?"

The plane began to taxi to the runway.

Connor lunged for her carry-on and pulled it to him.

"We have to wait until ..." Emily began.

"I'm not waiting." Connor rummaged through her bag, opening the zippered compartments and removing the neatly organized contents. "Here." He placed the earbuds into her hand.

The engines revved and the plane began to barrel down the runway before the wheels lifted from the ground.

"Thank you."

He pushed the contents back into her bag and tugged at the zipper. "It's stuck. Damn it. I'm sorry."

"Don't worry about it."

He shoved it under the seat in front of her with his foot.

The plane climbed and finally leveled out.

"Go," Emily said.

"You're sure?"

"Yes."

"See you when we land," Connor said as he unlatched his seat belt. "We'll get you help as soon as we get there." He leaned over, kissed her lightly on the lips, and was gone.

Emily connected her earbuds to her phone, rotated its position until she could see the screen in her narrow field of vision, and tapped to open her audiobook. Her vision wasn't any better, but it hadn't gotten worse. She closed her eyes and settled back to endure the long, lonely flight home.

R

The dinging of the intercom overhead roused Emily. She pulled the earbuds out of her ears. There was nothing but silence coming out of them, anyway. She must have fallen asleep somewhere over the Pacific. Her book had finished. She rubbed her forehead. She couldn't remember the last thing she'd heard before sleep had overtaken her.

"Hello, ladies and gentlemen. We're making our final approach into San Francisco. Stewards, please take your seats. We'll be on the ground shortly."

Emily opened her eyes slowly and with great trepidation. Her vision remained unchanged. She released the breath that she hadn't been aware she'd been holding.

She suddenly sat up straighter. Where was Connor? Then she remembered. He would still be at the back of the plane. She leaned out into the aisle and pointed her chin to the back to try to get a glimpse of him. It was pointless. The plane was too big and her vision too limited.

Emily's palms grew damp. How would she deplane without him? How would she find him in the terminal? She closed her eyes as she tried to swallow her rising panic.

The plane touched down, bounced up with a jerk, then settled into the runway.

She opened her eyes. Everything was the same. The jolt hadn't made things worse. She was home. She'd go directly to the eye clinic's retina specialist. He'd perform whatever surgery was necessary today. Her eyesight would be saved. She'd hang onto that thought.

"Sir! Remain seated until we're at the gate," a steward yipped into the microphone.

A moment later, Connor was stepping over Emily and throwing himself into the middle seat.

"You're here," Emily said, the relief evident in her voice.

"Of course, I'm here," Connor said. "I want to be with you when we deplane. Did you get any sleep?"

"I dozed off."

"How's ... how's your eyesight?"

"Unchanged. Not worse, which is a good thing."

"That's a relief," he said.

The plane lurched to a stop. The captain turned off the Fasten Seat Belt sign. Connor leapt to his feet and opened the overhead bin. He shifted suitcases and brought both of their bags into the aisle.

"Can you manage your bag?"

Emily nodded. She yanked the carry-on out of the tight storage space and stuffed her earbuds inside the open compartment. The zipper caught on the fabric as she tried to close it, and she jerked it back and forth until it finally cleared.

"I can't wait to get home to take a shower," he said.

Emily spun on him. "We can't go home. We need to head directly to the doctor's office."

"Will they be open this early? It's only six fifteen."

"They do all their surgeries this early. Someone will be there to let us in."

"You don't have an appointment. Shouldn't we go home to call first?"

Emily's jaw tightened. "They'll work me in. This is an emergency."

The people in the row ahead of them began to move toward the exit.

"Let's get a cab. We'll figure it out from there," Connor said as he extended the handle on his suitcase and headed down the aisle.

A woman from the row across the aisle stepped between Connor and Emily. She attempted to remove her suitcase from the overhead storage and, in the end, had to ask for help.

Emily cursed under her breath. She didn't want to lose contact with Connor.

She made her way out of the plane and through the jetway, into the terminal. Her field of vision was limited to the floor and a foot above it. She stepped to one side to get out of the way of the other deplaning passengers and felt panic rising in her. She was tilting her head back as far as it would go to expand her visual field when she felt a familiar hand on her elbow.

"I'm right here, sweetheart," Connor said. He took her carry-on bag and slung it over his shoulder. "Hold on to my arm and I'll lead us out of here."

Emily grasped his elbow and they wove their way through the crowded terminal. Connor turned to update her on their progress.

They settled into the cue waiting for a taxi.

"There are five people ahead of us," he told her. "It won't be long. The line moves fast."

Emily nodded. She pulled her phone from her pocket and tried to position it so she could read the time.

"It's six twenty," Connor said. "If that's what you wanted to know."

"Yes, thanks," Emily said. She paused, thinking, then murmured. "If you really want a shower, we can stop at home first. It might be a long day at the doctor's office. That way we can have our car."

"Really, Em? That would be great."

They shuffled forward. "We're next," he said.

A male voice with a thick accent said something Emily couldn't make out.

Connor responded.

She became aware that their suitcases were being loaded into a trunk. She stood, rooted in place.

"Come on, Em. Get in."

Emily extended her hands in front of her and leaned forward until she felt the frame of the open door. She could see the curb through her remaining sliver of vision.

She heard two doors on the other side of the cab slam shut. She lunged forward and into the backseat, hitting her head on the door frame with a resounding *thwack*. She brought her hand to her head.

"Ouch," said the driver from the front seat. He turned to Connor. "Where to?"

Connor recited their home address.

Emily ran her hand through her hair and blinked her eyes repeatedly. The sliver of vision in her right eye was gone. The bump must have jarred her retina, causing it to completely detach. She cursed, choking on the words.

"What?" Connor asked.

"I'm blind in my right eye." She shouted at the driver to turn around and gave him the name of the eye clinic. "We need to get there as soon as humanly possible."

Chapter 9

"I need to see Dr. David Anderson." Emily couldn't see the receptionist and hoped that she was pointing her face in the right direction to be addressing her.

"He's finishing up a surgery. Let's put you in an exam room, and I'll get word to him that you're here."

Emily heard the woman push her chair back. "Follow me," she said.

Connor took Emily's elbow and steered her after the woman's retreating steps. They entered a brightly lit room with laminate flooring. Emily could make out a paperclip on the floor against the baseboard. She couldn't see anything else.

Connor guided her to a chair.

"I'm sure the doctor will see you as soon as he's done with surgery. It may be a while. Please be patient."

"Should we make an appointment and come back later?" Connor asked.

"NO," the woman practically shouted. "Sorry. No, don't go anywhere. From what Emily's told me, I think you should wait here."

Emily heard the door to the exam room close. She clutched her purse on her lap and twisted and untwisted the strap. "Will you text my mother? Let her know we came home early—and what's happened with me?"

"Why don't I wait until after you've seen the doctor?" Connor said. "She's going to freak out, so I'd like to give her the latest information."

"Okay." Emily pursed her lips. "You're right. We'll wait."

They sat in silence, the tick of the clock on the wall marking the slow passage of time.

Connor swore under his breath.

"What's wrong?" Emily asked.

"I'm just reading emails from work. Nothing for you to worry about."

Emily was about to say that they had bigger things to worry about than anything going on at his office when the door opened and Dr. Anderson stepped into the room.

"Emily," he said.

She extended her hand in his direction, and he shook it. "This is my husband," she said, flushing with pride at her first time to introduce him this way, "Connor Harrington."

The two men shook hands.

"I understand that you're having symptoms of retinal detachment," the doctor said.

Emily heard him rustling papers. "I'd like you to tell me what's going on."

He listened carefully as Emily described her vision loss after she fell from the horse and, more recently, after bumping her head.

"Let's take a look," he said. "Give your purse to your husband, and I'll help you into the exam chair. I'm going to start with some drops that will allow me to see the back of the eye better."

Dr. Anderson left the room to allow the drops to take effect and returned with two other doctors in tow. The three of them took turns examining Emily's eyes.

The fiercely bright light and magnifier were giving Emily a blinding headache. "I never should have gone horseback riding," Emily said. "I knew better than that."

She heard one of the doctors clear his throat.

"We all do things that, in hindsight, we wished we hadn't," said Dr. Anderson. "You did the right thing by cutting your honeymoon short and coming home. These issues are most successfully treated right away. Unless one of my colleagues disagrees, I'm going to recommend that we perform surgeries on both eyes—immediately."

"I'm in agreement," said one of the other doctors.

"I thought you weren't supposed to operate on both eyes at once," Connor said. "Like when my grandmother had cataract surgery."

"We prefer not to do them both at the same time, but in this case, time is of the essence," Dr. Anderson said. "That's why I brought my colleagues in to consult with me. I believe they agree with me."

"We do," both men said in unison.

"There's absolutely no doubt that surgery in each eye is medically necessary—right now," said one of the other doctors.

"Is it the same procedure for both eyes?" Emily asked.

"No," Dr. Anderson said. "The damage to the left eye presents a relatively minor retinal tear. We can fix that with a routine procedure."

Emily didn't breathe. "And my right eye?"

"The damage there is more extensive. We have a variety of treatment options available to us. We'll decide on the best course of action once we get in there."

"But it'll work, won't it?" Emily's voice sounded shrill to her own ears. "I'll be able to see when you're done?"

"That's our goal, yes," Dr. Anderson said. "All surgeries have risks. We can't guarantee outcomes, but we expect a good result. If you agree to move forward, we'll get you prepped for surgery right away. You can ask your husband to sign the consent forms."

"I can still sign for myself," Emily said. "Just put the pen in my hand and direct me to the correct spot."

"I'll have the forms brought in," Dr. Anderson said.

"Will I go home afterward?"

"Yes. We'll send you home with detailed aftercare instructions and several eye drops." He turned to Connor. "Will you be able to stay with her? Not the honeymoon you'd planned, I'm sure, but at least you'll be together."

Connor cleared his throat. "I let my employer know that we came home early. They're expecting me in the office tomorrow."

"Why did you do that?" Emily asked. "Didn't you think that I might need you?"

"I'm sorry. It's just that —"

"It's okay. Call my mother. Tell her what happened and ask her to come. She'll take care of me." Emily addressed the doctor. "I'm supposed to go back to work on Monday. I'll be fine by then, won't I?"

"I expect that it'll take six to eight weeks for you to recover. You shouldn't expect to work during that time."

Emily sucked in her breath. "Oh … I had no idea. I need to call my office. We've been so busy—taking a week off for our honeymoon put a strain on my team. And now this?"

"We'll know more when we've finished the surgeries," Dr. Anderson said. "Don't make any definite plans just yet."

The door opened again, and the receptionist interrupted them. She gave Emily a pen and positioned her hand on the paper. "Just give me your John Hancock, and I'm ready to take you back."

"I'll let your boss know that you won't be in on Monday," Connor said.

Emily scribbled her name on the consent form. "Call my mom, too, Connor. I'm going to need her."

Emily allowed the woman to help her into a wheelchair.

Connor leaned over and kissed her cheek. "It's all going to be fine," he said. "They're going to fix this."

The nurse wheeled her out of the exam room and down the corridor. She heard Connor call, "Good luck," after her.

R

Emily sat in the recovery room, her face held parallel to the floor, as she listened to the nurse go over Dr. Anderson's aftercare instructions with her. Both eyes were protected with gauze pads that the nurse said must be changed every time she received drops. Her right eye also needed to be protected with a metal shield at night. She would only need the gauze pads for three days, but she'd have to keep her face directed to the floor for the next two weeks. Twenty-four seven. Her compliance was crucial to her recovery.

"I understand," Emily said softly after the nurse's advice to keep her head as still as possible. The next two weeks sounded like they would be a trip to hell, but she could get through them. She had to do everything she could to preserve her eyesight.

"You'll come back to see the doctor tomorrow afternoon at three," the nurse said. "Just remember to keep your face down in the car and at home. You can get up to go to the bathroom as long as you keep your face level with the floor."

"How do I sleep?" Emily asked.

"You'll need to lie on your stomach, with pillows arranged so that you can't roll over. Some patients have had success with wearing a backpack stuffed with towels. It prevents them from rolling over. It's also a good idea to set an alarm clock every two hours so you can correct your position if your head isn't down."

"Okay. I can do that."

"Don't worry if you can't see anything when your husband takes the gauze off to give you your drops. You've had a lot done, and it can take several weeks to see the effects of the surgeries."

Emily's shoulders sagged.

"This is the worst part," the nurse said, reaching over and patting Emily's hand. "I'm not going to lie. The next two weeks will be challenging. When you recover and can see again, all the discomfort will be worth it."

The nurse addressed Connor. "Unless you have any questions, you're ready to go home."

"No. I think I've got it."

"Our emergency number is printed on the instructions. Call us if you have any questions."

"Emily's mother should be at our place shortly after we get home. We'll be fine."

"I'll take her in a wheelchair to the door on the east side of the building. You can bring your car around there."

"We took a taxi," Emily said.

"I went home to get our car while you were in surgery. We're all set."

"Oh …" Emily said, slightly taken aback that he wasn't there at the hospital while she was in surgery. "Thank you."

A clattering noise on her right let Emily know the nurse had brought the wheelchair. With both eyes bandaged shut, Emily experienced what it must feel like to be blind. She shuddered involuntarily. She was glad that she'd only have to endure this for the next three days.

Chapter 10

"Your mother just texted," Connor said. "She stopped at the grocery, and she'll be here in fifteen minutes."

"That was nice of her," Emily said to the floor. She was sitting, bent at the waist in a sleek Danish recliner in the living room of their condo, with her elbows resting on the arms of the chair, her face parallel to the floor.

"She knew we wouldn't have any food in the house since we were just coming home from our trip."

"What she probably meant to say was that she knew we wouldn't have any food in the house because neither of us can cook, and we eat out all the time."

Connor laughed. "There's my girl. I expect that's exactly what she meant. Knowing Martha, we'll be eating like kings for as long as she's here."

"Mom always says a home-cooked meal can solve anything." Silence hung between them. "Well ... it won't solve this."

"No. I'm sorry." He coughed nervously. "Your eye drops start tomorrow. Do you mind if I let her take care of them?"

"Okay ... sure."

"It's just that I'm not good at ... she'll be so much better at it than I will be. Plus, she'll have to give them to you when I'm at work, anyway."

"You're still going to the office?"

"Yes. Why wouldn't I? You won't need both of us to look after you."

"I just thought ... with the alarm going off every two hours, won't you be too tired to go to work?" What a foolish thing to say. She knew once Connor was asleep, he was dead to the world. In fact, he barely budged. But she really had hoped, expected even, that her new husband would stay home with her, at least for the first couple of days.

50

"I'll stay in the guest room so that your mother can sleep in our bed with you." He knelt down next to her and put his hand on her arm. "You know what a restless sleeper I am. I'd be scared to death that I'd jostle you. They warned me about that."

Emily stared at the floor.

"You understand, don't you? I'd love to be with you, but it's for your own good."

"Of course," Emily said stiffly. "You're just thinking of me."

R

Martha lifted her head from the pillow and listened. The knocking sound repeated itself. Someone was at the front door.

She swung her feet over the side of the bed, taking care not to wake her daughter. She retrieved her glasses from the nightstand and peered at the bedside clock. Eleven twenty-three. Who in the world could be at her daughter's door at this hour of the night?

She padded around the foot of the bed.

"I'm not asleep," Emily said, her voice muffled by the ring of pillows supporting her face above the mattress. "Is somebody at the door?"

"Yes."

"Ignore them."

"I'm just going to look through the peephole."

"It's probably somebody too drunk to find their own front door."

"I'll let Connor deal with them if that's the case."

"You'll have to wake him. Nothing disturbs him once he's fallen asleep," she said as her mother left the room.

Martha placed her eye against the peephole. Standing on the other side was a stocky middle-aged man who looked vaguely familiar. Shopping bags loaded to the hilt hung from each arm. A tall plastic cup bearing the In-and-Out logo was in his left hand, and he gripped a gigantic plush puppy under his arm. Behind him was a black leather bench with a headrest that Martha recognized as a massage table.

The man looked directly into the peephole and raised his right hand, knocking more firmly this time. Recognition washed over her. This was one of Emily's employees. What was his name? Dhruv? Yes— it was Dhruv.

Martha slid the privacy chain out of place and opened the door.

Dhruv stepped inside without waiting to be invited.

"Hello," Martha said, extending her hand to him. "I'm Emily's mother. I believe we've met before?"

"We have," Dhruv said. He marched through the minimalist furnishings of the living room to the kitchen counter and deposited his bundles. "Emily needs this."

He retraced his steps to the front door and rolled the massage table inside, shutting the door behind him. Dhruv began pushing the table across the living room. "Where is she?"

"She's in her bedroom," Martha said, taken aback by his brusqueness.

"Which door?"

Martha stepped around him. "Over here," she said, directing him to the partially opened door.

Dhruv pushed the massage table into the bedroom. A shaft of light from the living room showed him that Emily lay motionless in the bed.

"I've got this for you to lay on."

"Dhruv?" Emily asked. "What in the world are you doing here?"

"They told us at work what happened to you. I researched what you'll need. A woman on YouTube said a massage table is much better than using pillows to position yourself in bed. She said that doctors should prescribe one for patients, but they don't. My cousin is a massage therapist, so I called her. She had this old table at her place. I picked it up after work."

Emily cleared her throat. "Did you try to call first? Do you know what time it is?"

"Why would I call? You just came home after surgery. I knew you'd be here. And I know you need this."

Martha stepped around him and stood next to the bed.

"This is awfully nice of you."

"This table," he said, patting it with his open palm, "is best."

"Is it the kind with the cutout area for your face when you're lying on your stomach?" Emily asked.

"Yes."

"Thank God. I'm getting claustrophobic with all these pillows around my face. And the air I'm breathing is hot and stale."

"I also brought special pillows from the home health supply store that you can put under your hips to immobilize yourself in the bed. And straws for drinking since you can't tilt your head back."

He turned and retraced his steps to the kitchen counter, returning with the cup and stuffed toy.

"I brought you a chocolate shake from In-and-Out. I know it's your favorite."

"Thank you." Emily's voice cracked.

"And a stuffed golden retriever puppy." He paused, shifting his weight from foot to foot. "I have a real golden retriever." He leaned toward her and placed the toy by her face. "I thought you could rest your forehead on him."

Martha crossed to him and put her arm around his shoulders. "This is the nicest, most thoughtful thing you could have done." She attempted to hug him, but he remained rigid in her arms.

"This is exactly like you, Dhruv. Researching what's necessary and then acquiring it." Emily raised herself onto her elbows so that her voice wasn't muffled. "I'm so grateful to you, Dhruv. Thank you— for all of it." This time a small sob escaped her lips.

"Okay, then." Dhruv turned and made his way out the front door, drawing it shut behind him.

"Well … for heaven's sake," said Martha. "I never …"

"Dhruv's on the autism spectrum, Mom. Don't you remember me telling you that?"

"Now that you mention it, I do."

"He doesn't pick up on social cues, but he's the best researcher I've got. Maybe the smartest on my team. Certainly the kindest—and with the biggest heart."

"I'd have to agree with that last statement," Martha said. "He put a lot of thought and effort into this."

"Can you get me one of those straws? I'm suddenly hungry and that milkshake sounds good."

Martha beamed. The thought of her daughter enjoying anything right now gladdened her heart.

"I'll also dig out those pillows he brought. Maybe we can make you more comfortable."

"If Dhruv thinks they'll help, I'm sure they will."

"I'm glad that you've got such a nice friend," Martha said. "He's a blessing to you."

"That he is," Emily agreed.

Chapter 11

The truck began to move. The other puppies in their crates were lying down. I did the same, stretching out and resting my nose on my outstretched front paws. I was glad for some downtime; I needed to think about what the woman had just told me. What was my destiny?

The vehicle rocked slightly as we sped down the road. The muffled sounds of calm human voices drifted to me from the front seat, punctuated occasionally by a louder male voice saying, "You're listening to NPR, National Public Radio."

I closed my eyes so I could concentrate.

The next thing I knew, the back doors of the van opened with a loud crack. The people from the front took us out on our leashes. We had a few minutes to stretch our legs and do our business.

I sniffed the small patch of grass under my paws, and the unmistakable scents of my kind—some recent and some ancient— filled my nostrils. I could have spent hours exploring it with my nose, but we were soon loaded back into the van and secured in our crates.

I resumed my position and resolved to stay awake to continue my inner journey but sleep once again overcame me.

When we stopped again, I was the only puppy taken out of his crate. The man from the front seat clipped the leash on me, and I jumped to the ground.

We'd only taken a few steps toward a two-story stucco house when the front door flew open and a tall young woman with a strange hairdo—that I later learned is called a "topknot"—ran down the walkway to us. She was followed by a tall man who looked to be the same age.

"Is this Garth?" she cried.

"It is," said the man holding my leash. "Are you Katie? And Jon?"

"We are," Jon said.

Katie dropped to one knee and held out her hand to me. "Hello, sweet boy," she said.

I sniffed her hand politely and looked up at the man holding my leash, wagging my tail.

"This is your new home," the man said, reaching down to pat my head. "Katie and Jon are puppy raisers. You're going to live with them and learn basic obedience skills while you grow up—before you come back to use and learn the skills you'll need to be a guide."

My ears perked up. There was that word again. Guide. I jerked my head and gave a short bark.

The man handed the leash to Katie. "Why don't you take him inside while I give Jon the supplies I've brought for you?"

Katie stood with me on her left side. She gave a slight tug on the leash and said, "Heel." She began walking to the house, and I followed alongside.

"Good boy!" she said, reaching into her pocket and producing a tiny treat for me.

I gobbled the snack. I wasn't sure what I'd done to deserve it, but I certainly wasn't going to turn down a treat. I was sure I was going to like it there.

We entered the house and walked through a room with a long, raised dog bed. I'd never seen anything like it.

Katie unclipped the leash.

I headed to the dog bed covered in a smooth black fabric called leather. The cushions were thicker than any dog bed I'd ever seen, and I knew it would be cool against my coat. I crouched, gathered myself, and sprang onto the cushion.

"No," Katie said firmly. I raised my eyebrows and looked at her. What was she talking about?

She pointed to the floor. "Off," she said in the same firm voice.

I sighed heavily and jumped to the floor. It must not be my bedtime yet.

"Good boy," she said, producing another treat. She snapped the leash back on me and hooked the loop onto her belt.

Jon came through the front door and walked into the kitchen, his arms full of the items that the man from the van had given him. He placed them on the counter.

"I see you're wearing him," he said, gesturing to the leash that connected Katie and me.

"Yep. We're going to have to. The first thing Garth did when we walked in was jump on the sofa."

Jon bent over and began to massage behind my ears. This was better than getting a treat. Almost.

"I'll bet he thought it was a giant dog bed." He continued to pet me.

I liked this Jon; he understood me.

"We're going to follow all of the instructions from the Guide Dog Center," Katie said. "We don't want to mess this guy up."

She squatted next to me and took my muzzle in her hands, staring into my eyes.

"You're going to be a guide," she said. "You're going to be someone's eyes and their friend and companion. You're going to enrich their life like no one else can."

I felt a familiar surge of energy through my system.

She leaned toward me and kissed the top of my head. "We're not going to fail you, Garth. I promise."

Chapter 12

"It's raining cats and dogs out there!" Gina said, standing her umbrella in the tray beside the door.

"I shouldn't have asked you to stop by." Connor shook his head.

Gina put her hand on his arm. "Are you kidding? Wild horses couldn't have kept me away. This is really serious. How is she?"

"She slept most of the day."

"Can she see?"

"Not yet. They told us it could take several months for her to fully recover."

"But they do expect her vision to come back, don't they?"

"That's what they say."

"Is she in any pain?"

"No, but she has to keep her face turned to the floor at all times. She can't look up."

"Good Lord. That sounds horrible. Not even to take a shower or … use the bathroom?"

"Nope. She has to sleep on her stomach, too."

"For how long?"

"Two weeks."

"That sounds like it'll be the hardest part. Can I see her?"

"Sure. Martha is with her now, helping her with dinner. You can go on in." He pointed to an open doorway at the end of a hall running off the living room.

Gina squeezed his elbow, then released it. "Try not to worry. She's going to be fine. I can feel it." She stepped around him and walked to the bedroom, knocking softly on the doorframe.

Martha looked up from where she was holding a plate of macaroni and cheese that Emily was picking at. "Well … look who's here." She leaned toward Emily. "It's Gina."

Gina entered the room. "Hey, Em," she said, crossing to sit next to Martha. "This is a fine mess you've gotten yourself into," she said, trying—and failing—to sound easy and breezy.

"I know," Emily said. "I've really done it to myself now. I win the award for being the stupidest bride ever."

Gina took the plate from Martha. "I'll take over here. Why don't you let us have some girlfriend time?"

Martha nodded and gave Gina a rueful smile. She mouthed "thank you."

"Do you want more of this?"

"No. I'm not very hungry these days. I think I'm still in shock over the whole thing."

Gina leaned over to set the plate on the nightstand.

"Did you hear what happened?"

Gina nodded, then stopped herself. Emily couldn't see her.

"I did."

"So you know what a complete idiot I was? Going horseback riding. What in the hell was I thinking? I knew better than that."

"It was your honeymoon. You were just trying to have fun. Sounds like it was a freak accident."

"It was. Connor was being so sweet and was so excited about riding. He wanted to take a picture of me on this huge white horse— he was going to enlarge it and hang it in his office."

"Who could say no to that? If I had a husband as handsome as Connor, I'd want my picture on display in his office. Hell, I'd make him get my picture tattooed on his chest."

"Stake my claim on him." Emily laughed dully.

"Anyone would have gone on that horse ride, Em."

"And now I may spend the rest of my life in darkness because of one dumb decision."

"Don't talk like that. You have no reason to say such a thing."

Emily moved her hand to her side, and the massage table creaked.

Gina cleared her throat. "Connor says that the surgery went well but that it may take several months for everything to be back to normal."

"I guess."

"Oh, Em." Gina took Emily's hand in hers. "I'm so sorry this happened to you. I'm sure it'll be fine in the end, but it's going to be tough getting there."

"I'm only on day two of keeping my face pointed at the floor, and I'm already so tired of it I could scream." Emily drew in a sharp breath and pulled her hand away. "And I have to do this for two weeks."

"That … sucks. There's no other way to say it."

"I'm bored, too. There's only so much television I can stand to listen to."

"You're the strongest person I know, Em. You can get through this. And you have your mom and Connor to help."

"I know—I'm lucky. Mom's great, but Connor's been sort of … weird."

"What do you mean?"

"He acts like he doesn't want to be around me. He lets Mom do everything—and … he's sleeping in the guest room."

"He's afraid that he'll hurt you. And he feels guilty because all of this happened on a horseback ride that he talked you into."

"Is that what he said?"

"He called me from the car while you were in surgery. He was so upset."

"Oh …"

"You can understand how he feels, can't you?"

"It makes me feel a little better about things between us."

"It should. Connor's a great guy."

"You're right—this isn't just happening to me. Will you keep checking in on him, too?"

Gina paused, studying her hands. "Sure. I can do that."

"Thanks, Gina. You're a wonderful friend—to both of us." Emily held her hand out to her.

Gina took it and squeezed. "Do you still want me to come over on Saturday? We were going to unpack your things, get you settled into your new home."

"I forgot all about my stuff! Out of sight, out of mind, I guess."

"You may want to wait to unpack your books and knickknacks, but you'll need your clothes."

"You're right." Emily nodded. "That would be nice—if you don't mind," she added hastily. "I won't be able to help with any of it."

"I know that. I can pull stuff out of the boxes and describe things to you. You can tell me where to put them."

"I can ask Mom to do that. You don't have to sacrifice your entire weekend."

"I want to help you, Em. It'll make me feel useful. I can give Martha a break. And I'll stop by the library and bring you an armload of audiobooks."

"That's a great idea. Plus, I'd like to have your company. You always make me feel better."

"Then I'll see you Saturday morning. I'll bring your favorite chai tea. We'll get your closet organized. And if I find that Hermès scarf you found at the thrift store, I can't guarantee that it won't find its way into my purse."

"So that's what you've got up your sleeve?"

"Just sayin'." Gina shrugged. "I've got meetings the next two nights, so I won't be able to stop by until then. But I'll call you every day. And you can call me anytime. Day or night."

"Thanks, Gina. You're the most faithful friend a girl could ask for."

R

"We're fine," Gina said, turning to address Martha from Emily's closet. "We've got this, don't we?" She turned to Emily who sat face down in a chair surrounded by a mountain of clothes. "Why don't you get out of this condo? Have lunch. Go run an errand."

"Well …" Martha stammered.

"Go on, Mom. You're probably going stir-crazy by now. No point in both of us having cabin fever."

"Take your time," Gina said. "It's a beautiful day out there. Rain's predicted for all of next week, so enjoy it while you can."

"Could you ask Connor to come in here before you leave?" Emily asked. "I want to check with him on which drawers he cleared out for me to use."

"Connor went to the gym," Martha said.

"When did he leave? Do you know when he'll be home?"

"He left early—before breakfast."

"What time is it?" Emily asked.

"Almost eleven," Martha said.

"Surely he's done at the gym by now. Was he going somewhere after that?" Her voice held a sharp tone.

"Not that he told me. I'm sure he's running errands."

"Or maybe he went to the office," Emily muttered to the floor, "because he can't stand to be around his blind wife."

Emily couldn't see the glance exchanged by Gina and Martha.

"He's doing the best he can," Martha said.

"Don't read things into his actions that aren't there," Gina said.

"All right," Emily said. They could say what they would, but she could sense a difference in her husband.

Chapter 13

Emily smelled his aftershave before he even opened their bedroom door.

"Em?" Connor's voice was barely above a whisper. "Are you awake?"

"I am," she said.

"Good. I just wanted to say goodbye. I'm going into the office super-early so I can leave in time to meet you at the doctor's office."

"You're not going to take me?"

"I already talked to your mom. She said that she's fine getting you there. I'll come from my office."

Emily tasted disappointment like sour milk.

"You understand, don't you?"

She could hear Connor shifting his weight from foot to foot.

"It's just that we're really busy right now. I figured it's most important that I'm at the appointment."

Emily didn't trust herself to speak without bursting into tears.

"Martha thought it would be fine."

She raised her right hand and made a dismissive gesture.

Connor stepped to the massage table where she lay on her stomach—as she had done almost every day for the past two weeks—and kissed the back of her head.

"I'll see you soon, darling."

She heard him turn and walk out of the room. Emily listened to him murmur a goodbye to her mother and shut the door as he left the condo. She brought her right hand to her left and felt for her wedding ring. She grasped it with her middle finger and thumb, twisting the ring around her finger, and allowed her tears to flow.

She must have cried herself to sleep because the next sound she heard was her mother calling to her from the doorway.

"We need to leave for the doctor in about an hour," Martha said. "Are you hungry? You haven't eaten anything yet today."

Emily pushed herself onto her elbows and swung her feet over the side of the table to sit up. She kept her neck bent and her face parallel to the floor. "I don't think I could keep anything down," she said. "I'm too nervous."

Martha came to sit next to her daughter. She put her arm around her shoulders. "I know that you'd hoped to have your vision restored by now, but they told us it could take more time."

Emily's tears began again, splashing onto her knees. "I'm so discouraged." Her voice was ragged. "Correction. I'm terrified."

"Stop imagining the worst," Martha said. "We need to see what the doctor has to say and that's all there is to it." She ran her hand over her daughter's back. "Why don't you take a shower and then we'll be on our way?"

"You're giving me something to do to take my mind off of things."

"What would be wrong with that?"

"Nothing. A shower would feel terrific."

"Do you need me to help you?"

"No. I can manage." Emily got off the massage table and shuffled, hunched over, to her bathroom. The sparse furnishings of Connor's modern décor hadn't been appealing to her before but proved advantageous now; there weren't many obstacles to watch out for. She felt her way along the wall to the shower and turned on the water. She reached toward her towel and found that it was in its place on the towel bar.

Emily got into the shower and adjusted the water temperature. She allowed the water to flow over her body, the sensation of warmth relaxing her tense muscles. She stood in the stream until she felt guilty about the water she was wasting.

She swung her right hand up to the shelf in the shower and reached for her shampoo. The shelf was empty. She ran her hand down the wall of the shower to the floor. She got down on her knees and swept her hand in front of her, searching for the bottle. Her hand found it in the corner, on its side. She picked it up and knew, from its weight, that it was the empty bottle she'd been diluting with water for the past several days, eking out the final drops of shampoo.

Emily groaned softly. Connor had promised her he'd put a new bottle in the shower when she'd told him it was empty. He'd kept forgetting and she'd kept reminding him. Was it too much to ask that he pay attention and do this one small thing for her?

She jerked the lever on the faucet to the off position. The stream of water stopped. She needed to dry herself off and get dressed. Her hair would have to wait. She'd ask her mother to make sure that she had what she needed in the shower. Connor excelled at many things, but being a caretaker wasn't one of them.

R

"The doctor is ready for you," the nurse said.

"My husband's not here yet," Emily said.

"I'll bring him in when he gets here."

"Can we wait for him?"

"The doctor is booked solid this afternoon."

"Mom—can you come back with me? In case Connor doesn't make it?"

"Of course," Martha said. "I'm sure he's doing his best. You know how much traffic we ran into getting here."

They followed the nurse to a room. Dr. Anderson was with them in another ten minutes and began his examination. He frowned at the answers Emily gave to his questions.

Dr. Anderson switched off the bright light and rolled on his stool away from Emily. Martha sat on a chair along the wall. He motioned for her to scoot it next to Emily. "Everything's healing as expected. The backs of both eyes look good."

"But I still can't see," Emily replied.

"Your recovery could take two to three months," the doctor said. "Most patients experience restored vision right away, but it's certainly not unheard of for it to take longer."

Emily turned her face to the floor and moaned.

"Do I have to keep on … like this?" She pointed to her face.

"No. The gas bubble we inserted has dissipated on its own. The retina of the right eye has reattached correctly."

Emily threw her shoulders back and sat up straight. "Thank God. Keeping my face to the floor at all times was torture."

"I'm sorry. Everyone hates that. You've been very compliant with our post-operative instructions. I can tell."

"So the fact that I only see light and shadow out of my right eye—and bright colors—isn't my fault? I rolled onto my back while I was sleeping day before yesterday and may have been like that for over an hour."

"No. You didn't do any harm to yourself. There can be a myriad of causes. Most likely, you suffered nerve damage when your retina detached."

"Will it get better over time?"

"We'll have to wait and see. You also might be developing scar tissue that's causing your retina to detach again. It's too soon to tell."

"Can you do anything to remove the scar tissue?"

"We can do an additional surgery."

"Would I have to keep my head parallel to the floor, again, like I just did?" Emily's voice caught. "I've never been so miserable in my life. Lying on my stomach on that massage table, with my face inside that special pillow, was becoming unbearable. I felt claustrophobic. I don't think I slept more than a couple of hours at a stretch during the entire two weeks." She balled her hands into fists. "I can't face that whole ordeal again."

"It's way too early to think about further procedures. We need to let your body continue to heal."

"What about my job? My right eye is useless, and I feel like I'm looking through a straw with my left eye. I can't work like that."

"You're nowhere near ready to go back," Dr. Anderson said. "You don't want to strain your left eye by trying to read or work on a computer."

"So what am I supposed to do?" Emily's voice was shrill.

"You should apply for benefits under the Family and Medical Leave Act. The FMLA will provide you with time off and your employer won't be able to terminate you. You're legally entitled to protect your job this way. I'll write the required doctor's report."

"Okay ... thank you ... but I mean what can I do to function in my life? I'm completely helpless."

"You won't have to keep your head lowered anymore. That should be a huge relief."

"It is, and I can navigate our condo pretty well. My muscles remember where everything is. But I'm stuck there all day long. My mother's been staying with us since the day of my surgery, but she needs to go back home, and my husband travels constantly for work. I'll be by myself and the thought terrifies me."

Dr. Anderson didn't respond, and the silence hung between them like a barricade. When he spoke, his voice was tinged with regret.

"I'm sorry, Emily, that the outcome isn't what we'd hoped for. And your sight might improve dramatically over the next few weeks, but I think we need to start moving forward from where you are right now."

He paused and Emily jumped in. "And where—exactly—is that?"

"My assessment is that you have eight percent of your vision remaining." He waited, allowing this information to sink in.

"But you still think I might get it back?"

"I think it's possible that it will improve, yes. But I also think that you've got to be able to live with what you've got right now. As you said yourself, you're currently a prisoner in your own home. You don't want that."

"So ... what do you suggest?"

"Let me connect you with a vision rehabilitation specialist at the state."

"What will this person do for me?"

"They can get you enrolled in programs that will help you."

"Like?"

"Training on assistive technology—programs that will read your computer and phone screens to you. There is a boatload of devices on the market that can help." He glanced at his chart. "You work for a gigantic technology company. They're required by law to provide you with reasonable accommodations when you go back to work, but my guess is that they'll voluntarily furnish more than the law requires. You'll be amazed at what you'll be able to do."

"That sounds good," Emily said. "I'm anxious to get back to my job as soon as possible."

"Assistive technology isn't the only thing you need," the doctor pressed on. "You'll need counseling and group support, training on how to perform the tasks of daily life …"

"What do you mean?" Emily interrupted.

"Personal hygiene. And how to make meals and clean."

"I didn't know how to cook before this happened—I don't think I need to learn now."

Martha, who had been sitting quietly next to Emily, interjected. "Everyone needs to know how to make a few basic meals. It'll be good for you."

"You won't be the first person who learned this way." His voice contained a smile. "Most importantly, you'll receive orientation and mobility training."

"What's that?" Emily asked.

"It's also known as white cane training."

Emily jerked back into her chair. "NO! I'm not blind and I don't need a white cane."

Martha reached over and took her daughter's hand.

Emily snatched it away from her. "As I said, I'm not going to be blind."

"I remain hopeful that your vision will improve and, as I've said, we can consider additional procedures if it doesn't. But right now—today—you are considered legally blind."

Emily recoiled further from his words. She choked on her breath and tears slid down her cheeks.

"I'm so very sorry. It's always a shock for people when they hear it out loud."

"I … I don't know what I'm going to do … how I'm going to live if my eyesight doesn't get any better than it is right now."

"That's why it's important to get you enrolled with the state program as soon as possible. In my experience, blind people who go through training lead lives as full and happy as anyone else."

"How's that possible? They're so many things they can't do," Emily said.

"To quote one of my former patients, the only things a blind person can't do is drive or fly an airplane."

Emily sat, motionless.

Martha reached again for her hand and, this time, Emily didn't pull away.

"Think about it," the doctor said. "I'll send the paperwork to the state this afternoon."

Martha cleared her throat. "In the meantime, can Emily come home to live with me? So that I can take care of her while she's recovering?"

"I don't want to be a burden …"

"You're my daughter—you'll never be a burden."

"How long does all this training take?" Emily asked.

"That depends on each person, but anywhere from eight to eighteen months."

"You see," Martha said. "It would work out perfectly."

"I don't know, Mom. I just got married. Connor's not going to want me to be away from him that long."

"Talk to your husband and let me know. I think it's the best next step for you, Emily."

R

"I'm so sorry I didn't make it to your appointment," Connor said, entering their bedroom. "I was in the middle of a meeting with this prospect that I've been working on for more than a year."

Emily stood on the other side of the room, her back to him.

"You didn't say anything about the meeting this morning before you left."

"They called right before lunch to say that they were ready to sign the contract this afternoon."

She spun on him. "You should have let me know. I kept waiting for you to show up at the doctor's office."

"I was so excited that they were finally going to sign that I ... I forgot to call." He blew out a breath. "I'm really sorry, Em. That was thoughtless of me. I knew your mom would be there and that you'd be okay."

Emily remained silent.

"I wanted to win this business because it'll make me the top sales rep in the West. I'll win us a spot on the trip to Costa Rica. It'll make up for our honeymoon."

She forced the words. "Congratulations. That's ... terrific."

"I hear Costa Rica is gorgeous. And I promise—we won't go horseback riding."

His mention of the incident that had caused her current anguished state felt like a slap in the face. "I won't be going to Costa Rica with you," she snapped.

"Why? It's not for another four months."

"I may not have recovered my eyesight by then." Her voice went up an octave.

"You said the doctor told you that your retinas are reattached and that it might take a couple of months for your vision to come back completely."

"That's what they said but it's not getting better. AT ALL." She screamed the last words at him. "The doctor said that everything looks normal but that I might have had permanent nerve damage when the retina tore. It may never improve."

"You didn't tell me that," he snapped back. He raked his fingers through his hair. "Damn, Em. I'm so sorry. Can they operate again?"

"Maybe. He didn't hold out much hope on that score."

"So what does he advise?"

"That we should give it time—and I should start learning to use a white cane in the meantime."

"You're … you're kidding, right?"

Emily couldn't block her sobs. "Of course I'm not kidding. I wouldn't be joking about this."

"I know. I … I'm sorry." He came to her side.

"I don't want a damned white cane. I want to see again." Emily continued to cry, giving way to her grief and fear.

Connor pulled her to him and encircled her with his arms. He rocked her gently as she cried. "I understand. But if the doctors recommend it, maybe you should try. How long will this white cane training take?"

"It's not just learning to get around with a white cane. I'll also train in the various assistive technologies. That'll help with my job. It'll take almost a year."

"That long? Maybe your eyes will get better before then."

Emily leaned her forehead against his chest. "That's what I'm hoping. So you think we should wait?"

"No. That's not what I meant. If the doctor thinks it's time, it's time. Where can you get this training?"

"The doctor is going to connect me with a rehabilitation specialist from the state. He works with blind people and will help me find a place. I hope there's one near us."

"Isn't the Foundation for the Blind near your mom's house?"

"Yes, less than a mile. I've driven by it my whole life."

"Do they teach this stuff?"

"Mom thinks so. But it's over an hour from our condo."

"What about your job?"

"I don't know, Connor." Emily sank to the side of their bed and cradled her head in her hands. "I don't know anything about my life right now."

Connor sat next to her, pulling her back into his arms. "You know you're married to me and that I love you."

"I'm totally dependent on other people. I hate this." She pounded the mattress with her fists.

He chose his words carefully. "We need to figure out how we're going to handle the logistics of … everything."

"You mean who's going to take care of me?" She spat the words.

"No … Em … I just meant that I have to keep on working. And I travel a lot. I'm out of town all next week." He laid a hand gently on her back. "Can your mom stay longer?"

"We talked about that on the way home from the doctor. If I get my training at the Foundation for the Blind, Mom suggested that I live with her. While I'm learning," her voice broke again, "to be a blind person."

"That might be best," Connor replied, barely able to conceal his relief. "This condo is too small for the three of us—especially if it takes a year. She has a nice yard, too. You'll be less cooped up with her."

"That's exactly what she said." Emily sniffled. "So, you don't mind?"

"I'll hate being away from you, but I think it's the best scenario." He smoothed her hair. "Since you didn't move in before we got married, I'm accustomed to living alone. I'll work like crazy all week and come out to spend the weekends with you."

"You promise? I'm so scared, Connor." Her voice was barely audible. "I need you to be with me."

"I promise," he said. "When will you leave?"

"She was hoping to go home tomorrow. We thought I'd be recovered by now. She has doctor's appointments scheduled that she'd like to keep."

"So go home with her tomorrow."

Emily slumped against him. "I guess that's best. We'll need to pack my clothes."

"I'll ask Martha to do that."

"Don't you think you could help me?"

"She'll be better at it than I am, Em." He cleared his throat. "I remembered when I was driving home that I forgot to put a new bottle of shampoo in the shower. Did you notice? Was that a problem?"

Emily drew a deep breath. "It … was …"

"A problem, wasn't it? I'm a crappy caretaker, Em. That's all there is to it. I'm so sorry." He dropped his hands to his knees.

She swallowed the rebuke on her tongue. "It's not your strong suit, but you never had anyone show you how. Your parents didn't take very good care of you. Don't worry—you'll learn. And, hopefully, I'll get my sight back, so it won't matter."

"You'll definitely be better off with your mom."

"But we'll be together this weekend?"

Connor cleared his throat. "This weekend may be a problem. I've been invited to play in a golf tournament on Saturday that our new client is sponsoring, and I fly out to the East Coast on Sunday morning."

Emily swallowed hard. "Sounds like you need to keep these commitments."

"I do. It's just this weekend," he said. "I'll keep my calendar clear for all the others. And we'll talk on the phone every night."

"Okay," Emily said, choking back tears. "Can you ask Mom to come in so she can pack for me? I'm exhausted. I'd like to get some sleep before we leave in the morning."

Chapter 14

My new favorite time is After School. It happened for the first time on the day I arrived at Katie and Jon's, and most days after that.

I'd spent the rest of the morning connected to Katie. She took me to my water bowl and to a patch of grass in the backyard that I came to learn was my own special area. Before long I had it smelling just the way I wanted it to.

During that first day, Katie did something she called working from home. I lay on a cushy rug under her desk and—although I tried to resist it—fell asleep.

I woke up when the front door crashed open and two smaller versions of Katie and Jon ran into the house, hollering, "Is he here yet?"

"He sure is," Katie called to them. "Lower your voices and calm down. He's just a puppy." She picked me up and pressed me tightly to her chest. "He's all tuckered out from the journey here and he's been asleep almost from the moment he got here."

I knew that last bit wasn't quite true but didn't hold that against her. She smelled good and gave me treats. I'd overlook the exaggeration.

She knelt on one knee and the two small humans went to her. "This is Garth," she said, ruffling my ears. "Garth—these are my children, Abby and Alex."

Alex began to pet my back.

Abby threw her arms around me.

I wagged my tail and whipped my tongue out, licking whatever was in its path.

Abby squealed.

"Can we take him out and play with him?"

"Sure. For a little while. Remember—Garth's not like the other dogs we've had. He's going to be a guide when he grows up.

My ears perked up.

"We've got to follow all the rules of puppy raisers. No chasing a ball, no table scraps, no aggressive play."

"We know, Mom," Alex said.

"Eat your snacks and then you can take him out back for fifteen minutes. Before you do your homework."

Alex and Abby turned on their heels and headed to the kitchen. Katie set me on the floor, and we went with them.

What followed was a tsunami of delicious scents and crumbs dropping to the floor. I traced the trajectory of a bright orange cylinder rolling off the countertop toward me, and I lunged for it—in one beautiful, graceful motion—and caught it in my open mouth and swallowed. In that moment, a true love was born. Cheetos. Crunchy Cheetos. I would love this forbidden fruit all my life.

I'd no sooner swallowed when Katie corrected me and told me no.

Why in the world not? They are delicious—really. And, as I later learned, people won't eat food that falls on the floor. One of them will get down on their hands and knees to clean it up, but I'd be happy to do that for them—whether it's a Crunchy Cheeto or not. It makes no sense that they won't let me, but I've never been able to convince them otherwise.

After the Cheetos business, I sulked under the counter, but no one seemed to notice. When Alex and Abby had finished their snacks—and Katie had laboriously completed the cleanup tasks that would have taken me a nanosecond—she unclipped the leash that kept me tethered to her. I was free to go into the backyard with the kids.

Besides my special area, there was a swing set and two boxed-off areas. One was filled with sand. The other one was full of wonderful-smelling plants. A row along the back was decorated with heavy and fragrant soft red balls.

Surely it would be all right if I tried one? I poked at them with my nose, looking for the softest one. I tugged at it and the ball came loose from the plant.

Katie was standing in the doorway. I figured I'd better check. I trotted over to her, the red ball held loosely between my teeth. I looked up at her and wagged my tail.

"Garth," she said. "No! That's a tomato—one of my prize tomatoes. Those aren't for you."

I set it gently at her feet. I was beginning to get the idea that most stuff around here was not for me.

"Good boy," she said and reached into her pocket and gave me a treat. I almost forgot my disappointment over the tomato.

Abby approached with a large mallard duck sewn out of heavy fabric. "Is this one of his toys?" she asked, pointing to me.

"It sure is."

"Can I give it to him?"

"You certainly can," Katie said. "This one's got a real instinct for finding things that aren't his." She bent and petted my back. "Let's offer him something he's supposed to have and give him plenty of love and praise at the same time."

"I can do that," Abby said. She held the duck out to me. I'd never seen a more unappealing thing in my life, but she was a sweet girl. I wanted to humor her, so I grabbed the duck firmly between my teeth and bit down. The duck squeaked.

Abby chortled.

I wagged my tail and squeaked it again.

Abby clapped her hands. "That's a good boy," she said. "A very good boy."

In the end, being "a very good boy" was enough for me.

Chapter 15

Emily lowered her foot to the uneven wooden slats that formed the floor of her mother's front porch. She stopped the motion of the glider, as she'd done countless times growing up in the comfortable Craftsman-style bungalow. She bent forward, listening hard, while the old contraption rattled to a stop.

She sat motionless, turning her left ear toward the steps leading to the porch. Everything was quiet. A truck rumbled by at the end of the block.

Emily was relaxing into the back of her seat when she heard it, again. A soft footfall—she was sure of it. Someone else was on the porch.

"Who's there?" she almost screamed. "I know you're there!"

"It's me," came a small voice from the area at the top of the steps. "Zoe. From next door."

Emily swung her face toward the voice.

"I live with my grandma now," she said, as if that explained everything.

Emily swallowed hard. "Hi, Zoe. You scared me."

"I didn't mean to. You're blind. Gramma told me."

Emily felt her face flush. Was that what she was now? The blind woman?

"I'm real sorry. I saw you sitting out here, so I decided to come over to cheer you up. Gramma says you're sad."

Emily heard Zoe walk to the glider. Her mother had told her about the little girl whose parents were killed in a car accident and now lived with her grandmother Irene, next door. There wasn't another child for her to play with in this neighborhood of mostly retired people, and Zoe rode her bike up and down the street every afternoon until dinner time. It seemed Emily wasn't the only one on this street who was coping with tragedy.

Zoe bounced against the glider with her thighs.

Emily scooted over and patted the cushion next to her.

Zoe climbed onto the glider.

Emily pushed off with her foot and the glider creaked into motion.

"This is fun," Zoe said. "Is that why you sit out here? What do you do all day when you're blind?"

Emily lifted one hand to her temple. Did she really have the energy for this conversation? "Don't you have homework to do?"

"All done. It was simple. I'm in all the advanced sections. Third grade is really easy."

"I get that. School was always easy for me, too."

"Gramma said you had an accident and got blind."

Emily felt her throat contract. Could she say the words? "Yes. That's what happened."

"That sucks. What will you do now?"

"I had an operation on each eye and they'll probably get better. In the meantime, I have to learn to live as a blind person."

"How do you do that?" The glider was slowing to a stop, and Zoe thrust her foot against the floor, giving it a big push.

"There are schools that teach you things, like how to walk with a white cane and how to use special computers."

"That's supercool! So you'll be going to school, like me?"

Emily hesitated. "I guess I will."

They rocked back and forth in silence.

"So … what's your favorite subject?" Emily asked.

"Math," Zoe said. "I'm the best in the entire third grade. Gramma says that's really good—that the high-paying jobs are for people who know math."

"I was good in math, too," Emily said. "I'm a computer programmer." Or at least she had been a computer programmer. "Do you know what that is?"

"Nope."

Emily explained. "So I head up a team of other programmers. I love my job and have the best team in the business."

"Can you go back to work?"

Could she? "I hope so."

Zoe put her hand over Emily's, and they continued to swing.

"What do you want to be when you grow up?" Emily asked.

"Either an engineer or an ice cream maker," Zoe said.

"Those are ... two very good options."

"I think it would be supercool to come up with ice cream flavors," Zoe said. "You'd get to eat a lot of ice cream to do that."

"I'm sure you would," Emily said.

They were interrupted by Irene, Zoe's grandmother, calling to her from their front door.

"It's dinner. I gotta go. Can I come over tomorrow, when I'm done with my homework? If you're out here? I like talking to you."

Something in the plaintive voice touched Emily's heart. "On one condition," Emily said. She swiveled to turn her face to Zoe. "That you tell me that it's you when you start coming up the stairs."

"Okay."

"It's scary when someone enters a room when you're blind. You can't tell who they are."

"I understand. I'll yell my name when I'm at the bottom of the steps," Zoe said.

"That'll be perfect," Emily said, stopping the glider to allow her new friend to slip off and run home.

R

A car pulled into Martha's driveway shortly before dinnertime on Friday.

"Who's that?" Emily asked Zoe as they sat on the glider.

"I dunno," Zoe said. "Some man. He's handsome."

Emily's heart skipped a beat. "How old?"

"Old," Zoe said. "Maybe your age."

Emily laughed. "That old, huh?" She put her foot down and stopped their swinging. She recognized the cadence of his footsteps before he called her name.

Emily held out her arms, and Connor lifted her to her feet and into his arms, kissing her firmly and long.

Zoe tapped her foot on the floor.

Emily pushed back from Connor. "This is Zoe," she said. "She lives with her grandmother next door. Zoe, this is my husband."

"Connor," he said. "Nice to meet you. Emily told me you've become friends."

Zoe scooted to the edge of the glider and stood. "I've got to go home. See you, Emily."

"Okay, sweetie," Emily said. "Have fun tomorrow at that birthday party you were telling me about. And don't worry about not knowing many of the kids. You'll be fine."

Zoe slipped around Connor and raced down the steps.

"What're you doing here?" Emily asked. "I thought we agreed you were going to play in your client's golf tournament tomorrow."

"I am. I couldn't stand the thought of not seeing you all weekend, so I decided to sneak out of the office early and drive down. Take you out to dinner. I've got my clubs with me. I'll get up early to make my eight o'clock tee time."

Emily ran her hand up and down his arm. "That's very … thoughtful of you."

"What's wrong? Aren't you glad to see me?"

"Of course I am! It's not that."

"Then what?"

"I haven't been out anywhere—other than the doctor—since …"

"I thought you might be going stir crazy. We don't have to go anywhere fancy. Maybe just grab a burger? A place close to here offers one that's supposed to be in the top ten in the country—it uses bison. I read about it."

She inhaled slowly. "I guess that'll be fine."

"You'll be with me the whole time. What could happen to you?"

"You're right. I'll be fine."

"I'll go say hi to your mom—let her know that we're going out."

"Ask if she wants us to bring her something back," Emily said.

"Good idea. Do you need anything from inside?"

"No. I'm good. I'll wait here."

Connor returned to the porch a few minutes later. "Your mom said to go and have a good time. She's going to warm up some leftovers and go to bed early."

Emily positioned Connor on her right and put her hand on his left shoulder. "Good. I know that she's exhausted, taking care of me."

"She didn't say that," Connor said.

"Still—I know it's true."

He led them to his car and helped her get seated. "She's happy to do it."

"I hate being so dependent."

"It isn't going to be like this forever," he said. "Going out to dinner with me is a good first step."

R

Emily turned her face to the right. She couldn't see the window, but she could feel the sun on her face through the glass.

Connor made the short drive and left his car with the valet.

"I guess they're really busy tonight," he said. "I hope we don't have to wait long for a table."

Emily clung to his shoulder as he angled his way into the crowded restaurant. She couldn't hear whatever Connor was saying to the host.

He turned back to her and took her hand in his. He steered her a short distance until she felt a wall behind her back. Connor put his lips against her ear. "I gave the guy a twenty. We'll get the next table."

Emily squeezed his hand. Someone brushed by them, treading on her toes. She yelped and pulled her foot back.

"Hey," Connor said. "Watch it. Are you all right?" he asked Emily.

"Fine. No big deal," she replied. She grasped her hair with her left hand and held it away from her neck. Sweat was beginning to trickle into her collar. The sooner they got out of this hubbub, the better.

A male voice called, "Connor?"

He placed his hand on the small of her back, and they followed the host to their table.

Connor held a chair for her. Emily ran her hands over the back and the seat, then settled into it.

A waiter approached their table with menus.

Connor reached for both of them as the waiter began to offer one to Emily. "I'll take that," he said. "She's …" He stopped abruptly.

Emily tilted her face to the table.

"We don't need menus," he said, handing them back to the waiter. "Shall we have the award-winning bison burger?" he asked Emily.

"Sure," she said. Their table was in a quiet section of the dining room. She began to relax. "I'll have a Diet Coke," she told the waiter.

Connor ordered the same.

"Is this okay?" he asked.

Emily smiled. "Yes. You were right. I need to learn to go out."

Their drinks arrived, and she took a sip. "Tell me about work," she said. "We've only been talking about me when you call."

"That's understandable," he said.

"I want to hear all about you," she said.

Connor filled her in on the prospects he had in the pipeline and a new deal he was hoping to close.

Their burgers arrived, the rich aroma of caramelized onion rising from the plates. They dug in.

"The company's opening an office in Tokyo," he said. "Later this quarter."

"That's promising," she said. "They must be doing well. Who's going to staff it?"

"Nothing's been announced."

"I'd like to go to the ladies' room," Emily said. She extended her hand to him. "You'll have to take me."

Connor stood and guided her to the door. "Do you need me to get someone to go in with you?"

"No. I can feel my way along the wall to the stall."

"Okay," he replied.

Emily entered the small restroom to find that there were two women standing right inside the door, chatting.

"Are you in line?" she asked.

"Yes," one of the women said.

Emily stood behind them.

When she emerged from the restroom, holding her hands out in front of her, she swung her head from side to side, searching for Connor in the dim interior. The pinhole of vision was useless.

Her pulse began to race, the noisy restaurant drowned out by the pounding of her heart. She was growing lightheaded and reached a clammy hand behind her, feeling for the wall. A wave of nausea swept over her. She gulped for air but couldn't get her breath.

She turned sharply, searching for the way back to the restroom when a strong pair of hands grabbed her. Her name floated out above the roaring in her ears.

It was Connor. Connor had her.

He put his face in front of hers. "Sweetheart! Are you all right?" He swept the hair off her damp forehead.

She shook her head.

"What's wrong?"

"I felt like I was going to die."

He looked into the eyes that couldn't see him. "You're not going to die. Do you want to get out of here?"

She nodded.

Connor put his arm around her shoulders and held her to him as they made their way out the door. They paused at the hostess stand. "My wife isn't feeling well," he said. "I didn't have time to get our bill. This will take care of it," he said as he handed the hostess a small stack of bills.

"Thank you," she said, but they were already out the door.

Emily leaned against Connor as they waited for their car to be brought around.

"Feeling better?" he asked as she gulped the cool night air.

"A little."

"I think you had a panic attack," he said quietly when they were on their way home.

"I think you're right," Emily said. "I've never had one before, but I've heard about them. God, it was horrible. I was certain I was going to die."

"But you didn't."

"I know. But I don't think I can ever go into a restaurant again."

"That's not true," he said. "I shouldn't have taken you out. It was too soon."

"Don't blame yourself," Emily said.

"But it's my fault. I moved because I was standing in the way of the kitchen staff. I should have stayed where I was. I should have been there when you came out of the restroom. I'm so sorry, Em. I'm so sorry."

"Let's just go home and go to bed. I'm exhausted. All I want to do is go to sleep."

"Whatever you want. I'm sorry I made things worse."

Chapter 16

"You've got a visitor," Martha said, leading the way to her living room.

"Hi, Emily," came the familiar voice as he stood in front of the chair where she was reclining and listening to a cooking show on television.

"Dhruv! What in the world are you doing here?"

"They said you're on FMLA, and they don't know when you'll be back. We all have to work extra hours to make up for your being gone."

"I'm sorry about that," Emily said. "Won't they give you a temporary manager or someone else to share the workload?"

"No. We don't want anyone else."

"You may have to, Dhruv."

"We don't want anyone else."

Emily sighed. She'd worked with Dhruv long enough to realize that he couldn't be moved off of an idea once it had taken root in his mind.

"How did you know I'd be at my mother's house?"

"I asked Connor."

"Okay. That still doesn't tell me why you're here." Emily sucked in a breath. "I can't see a computer screen. If you need help with something, you'll have to go to someone else."

"I don't need help. I talked to your mom. She says you do."

"There's nothing you can do."

"You need training for the blind. I researched it online, and there are several top-notch programs in our area."

"The state will make those connections for me."

"The state will take too long. You need to start learning now. I called all the places in the county."

"That wasn't necessary."

"The best one is the Foundation for the Blind."

Emily pulled a strand of her hair out of her messy bun and began to twirl it. "The foundation is right down the street—I've driven by it for years—but we have to wait for the state to set things up."

"No, we don't."

"I can't just march in there and demand training."

"I called and found out. You can start any time. And their assistive technology program is state of the art."

"Thank you for all of this information," Emily said, raising from her chair. "You could have called me with it."

"I'm going to take you to visit."

"Who?"

"The Foundation for the Blind. I asked Martha, and she said that would be helpful. She said you're depressed, and you don't want to do anything."

Emily prickled with irritation. "I'll check them out when I'm ready."

"Are you ready now?"

"No. I'm … busy. And I'm sure we'll need an appointment."

"I made an appointment."

"For today?"

"Yes. For after work. I went in early today and worked through lunch."

"That was very nice of you—but not necessary."

"Let's go."

"I'm not going. I don't want to. This is a lot to adjust to. I need more time." Emily was on the verge of tears.

Dhruv made his way back to the door. "Okay. I'll call them. We'll go tomorrow after work."

"No. Don't make any more appointments. I said I'll go when I'm ready."

"That's taking too long. What did you always tell us at work? Sometimes you have to push a project through."

"That doesn't apply to me and my situation," Emily said in exasperation. "I'm not your project."

"See you tomorrow," Dhruv said as he walked to the door.

"It takes you at least an hour to get here in rush hour—probably longer. Don't waste your time."

"I'm coming back," he said and shut the door behind him.

"What the hell, Mom? Why did you let him come here?"

"As you once told me, that is one very determined man."

"This isn't his business. And he's a programmer, not a retina specialist."

"He's a brilliant man who's concerned about you. He's being a good friend. You need someone to help you."

"I've got you, Mom."

"And you're not listening to me."

Emily sank back into the chair and turned away from Martha toward the television set. She wondered if her mother thought that Connor should be doing the investigation that Dhruv was doing for her. At this point she didn't have the energy or interest to fight with her mother.

"He'll be back tomorrow."

"I'm still not going," Emily said to the screen.

Her mother placed a hand on her shoulder. "That's your choice, but I think he's going to keep coming back until you do."

Emily shrugged her off and sighed.

"My dear, I think you've met someone who's more tenacious than you are. And … for the record … I think he's right. You should start training as soon as possible."

Chapter 17

I did not eat Alex's homework. At least, I didn't intend to. The whole incident was blown way out of proportion. I circled the inside of my crate twice, then lay down—with my back to all of them. My feelings were hurt, and they needed to know it.

Here's what really happened.

Alex was sitting on a tall stool at the kitchen island. He was supposed to be doing his homework, but he was mostly eating those crackers that look like little fishes and drinking something fizzy from a tall glass filled with ice.

I wedged myself between his feet and the island, my attention focused on the edge of the counter. Just in case one of those fish crackers needed to be cleaned up from the floor.

Katie warned him about that fizzy stuff—to move it out of his way.

Alex mumbled something back to his mother and kept on slurping and eating.

Katie left the kitchen.

Abby ran in, snatching the bag of crackers from the counter and tearing out of the room.

"Hey," Alex shouted, "those are mine!" He shoved his stool back from the island and tore after his sister, scattering his homework papers and overturning his drink. Fizzy liquid flooded the countertop, sending ice cubes and paper over the island's edge like barrels going over Niagara Falls.

I started to get out of the way but then realized I could be helpful. I lapped up the sweet liquid from the floor. The fizziness burned my tongue—but in a way I found oddly appealing.

I ran my tongue along the edge of the island, but I didn't raise up on my hind legs to lap up the pool of fish crackers on the counter. I knew I wasn't allowed to do what Katie calls "counter surfing."

When I finished cleaning the liquid from the floor, I turned my attention to the ice cubes. They were terrific! The coldness felt wonderful on my gums, and they crunched with a satisfying *thwack* that resulted in a refreshing sip of water. Brilliant invention, ice cubes.

I was moving the papers—Alex's homework papers—aside, looking for more ice cubes, when Katie and Alex returned to the kitchen.

Alex rushed to me and dropped to his knees, tearing the papers out of my teeth. "Garth! You stupid dog!" He rocked back onto his heels and held the papers out to me. "Bad dog, Garth. Bad dog."

Katie came to his side and took the papers from him. "Not yours," she said to me, holding them under my nose. "Not yours."

I slunk backward. I knew they weren't mine. I was looking for ice cubes. I'd been cleaning up Alex's mess. In my humble opinion, I'd been a very good dog.

"And you, young man," Katie stood and pulled Alex to his feet, "shouldn't have had that drink where you could knock it over and ruin your homework."

"Now what'm I going to do?" he cried.

"You're going to clean up this mess on the counter and do your homework again."

"All of it?"

"Let's see what we can salvage," Katie said, grabbing a roll of paper towels. She and Alex set to work.

If that's all the thanks I was going to get, they could do it themselves. Back in my crate, I put my head on my paws and let my eyelids grow heavy. I was almost asleep when I heard a tinkling sound and opened my eyes.

Katie deposited a handful of ice cubes near my nose.

"Here you go, Garth," she said. "This wasn't all your fault. Sorry you got the blame."

I lifted my eyes to hers and wagged my tail to let her know I understood that some things can be difficult to sort out. I snatched one of the delicious frozen treats with my teeth and began to chew.

Chapter 18

Martha walked Dhruv to her front door.

"Dinner was good." Dhruv smiled at her. "I like chicken."

"I'm glad. Feeding you is the least I can do, since you've come out here every night for the last two weeks."

Dhruv reached for the doorknob.

"I … I don't think she's going to go with you," Martha said.

"She will."

"I don't know why you say that. She hasn't come out to see you this entire week. She barely leaves her room at all. She sleeps and listens to the television all day long."

"That's not good."

"I know that," Martha said. "I've talked to her until I'm blue in the face." She sighed heavily. "Her rehabilitation specialist from the state gave me a list of resources that could help her. I've read them to her, and it's like she doesn't hear me."

Tears began to spill down Martha's cheeks. She fished in the pocket of her apron for a tissue. "She's depressed, and I don't know how to get her out of it. I feel so helpless." She lifted her eyes to his. "I'm scared."

"What about Connor?"

Martha sucked in her breath. "He calls her everyday—that's the one thing that she looks forward to. But they only talk for a few minutes. He's always so busy, racing from meeting to meeting. I think he's in denial about how serious this is."

Dhruv remained still, his focus on Martha.

"I don't think he's once asked her about how she's coping with all of this. He came out here the first weekend, and it was a disaster. Emily had a panic attack while they were out, and it scared both of them. It's like they both want to ignore what happened." She dabbed at her eyes and blew her nose. "You're a good listener," she said. "Thank you."

Dhruv shuffled his feet. "Tell Emily I'll be back tomorrow."

Martha opened the door and shook her head slowly as she watched him walk to his car.

R

Dhruv stepped into Martha's living room at the same time the following day.

"I'm here for Emily," he said, as he had done every day for the past two weeks.

"I'm afraid she's not going to see you," Martha said. "She said to tell you to stop coming. And she gave me this—to give to you." She handed him a sealed envelope. "She asked me for paper and a pen this morning."

"Do you know what this is?"

Martha shook her head. "I tried to see but she was very guarded with it. Took her almost all morning. She asked me for an envelope when I brought lunch to her. She'd folded it up and put it right into the envelope and sealed it."

Dhruv tapped the envelope against his open palm.

"She said you're to give it to her boss."

Dhruv nodded. "Okay." He turned back to the door.

"Would you like to stay for dinner? I've got plenty."

"No. Tell Emily I'll be back tomorrow."

Chapter 19

Martha opened the front door before Connor had a chance to knock. She stepped onto the porch and threw her arms around him, drawing him in for a hug. "I'm so glad you're here," she whispered into his ear.

Connor wasn't entirely comfortable with the American penchant for hugging but did his best to reciprocate. "Is she still holed up in her room?"

Martha nodded against his shoulder. "Yep. She gets up to use the bathroom and goes right back to bed. I thought maybe today would be different because she took a shower. She doesn't most days, you know. I think she wanted to clean herself up because you were coming." She leaned back and looked into the face of her son-in-law. "I intercepted her on the way back to her room and tried to convince her to spend the day with me on the front porch. The weather has been beautiful."

"No-go?"

Martha shook her head again. "No-go. She didn't even answer me. Just went right back to bed."

"Is she taking the medication they gave her for depression?"

"I give it to her every day. I think she's taking it—unless she's hiding it under her tongue and spitting it out later."

"That doesn't sound like something Em would do."

"I don't think so, either."

"I've had an idea," he said, stepping back and rubbing his hands together. "I'm hoping it will cheer her up."

Martha's eyebrows shot up. "What have you got up your sleeve?"

"We never opened our wedding presents. Doesn't every bride love to open gifts?"

"I would think so! There was quite a pile of them in the corner of your living room. I remember seeing them while I was helping Emily after her surgeries."

"I loaded them all up and brought them with me. I thought it was high time we opened our gifts and sent out our thank-you notes."

"Terrific idea!"

Connor turned back to his car. "I'll start bringing them inside."

"Do you need help?"

"No. I've got it. Can you tell Em that I'm here?"

"Will do," Martha said. "I'll let you tell her about your surprise."

Martha stepped back into the house and headed for Emily's bedroom.

"Mom," Emily said from her perch on the living room sofa.

"When did you get up?" Martha asked, clutching her chest. "You scared the daylights out of me."

"I heard Connor's car in the driveway," Emily said. "I came out here to meet him."

"Did you hear our conversation?"

"About the wedding presents?"

"Well … what do you think? Doesn't that sound like fun?"

"Running my hands over all the beautiful things I'm never going to see? Yeah … that sounds like fun."

"Oh, Em. Please don't be like this. Connor's trying so hard to do something nice for you. Don't spoil it for him."

Emily jerked her face away from her mother.

"I'm sorry. This is hard on all of us."

"But mostly me," Emily said quietly.

Connor, arms loaded with elaborately wrapped gifts, lumbered up the steps. "Martha—can you open the door?" he called.

"I'll be nice, Mom. I know he's trying. You both are."

"Good," Martha said as she stepped to the door and held it open.

"Hi, sweetheart." Connor placed the packages on the floor next to the sofa and sat next to Emily, drawing her to him. He lifted her chin and kissed her tenderly. "I've missed you."

"Oh, Connor," she whispered. "Me, too."

"We've got all weekend together," Connor said. "And we don't have to leave the house unless you want to. In fact, we may be too busy to leave the house."

Emily gave a dry laugh. "What're you talking about?"

"Remember how you told me that you always prided yourself on sending out timely thank-you notes?"

"Well ... yes."

"We've got a whole stack of unopened wedding gifts that need to be dealt with. We wouldn't want the etiquette police to throw you in manners jail."

"That's for sure," Emily said with a hint of her old cheerfulness.

"So I packed them all in the car and brought them with me. I thought we could unwrap them together. You can dictate thank-you notes, and I'll have them transcribed. I'll sign our names and pop them into the mail. Voila! Your reputation as a thank-you note writer remains untarnished."

"That works. Very ingenious!"

Martha had been standing to one side, taking comfort in her daughter's more cheerful countenance. "I've got some paperwork to catch up on. I'll be in my room if you need me," she said.

"Why don't we open a few of them now?" Connor asked. "Would you like to stay for that? Isn't it an American custom for close family to be present when the bride and groom open their gifts?

"I wouldn't want to intrude ..." Martha said.

"We want you to stay, Mom. You can make sure Connor doesn't throw away any instruction booklets as he is so prone to do." Emily poked him in the ribs with her elbow.

"I have no idea what you're talking about," Connor retorted playfully. "I haven't done that more than a dozen times."

"If you're certain I won't be in the way," Martha said. "I'd love to see what you got. I'm sure they're all the latest things."

Connor scooped up a large box and put it on the coffee table in front of Emily. "This one's really heavy. I'm curious about what it could be."

Emily extended her hand and felt around the package for the bow. She tugged at the ribbon but couldn't get it to budge.

"I'll get scissors," Martha said, hopping up and heading for her sewing basket on an end table across the room. "Some people wrap so securely that it's like breaking into Fort Knox to get the package open." She extended the scissors toward Emily.

Emily reached toward her mother.

Connor intercepted the scissors. "Here. Let me do that," he said, cutting the ribbon.

"I can still operate a pair of scissors," Emily snapped.

"I know that," Connor said. "I was just trying to be helpful."

Emily tore the wrapping paper off the box. "What is it?"

Connor lifted the box onto his lap and turned it around. "It's that fancy espresso maker we registered for," he said.

"Really? That was so expensive. It must be from a group of people."

Martha retrieved the card that had fallen to the floor and handed it to Connor.

"It's from my office," he said, reading the card aloud.

"That's very nice of them," Emily said. "I remember it being complicated to operate. I may never …" her voice cracked, "learn to operate it now."

"Nonsense," he said. "You'll be barista-level proficient before you know it."

Emily turned her face aside.

"How about this one?" Martha said, holding out a rectangular box in the signature blue color of a famous jeweler. She told Emily about the box. "I can't wait to see what's in here."

"Who's it from?" Emily asked.

Connor opened the small enclosure card. "It's from Dhruv."

"Wow … that's so nice!" She untied the ribbon and opened the lid. Nestled in a molded foam interior was an exquisite crystal vase.

Martha gasped. "Oh, my. It's stunning."

Emily ran her hands over the object. "A crystal vase, right?"

"Yes," Connor and Martha said in unison.

"He's always noticed the fresh flowers on my desk at work," Emily said.

"That's what he said on the card," Connor said.

"How thoughtful," Emily said, pulling it carefully from the box. She let the wrapping slip from her lap and leaned over to place the vase on the coffee table. She didn't notice that she caught the tip of the scissor blade under the bottom of the vase. It teetered precariously.

Connor lunged for it but wasn't in time. The beautiful vase fell to the tabletop and crashed into a million pieces.

"NO!" Emily screamed. "NO!" She lunged at the tabletop.

Connor forced her back into the sofa. "Don't!—you'll cut yourself."

Emily put her face in her hands. "I can't believe I did that."

"It was an accident, honey," Martha said. "I'll get the vacuum cleaner. Don't worry about a thing."

"We'll get another one—exactly like it. We know where he got it. I'll go online tonight to order a new vase. He'll never know."

Emily began to cry. "What's the point? I'll just break it again. And I can't see it anyway. I can't have nice things anymore."

"You're blowing this out of proportion. It was just an accident. That scissor was hidden under discarded wrapping paper. I could have done the same thing."

"But you didn't," Emily said.

Martha returned with the vacuum. "There—all cleaned up. Let's get back to work."

Emily raised her hands in protest. "I'm done. I don't want to ruin anything else."

"Let's stop for tonight," Connor said. "We can do the rest tomorrow."

"No! Don't you listen? I'm not going to open any more of these stupid gifts." Emily stood and stepped around him, heading to her room.

"What about the thank-you notes?" Connor asked. "I can open them, and you can dictate ..."

"I don't give a damn about any of this," Emily said. "If you need help, ask Gina. I'm sure she'd dictate them for you. In fact—why don't you give all of this stuff to her? I can't see any of it, anyway."

"You don't mean that," he said.

Emily continued to her room in silence.

R

"You're sure she wants us to open these?" Gina asked Connor.

"You talked to her yourself, didn't you?"

"Yes ... but I can't believe it. She's still recovering, and there's a chance that she'll get her sight back. Why don't you wait a while longer?"

"That's what I said. I tried to talk her out of it the rest of the weekend, but she was insistent."

"I just don't know. Even if she doesn't recover her vision, she could open these. The vase sounds like a freak accident."

"Exactly. But she kept saying that it made her feel incompetent." Connor raked his fingers through his hair. "Honestly, Gina, all I want to do is be helpful and make Em feel better, but I always end up doing the exact opposite. It's like I can't do anything right."

"I'm sure that's not true. This is a confusing time for all of us."

"Martha says the same thing," Connor said.

"There—you see. We're all in the same boat."

"Except we're not all in the same boat. You don't seem to do or say the wrong thing."

"That's only because I've known her for so much longer than you have, Connor. You're newlyweds. Isn't there an adjustment period? You've got that, plus the tragedy of her vision loss. There's bound to be stress associated with all of it."

"I can see why Emily loves you so much, Gina. Your words always comfort me."

Gina felt herself flush.

"One thing I'm sure of," she said, "the Emily I know would be appalled if her thank-you notes weren't out on time. I think we can proceed on that basis alone."

"Okay—let's get started. I've stashed the gifts in the hall closet."

"Why don't you bring them to the middle of the living room? We'll move this coffee table aside and sit on the floor. There's plenty of room. You open the card and read it to me while I tear into the gift. I'll dictate each thank-you note as we go."

"Sounds efficient."

"Yep—entirely paperless. We'll be done in no time."

"You haven't seen the stack."

"No matter. I'm here until we finish."

Connor and Gina worked their way through the gifts until the last item was displayed on the kitchen counter and all of the wrapping paper and bows had been deposited in the trash.

"I have no idea what some of this stuff is," Connor said. He held up a chrome device with a red wooden handle. "It looks like a clamp I have in the garage."

"That's an apple peeler. Perfect for someone who's never baked a pie. Esoteric kitchen gadgets are an odd gift for two people who don't cook," Gina said.

"My favorite is that deluxe espresso maker. I'll figure that out tomorrow night. The next time you come over, you can count on a fancy coffee drink."

Gina concentrated on tidying the cards into a stack and tying them with a piece of ribbon rescued from the trash.

"What a haul!" Gina said. "I hope I get some of these things when I get married. If I ever get married."

"What are you talking about? You're going to get married. Some guy will come to his senses and snatch you up. I'll just want to meet him to make sure he's good enough for you."

Gina felt her cheeks flame. She stepped to the front door and retrieved her jacket from the chair where she'd tossed it when she'd arrived, four hours earlier.

"It's late, and I've got an early meeting. I'd better go. Are you going to tell Emily about all of this?"

"I don't know. Now I'm afraid it'll tick her off. As I said, I can't seem to put a foot right with her." He took Gina's jacket and held it for her to slip into. "Why don't you call her and tell her? She'll have more fun talking to you about all of this than she would with me."

Gina turned back to him and put her hand on his elbow. "This will get better, Connor. I promise. You've hit a rough patch, but it won't last. You love each other—hang on to that."

He put his hand over hers and gave it a squeeze. "Thanks for the encouragement. And you'll call Em?"

"I will. Tomorrow."

"Thanks for everything, Gina. You are one of a kind."

Gina ducked her head as she exited the condo so Connor couldn't see the tears stinging her eyes.

Chapter 20

Martha looked at the clock on the kitchen wall. Dhruv would undoubtedly be here in the next ten minutes. She'd come to look forward to his visits. They often provided the only human contact she had during the day—other than Emily.

Martha made weekly trips to the grocery and drug store, but was anxious about leaving Emily alone. That anxiety increased as Emily slipped deeper and deeper into hopelessness and depression. Without realizing it, both mother and daughter were isolating themselves. Martha missed her late husband more than ever—he'd know what to do about their daughter. Martha certainly wasn't getting through to her.

She checked the enchilada casserole in the oven. The cheese on top was nicely browned. She turned off the heat and left it to stay warm in the oven. She'd chopped lettuce and tomatoes for toppings, and they were chilling in the refrigerator. She wasn't going to let that kind man leave tonight without a decent meal. It was the least she could do to repay his faithfulness.

She wiped her hands on her apron and stepped to the front door. The heat of mid-day had given way to a lovely late afternoon. She opened the door to let fresh air into the house.

She was latching the screen when Dhruv's car pulled to the front curb. He was followed closely by six other vehicles.

Dhruv got out of his car and gestured to Martha's house.

The other cars parked on the street.

Dhruv waited on the sidewalk as four men and two women got out of the other cars and joined him. Dhruv turned and led the group up the walkway to Martha's front door.

Martha stepped outside to greet the group.

"My goodness, Dhruv, you've come with an entourage."

"We're her team," Dhruv said simply, as if this explained everything.

Martha took a step back. "Won't you come in?"

The group of seven filed into the living room.

A woman closer to Martha's age stepped forward. "I'm Rhonda," she said and introduced the others. Martha recognized Dhruv and Michael Ward. The rest were complete strangers to her.

"We came to see Emily"—Rhonda swung a large tote off her shoulder to rummage through it and pulled out the envelope Martha had given to Dhruv the night before—"about this."

"Oh, dear," Martha said. "I don't think she's up to seeing all of you. She's still not …"

"We know all about it," one of the men said. "Dhruv's filled us in. And you can tell Emily that we are prepared to camp out here until she comes out to see us. We don't care how long it takes."

Martha looked at each of them in turn. A bubble of hope began to form in her chest.

"Would you go tell her, please?" the other woman said. "We won't take long, but we're not leaving here until she hears what we've come to say."

"She owes us that much," Michael said.

"All right," Martha said. "Please sit down and make yourselves comfortable. There are water bottles in the fridge—Dhruv can show you. Help yourselves."

Martha headed to Emily's room. The door stood slightly ajar.

"Did you hear that?" Martha asked. The room was dim, but she could see that Emily had propped herself on her elbows. Martha waited.

"I did."

"Well? Are you going to go out there?"

"No, I'm not. They'll get tired and go away."

"I don't think so," Martha said. For the first time since her daughter's tragic injury, anger welled up inside her. "These people have come out here—after a long day's work—because they care about you. They're your employees for heaven's sake, Emily."

"Not anymore, they're not."

"What do you mean?"

"That envelope you gave Dhruv? That was my resignation."

Martha gasped. "You never said anything to me about that. You love your job. Why in the world … ?"

"Why in the world would I quit a job that I can't do anymore?" Emily shot up in bed. "Would it be better to wait until my FMLA runs out—string them along—and then let them fire me? Would that be better for me, Mom?"

Martha remained silent.

"I'm lost, Mom. I don't know what I'm going to do. Believe it or not, I love those people that are camped out in your living room. They are the best group of co-workers anyone could ever ask for. Especially Dhruv." Emily's voice cracked. "We had a crushing workload before I left. You know that I worked crazy hours."

"Yes—I remember."

"I'm sure they've been working twelve- to fourteen-hour days since I've been gone. That's not fair to them—especially since I'm not sure I'll ever be able to do my job again." Her voice held a new resolve. "Resigning was the honorable thing to do. They need to move on—without me."

"I see."

"Do you?"

"I don't agree with you, but I understand why you did it."

"I wanted to set them free—to bring an end to this."

"Maybe that's why they're here. Maybe they need to say goodbye to you."

Listening to Emily's heavy sigh, Martha thought her daughter might be considering what she'd just said.

"I'm a mess," Emily said. "I don't want them to see me like this."

Martha flipped on the overhead light and walked to the edge of the bed. She picked up a comb from the nightstand and handed it to her daughter.

Emily grasped the handle and brought the comb to her chest. "You really think I should talk to them?"

"Yes."

Emily tugged the comb through her hair and got out of bed, smoothing her T-shirt into place with both hands. She searched for her slippers with the toes of first one foot, then the other. "Okay," she said. "I'll give them five minutes."

Martha turned and waited for Emily to put a hand on her shoulder, then she led them into the living room.

The quiet chatter between colleagues ceased as they entered the room.

"Emily," Rhonda said, crossing the room to where Emily stood and leaning into her with an awkward half-hug. "We're all so glad to see you."

Emily stepped back. She tried to force a smile but couldn't manage it. "I want you to know that you've been the most talented, creative, and supportive team I've ever worked with. You were a dream come true, and you made me the envy of every other programming manager in the country. I'm sorry that my absence has increased your already insanely heavy workload. Dozens of people will apply for my position. You'll have a new lead in no time."

"No. We won't."

Emily turned to Dhruv. "What do you mean? They'll post the job immediately. Finding my replacement shouldn't take more than a couple of weeks."

"That's just it," Rhonda said. She put the envelope into Emily's hands. "We're all in agreement. We're not going to accept this."

"You can't do that," Emily sputtered. "You have to accept it." She thrust the envelope back at Rhonda.

Dhruv intercepted it. He meticulously folded the envelope in half and tore it along the fold. He repeated the process until Emily's resignation letter was in tiny pieces.

Dhruv took Emily's hand, opened it, and placed the pieces in her palm. "No. We don't."

"I ... I can't ... do it." Emily flung the pieces onto the floor. "I can't see ... I'm blind." She spat the last word. "I'm not going to get better. There's no hope for me."

"That's not true," Dhruv said. "About no hope. I've been to the Foundation for the Blind. They say you can learn to do your job again. You just won't try."

Emily lowered her face to the floor. "It'll take too long. You're working too hard. You need to go on without me."

Rhonda cleared her throat. "We've decided that we can keep things going until you return."

"It could take a year."

"We talked about that. It doesn't make a difference. We're all agreed." She turned to her co-workers. "Aren't we?"

Each of the assembled members of her team took their turn and responded with a firm yes.

Emily's throat constricted and hot tears pricked the back of her eyes.

"We're going to keep working overtime until you return. You said it yourself. We're a dream team—and you're an irreplaceable part of that team."

Tears splashed onto the front of Emily's T-shirt.

"No matter how long it takes."

"Even a year?" Emily's voice was small.

"Even if it's more than a year," said one of the men.

"We all love you, Emily," Rhonda said. "And we're behind you. Dhruv's done the research—of course—and we know that you'll be able to do your job again. Just like you did before."

"I'm not sure I believe that," Emily said.

"Then believe in our belief," said Michael.

Emily brought her clasped hands to her chest. "I ... I don't know if I can do this."

"You can at least try," Rhonda said. "Like you always say, 'There's no excuse for not trying.'"

Emily smiled. "My words are coming back to haunt me. I can't guarantee anything."

"We're not asking for a guarantee," Michael said.

The room grew quiet, the only sound the breathing of the group of determined people.

Emily broke the silence. "I'll … I'll try."

"That's what we wanted to hear," said Rhonda.

"I don't want to let you down," Emily said.

"We're not worried about that, so don't you worry about it," Michael said.

Martha pulled a tissue from her pocket and removed her glasses to dab at her eyes. She swallowed hard and found her voice. "Would you like to stay for dinner? I've made plenty."

Rhonda turned to her. "That's very kind of you, but we wouldn't dream of imposing."

"It'd be no imposition."

"It's late. We'd better get going."

Her co-workers took turns hugging Emily and squeezing Martha's hand. The last one in line was Dhruv.

Emily grasped his arm with a shaking hand. "Will you take me to visit the Foundation for the Blind?"

She could hear the smile in his voice. "See you tomorrow, Emily."

Chapter 21

Martha fumbled in her purse and brought the tissue to her nose just in time to catch an enormous sneeze. She wiped her nose and crumpled the tissue, thrusting it into her pocket. "Sorry about that. I may be coming down with something."

"You're sick," Dhruv said.

"I'm fine," Martha said.

Emily stepped toward her mother. "You've been sneezing and coughing all day, Mom. It sounds like you're getting a humdinger of a cold. You need to be in bed."

"We've got an appointment at the Foundation for the Blind. We're not going to miss it. I can go to bed when we get home." She inhaled sharply twice and sneezed again.

"We can go without you," Dhruv said. "We'll tell you about it when we get home."

"Emily's only been out of the house with me," Martha said. "She needs me to guide her."

"I can do it. I read how online." Dhruv stepped in front of Emily and turned his back to her. "Here," he said. "Put your left hand on my shoulder."

Emily did as he directed.

Dhruv led her through the front door. "We're coming to steps," he said. "Take a step down."

Together, they made their way to his car. Martha followed close behind.

Dhruv opened the front passenger door and helped Emily into the seat, making sure she didn't bump her head. He handed her the retractable end of the seat belt.

Martha reached for the rear door and erupted in a fit of coughing.

Dhruv stood, staring at her.

"Okay. You're right. I shouldn't come with you. I don't need to be spreading my germs around."

"Yes. We'll see you later. Don't worry. We're fine."

Martha stepped back and watched him get into the driver's seat. She had to admit—Dhruv's matter-of-fact attitude was calming. Martha was tied up in knots all day, every day, over how her daughter was going to live her life if she didn't regain her eyesight. Would Emily lose her independence? Thank goodness she had Connor. But would they be happy together now that their lives had changed so drastically?

Martha watched as Dhruv's car backed out of the driveway, turned the corner, and disappeared from sight. She sneezed again and returned to the house. She'd make herself a cup of hot tea and settle herself on the sofa until they got back.

R

The hallways of the Foundation for the Blind were filled with people making their way purposefully in one direction or another. Some were assisted by a white cane, others by a guide dog, and some were walking without any assistance. Based on the speed and surety of their steps, you wouldn't guess that anyone was visually impaired.

Dhruv and Emily came to a stop outside of the office of Counselor Julie Ross. Julie and her guide dog Golda had just given them a tour of the facility. Emily kept her hand on Dhruv's shoulder.

"You've done your homework, Dhruv," Julie said. "You've got a thorough understanding of our program for adults here at the Foundation for the Blind."

Emily could feel his shoulder relax, and she could picture the open smile that would be spreading across his face. Dhruv was justifiably proud of his research abilities.

"What do you think, Emily?" Julie asked. "Are you ready?"

Emily tightened her grip on Dhruv's shoulder. "I … I think so."

"I'd like to take you to one more place," Julie said. "Do you have time?"

Emily shook her head. "Dhruv's got to get back—"

"We have time," he said.

"Good. I've got some people I want you to meet."

"Find the lounge, Golda," Julie said, and the dog, who had been waiting patiently in his harness, took off down the hall at a brisk pace.

Golda led them to a set of double doors. "There's a student meeting going on right now. I'd like to introduce you," Julie said. "These students are at different stages in our program. You'll be part of this group if you join us."

"I don't know …" Emily began as Julie opened the door.

"Follow me inside," Julie said.

Dhruv and Emily filed in after Julie and Golda and stood against the wall.

"Hey, everybody," Julie said in a teacher-in-charge-of-the-classroom voice, "I want you to meet Emily Main."

"Hi, Emily," came a chorus of a dozen or so voices.

"She's considering joining us. I want to go around the room so you can introduce yourselves. Tell her what brought you here and how long you've been in the program. And introduce your guide, too, if you have one."

"I'll start," said an older man with a radio announcer's voice. "I came here about eight months ago. My macular degeneration had gotten to the point several years ago where I couldn't function independently outside of my own home. I relied on my wife to take me places. She died year before last. I'm retired and didn't have anywhere that I had to go so I just stayed in the house. I'd become a prisoner in my own home. I was depressed and wasn't taking care of myself. My kids were worried and wanted me to come live with one of them. If there's one thing I never want to be, it's a burden to my children. My daughter found the foundation. My training," his voice cracked, "will let me continue to live independently. I'll be graduating next week."

"I'm Shirley," said the next person to speak. "I've only been here for three weeks, but I took my first walk outside with my cane today—by myself. I walked two blocks up to the next main street and walked back. I was terrified—they had to really encourage me to do it—but I made it just fine. I have to tell you—I experienced such a rush when I got back to my counselor's office on my own."

A smattering of applause broke out in the room. Emily joined in.

"They told me in orientation that I'll be able to go anywhere I want with my cane—even board an airplane," Shirley said. "Travel overseas. They have alumni who have climbed mountains and swum to the mainland from Alcatraz. They can teach us to do all of this." Her voice was thick with emotion. "I wasn't sure I believed all of that, but after today, I can see my life expanding."

Emily swallowed the lump gathering in her throat.

"I've only been here three days," said a young-sounding man. "I was holed up in my childhood bedroom, drinking too much and wondering if I even wanted to be alive. Being here has given me hope."

"Roman—he's my guide—and I have been together for four years. He's my third service dog. I can't imagine my life without my guides. I'm shy by nature and losing my sight in my late thirties caused me to go further into my shell. As I'm sure you've found out, people don't know what to say to a blind person, but everyone wants to say hello to you when you have a dog." The speaker chuckled. "I'm here so I can upgrade my skills with the latest computer technology. I'd like to get a promotion at work, and this will help."

The introductions continued until everyone had spoken.

"Thanks, everyone," Julie said. "I'm sure this has given Emily a lot to think about."

The man with the radio-announcer voice spoke again. "Don't be like me and waste time thinking about joining this program," he said. "Jump in and take charge of your life."

"I … thank you," Emily stammered.

"Have a good afternoon," Julie said to the group. "Find the front door," she said to Golda. Her guide took off.

Dhruv found Emily's hand and put it on his shoulder. They stopped at the entrance.

"I appreciate your time, Julie," Emily said.

Julie waited.

"I'm not sure I'm going to need all this," Emily said. "My eyesight might come back."

"If it does, we'll be delighted for you," Julie said. "Dhruv said your doctor referred you to the state rehabilitation department and recommended training."

"He did."

Julie remained silent.

"You should start," Dhruv said.

"You're right. I'm miserable at home and those people—in there—all seemed—so—happy."

"They are happy," Julie said. "All this training will be exhausting. You'll be challenged. But it's essential. And I have a hunch that you're going to be very good at it."

"She'll be a star student, for sure," Dhruv said.

Emily smiled for the first time in a very long time. "All right. I'm in. How do I sign up?"

"Can you spend another half-hour with me to start the paperwork? I'll call your rehabilitation specialist tomorrow. With any luck, you'll be able to start on Monday."

"We can stay," Dhruv said.

"Golda, find my office."

As she and Dhruv followed, Emily's footsteps felt lighter than they had in weeks.

Chapter 22

It was toward the beginning of my time with my family when I learned that "We've overslept!" is not a good thing.

I was lying in my crate in our bedroom—Katie's, Jon's, and mine—waiting patiently for Katie to get up. I knew that things weren't running on our usual schedule. One thing that humans don't know—but that all dogs are aware of—is that we have a perfectly calibrated sense of time. Particularly dinnertime. You can set your watch by when we tell you it's time to eat.

Anyway, I was awake and watched the room grow lighter and brighter as sunshine began to force its way between the slats on the window blinds.

I watched Katie stir and brush the hair off of her face. She suddenly sat bolt upright and stabbed a finger at her phone. "We've overslept!" were the next words out of her mouth.

Jon turned over in bed and uttered a word that I later learned would get him in hot water with Katie when he said it around the kids.

They both leapt out of bed and began racing in and out of the bathroom and their closets.

I waited anxiously in my crate. The first order of the day was to take me outside to do my business and then feed me my breakfast. I liked the usual order.

"Can you take Garth out and feed him?" Katie asked. "I need to get the kids up and pack their lunches."

"Sure." Jon opened my crate. "Come on, boy. You're stuck with me this morning."

He led me outside and then fed me. I thought he did an admirable job. He didn't hook my leash onto his belt, like Katie did. As soon as he put my food bowl on the kitchen floor, he raced off in another direction.

The kitchen was chaos. Katie was jerking open the refrigerator door and slamming drawers, all the while yelling for the kids to "Hurry up! We leave in five."

I didn't want to get in anyone's way. I knew enough to steer clear of the living room and its big leather dog bed, but there were other rooms I wanted to explore—particularly the one at the end of the bedroom hallway. There was a peculiar smell emanating from behind that door. I found it compelling, almost irresistible.

I sauntered down the hallway, hugging the wall—concentrating on making myself inconspicuous. The scent grew stronger with every step. I was almost to the door.

"Now!" Katie yelled from the kitchen.

The door flew open against the wall, nearly catching me on the nose, and Abby tore out of the room.

My nostrils twitched and flared with the scent. I looked back over my shoulder. I was alone in the hallway. No one had ever told me not to go into Abby's room.

I walked in, and there, on the floor, not more than ten feet from me sat a lumpy mass of long white fur. A pair of green eyes were fixed on me, tracking my every move. Those eyes were cold and devoid of any decent emotion.

I contemplated my next move very carefully.

The whiskers on the furball twitched. Its long tail snaked out, jutting toward the ceiling like a flag waving hello.

I took the invitation and bounded up to her in my cutest puppy fashion—the one that garnered praise and petting from humans— but the furball erupted, hissing and spitting at me. Then she turned and bolted to the back of the room.

I was perfectly happy to get acquainted right where we were, but if that wasn't the plan, I was prepared to follow. She was fast.

When she reached the bedroom's back wall, she spun around and we were nose-to-nose again. Razor-sharp claws extended from her paws. Her tail ballooned to twice its size, every hair standing on end.

As if that wasn't bad enough, she reached out and swatted at me with lethal intent.

I yelped as her claws connected with the soft flesh of my tender nose. I smelled blood—my own! I lunged backward, tripping over my own feet.

The evil furball hissed again and darted under the bed.

For a crazy moment, I thought about following it, but I quickly came to my senses. I turned my back to the furball—with grave misgivings—and retreated from the room without incurring further attack.

I rubbed my sore nose on the carpet in the hallway. No permanent damage had been done—other than my hurt pride.

I made my way slowly back to the kitchen where Jon was sitting at the table, drinking a cup of coffee in solitude. Katie and the children were nowhere to be seen. He glanced in my direction.

"Where have you been, boy?" He dropped his hand toward the floor and waggled his fingers at me.

I recognized the gesture and walked over to him.

He stroked the top of my head, then cupped my muzzle with his hand and leaned over to inspect my nose.

"Met Liloh, have you?"

I wagged my tail. So the she-devil's name was Liloh.

"It didn't go so well, did it?" He scooped me up into his lap. "I'm sorry. We were going to introduce you gradually. Cats—especially this one—don't like dogs they don't know."

Tell me about it.

He began to massage my ears. "Give it time. You and Liloh will become best friends."

I rolled my eyes up to look at Jon. He was a nice guy, and he certainly knew how to massage ears, but I thought he had a completely unrealistic expectation of my future with Liloh.

Chapter 23

"Emily?" Spencer Chamberlain called from the door to the student lounge. "I'm here to take you to your first mobility training session."

Emily rose from her seat at the table and gathered up her empty paper lunch bag. "Where can I toss this?" she asked, turning in the direction of Spencer's voice.

"I'll show you on the way out," he said, coming to stand next to her. "The trash can in this room will become one of your landmarks."

Spencer turned his back to Emily. "I'll be your sighted guide. Reach out your left hand directly in front of you."

Emily did as instructed and found his back.

"Slide your hand up to my left shoulder. We're going to tour the adult training building and then get you fitted for a cane."

Emily grasped his shoulder.

"We'll start with the restrooms."

Emily took a step forward and turned to her left.

"That's right," Spencer said. "How did you know that the restrooms are this way?"

"Julie and I stopped there before she brought me here."

Spencer began to walk, with Emily following behind. "You have a good memory."

"I've always been able to tell which direction I'm going. At least until this … happened."

"Your orientation skills should stand you in good stead. You'll need to learn new techniques." He stopped. "To our right, are the restrooms."

Emily ran her hand along the wall until she came to the doorway.

"There's a sign, with braille, that tells you whether it's men's or women's."

Emily felt the words on each sign. "The word 'women' is longer and easy to distinguish from 'men.'"

"Good. That's right. We're going to continue down this hallway, past a series of six classrooms. When we come to an intersecting hallway, we will turn right and go to my office. It'll be the third office on the right after we make the turn."

They started walking again. "How do you get along at home?"

"Pretty well. I started out memorizing the steps between pieces of furniture and different rooms. After a while, I didn't have to count anymore. Muscle memory took over."

"That's what most people do," Spencer said. "That works fine at home—provided no one moves things around on you."

"That's for sure. My husband moved the shampoo in the shower. I was so mad; I was ready to kill him. I'm staying with my mom right now. She's very conscientious about keeping things in the same place."

"Good. I know how frustrating mobility can be for someone with visual impairments. Counting steps is way too cumbersome when navigating outside your own home, and it can't be used in areas you've never been before. You'll find our training will be tremendously helpful."

They reached the intersecting hallway and Spencer turned them to the right. "See if you can find my office, based on what I told you. I have a feeling you're going to be really good at this."

Emily held his right shoulder with her left hand while she swept her right hand along the wall as they moved forward. When they came to the third doorway, Emily stopped.

"This should be it," she said. "Your office."

"Well done," Spencer said. "We're going to get you fitted for your cane and we'll explore more of this floor."

"Fitted?"

"Yes. One size does not fit all. The top of the grip should come up to your armpit when the tip is on the ground."

He led her into his office and opened a cabinet. "I think you'll want a folding cane. They're easier to take with you," he said. "And I'm going to give you a ball tip. It's designed to sweep along the floor. There are several types of tips, but we start beginners off with this one."

Emily heard the sound of metal snapping together. Spencer pressed a rubber grip into her hand. She closed her fingers around it and tapped the cane tentatively on the floor. She felt herself flush. She was really going to be using a white cane.

"You all right?"

Emily swallowed hard and nodded.

"This one is a good fit," he said. "Swing it in front of you, in a shoulder-width arc, so that the cane is tapping in the space that you'll be stepping into."

Emily began sweeping the cane.

"That's it," he said. "When your cane is on your left side, your right foot is stepping forward and vice versa. Are you ready to try it?"

"Sure," she said with more confidence than she felt.

"You'll start by going up and down the hallway. Then we'll learn how to identify doorways, stairs, and intersecting corridors."

They moved into the hallway, and Emily proceeded slowly to her right.

"That's perfect. I think you're a natural," Spencer said. "Over the next week, we're going to identify certain permanent landmarks in this building: the front door, the stairway, the student lunchroom, and a large photocopier. None of these things move."

Emily halted. "Is there a doorway on my left?"

"There sure is. How did you know?"

"I've been walking close to a wall on my left—hitting it with my cane. All of a sudden, the tip didn't hit anything."

"That's exactly right! Good job. Now, explore the opening with your cane."

Emily moved her cane in small arcs. "There's a door here, and it's closed."

"Yes. Is there anything you could do to identify what's behind the door?"

Emily began running her hand over the wall next to the door frame. She found a sign and examined it with her hand. "I think these must be braille bumps," Emily said, "but it feels like there is a raised number '6' too."

"Right on both accounts," he said. "You've identified classroom 6."

They continued down the hallway. "You're going to learn to identify places by mapping their location in relation to certain landmarks. By the time you go home today, you'll be able to enter our front door and find my office using your cane, without any human assistance, by counting the number of doorways past the front door." He paused. "What do you think of that? Does that seem doable?"

Emily drew a deep breath. "Yes. I think I can do that." She continued down the hall.

"You'll always be able to find the front door from anywhere. If you get lost, you just find the front door and start over from there."

"Makes sense."

"How are you feeling about your cane now?"

Emily stopped and turned toward his voice. "I'd say I'm … encouraged. Two parts hopeful, one part terrified, actually."

"That sounds about right," Spencer said. "It's a lot to take in. Most people report being overwhelmed at first. In time, people find that cane travel gives them back their independence. If you put in the effort to become proficient, you'll be very glad you did."

"You're sure I'm going to get the hang of it?"

"Emily—I'm sure you're going to master cane mobility in no time."

R

Martha sat in one of the reception chairs near the front door of the foundation. She was twenty minutes early. She didn't want to be late for Emily. Not on her first day.

She'd been overjoyed—and a bit surprised—when Emily had gotten herself ready that morning and hadn't come up with an excuse to postpone her first day at the foundation. The feelings were similar to those she'd felt years ago when she dropped Emily off at kindergarten for the first time. Martha knew then her fears for her small daughter weren't rational, and she knew the same thing now. Understanding there was nothing to worry about, however, didn't prevent her from doing so. She'd spent the day glancing at the clock and paying scant attention to any of the myriad of tasks she'd tried to accomplish. Thoughts of Emily crowded out everything else.

A tapping noise from behind her drew Martha out of her reverie. She looked over her shoulder to see Emily moving steadily toward her, swinging a white cane in front of her. A tall young man followed close behind her, but Emily was making the journey on her own.

Martha got to her feet.

The receptionist looked up from her computer screen and held up a hand to Martha. The woman gestured to Emily with her head and put her index finger to her lips.

Martha nodded and remained silent.

Emily walked to the door with her cane, turned around, and found the reception desk.

The young man hung back.

"I'm waiting for Martha Main," Emily told the woman.

"She's waiting in the chairs to your right," the woman replied.

"Thank you," Emily murmured. She extended her cane to the right and moved in that direction. "Mom?" she said softly.

"I'm … I'm here." Martha said, her words catching in her throat.

"Me, too," Emily laughed.

Martha looked at Spencer, her eyes wide.

"She's done extremely well," he said, turning to Emily. "Emily's got an innate sense of orientation, and we had a great first day."

Emily turned to him. "That's because I've had such a terrific teacher. Thank you, Spencer."

"You're welcome. Go home and get some rest. Don't forget to use your cane around the house, too. See you tomorrow?"

"Yes, you will," Emily said.

"Do you want me to guide you to the car?" Martha asked.

"Yes. We haven't learned curbs and outside mobility yet."

Martha took her daughter's left hand and couldn't resist giving it a kiss before she put it on her shoulder. "Tell me all about your day," she said. They stepped through the automatic doors and into the parking lot.

Emily launched into a description of the four different classes that made up her day. "The technology class was super interesting. I'm starting to believe I'll be able to do everything on a computer that a sighted person can do."

"You'll be able to go back to work at your old job?"

"Eventually. I want to become very proficient at mobility, first. It's obvious to me that's going to be crucial to living an independent life."

She hadn't heard this much hope in her daughter's voice since the accident. A small sniffle escaped her, and she was glad Emily couldn't see the tears rolling down her cheeks.

Emily, however, didn't need to see. Martha's erratic breathing seemed to clue her in. "Are you crying, Mom?"

"Maybe a little. It's just so good to see you so …"

"Not depressed?"

"Well … yes."

"I got a lot out of the group counseling session, too. It turns out everyone feels anxious and overwhelmed all the time when they're newly blind. And panic attacks are common. I didn't feel like such a freak."

"Oh, Em," Martha said. "I'm sure it will get better."

"It does. I met other people who are further along in the program, and they say it gets much better. Most of my teachers are blind, too, and they're getting along just fine. I'm exhausted and still scared about the future, but I have … hope."

Martha reached across and squeezed Emily's hand.

"And one more thing, Mom."

Martha glanced at Emily. "What?"

"I loved the lunch you packed."

Martha smiled. "That's the same thing I packed you on your first day of kindergarten. I wasn't sure if you still liked all that stuff or not."

"I do," Emily said. "It was great. Like a big hug from you delivered in a paper lunch sack."

They both laughed.

"But I don't think I'll want Crunchy Cheetos and Little Debbie cakes every day. I still need to watch my calories."

"Duly noted," Martha said as she pulled into the driveway. "Turkey on whole wheat with carrot sticks is on tap for tomorrow."

"Thank you," Emily said as she opened her door and extended her cane.

Martha came around the side of the car to assist but was intercepted by Zoe.

"Hi, Emily. It's me, Zoe. I've been looking for you on the porch every day after school. Gramma said you were sick. I wanted to come over, but she said no."

Thinking about the deep, immobilizing depression her daughter had been in, Martha looked to Emily.

"You look all better now."

"I'm … I'm fine," Emily said. "I've just started classes at the Foundation for the Blind."

"Wow! Did you learn to use that today?" Zoe asked, pointing to the cane.

"I'm beginning to."

"Is it neat?" Zoe asked. "Can you show me?"

"Watch." Emily began to sweep her cane along the pavement in front of her. "Have you ever seen anyone using a white cane?"

"Not up close," Zoe said. "Will you let me try it, too? I'll shut my eyes."

"Sure," Emily said. "We'll go to the porch and I'll show you there."

"This is so neat," Zoe said. "I'll bet your classes are cooler than mine."

"I don't know about that," Emily said. "What did you do in school today?"

"Why don't I bring the two of you some lemonade?" Martha asked. She hurried to the kitchen, her steps light, smiling at the unlikely friendship blossoming on her porch.

Chapter 24

Connor stood up from the table and waved at the petite blonde who'd just entered the restaurant. She made her way through the sea of tables and sat in the chair he held out for her.

"Thanks for agreeing to meet me, Gina."

"No problem. I wanted to get these new audiobooks to Emily." She placed a large paper shopping bag at his feet. "I've also got a candle in her favorite scent in the bag, too. The candle's breakable, so you'll have to be careful with this."

Connor looked at his hands resting on the table, his fingers intertwined.

A waiter came over to take their drink order.

"Iced tea for me," Gina said.

"Bourbon and water," Connor said, his words slightly slurred.

Gina knitted her brows. "At lunch?"

Connor shrugged. "I'm not going back to the office."

"Are you heading to Martha's early?"

"I'm not … I'm not going to Martha's this weekend."

"What? Why not?"

The waiter arrived with their drinks. "Are you ready to order?"

"Get whatever you'd like," Connor said. "It's on me."

Gina scanned the menu. "I'll have the field greens salad. Dressing on the side."

"That's not much."

"I'm on a diet."

"You certainly don't need to be. You look fabulous," Connor said. He turned to the waiter. "I'll have a Reuben."

"So … you're not going to see Emily at all this weekend?"

"No. I got a last-minute invitation to my boss's bachelor party in Vegas. I don't want to go—you know how much I hate Vegas."

"I remember Emily telling me that. So odd, Connor. Makes me wonder about you," Gina said with a playful gleam in her eye. "I'd be happy to take your place."

"I wish that would work. I feel like it would be career suicide if I didn't go. I'm in line for a promotion next year. With Emily's career on hold, we could really use the extra money I'd get with the increase in my salary."

"Surely it's not as bad as all that? I thought the two of you made a ton of money."

"Condos in San Francisco—even small ones—cost a fortune. We've got some pretty steep medical bills, and I'm not sure what other expenses we may be facing." He took a swig of his drink. "I want this promotion."

"I'm sure Em understood when you told her."

Connor flinched.

"You did tell her, didn't you?"

"Not yet. I wanted to see you, first." He held her gaze. "Would you be able to go out to Martha's? Spend the weekend with Em?"

Gina drew in a sharp breath. "She told me you were going to be with her, so I made other plans."

"Of course," Connor said. "It was just a thought. I didn't want her to be too disappointed."

"Hold on," Gina said. "I don't want her to be disappointed, either." She pulled her phone out of her purse and began scrolling. "I'm sure I can reschedule all of this." She lifted her eyes to his. "Yes. I'll go."

"I'd really appreciate it."

She slid the paper bag of goodies for Emily back to herself. "You won't be needing these."

Connor took both of her hands in his and squeezed them. "Thank you so much, Gina."

Gina quickly pulled her hands away, making Connor feel slightly awkward.

"I've got some of her clothes and toiletries with me. Can I transfer them to your car after lunch?"

"Sure," Gina said. "I'd be happy to take them. When will you tell Emily?"

"She's in those classes at the Foundation for the Blind right now. I'll be on the plane by the time she gets out, so I'll leave her a voice mail."

Gina grimaced. "When does she get home from the foundation?"

"Martha picks her up at four-thirty."

Gina checked her watch. "I can leave work early today."

The waiter approached their table with their meals.

"Can you box this up for me?" she asked the waiter. "If I head back to the office now, I can leave by two. I'll swing by my place to pack a bag and be on the road by three. With any luck, I'll be waiting in Martha's driveway when they get home."

"That's incredibly kind of you, Gina," Connor said. "You're the best. Some guy is really missing out."

R

Gina pulled to the curb outside of Martha's home at ten minutes after four. Traffic on the bridge had been unexpectedly light, and she'd made good time. She climbed the steps to the front porch where she and Emily had spent hours discussing boys, makeup, hairstyles, and their hopes and dreams.

She rang the doorbell and waited. When no one answered, she sank onto the old glider and looked at her phone. Martha and Emily should be home soon.

Gina started to text them when Martha's car turned into the driveway.

"Hey," she called as Martha stepped out of the car. They exchanged a glance across the roof of the car. Gina raised her eyebrows and shrugged.

Martha furrowed her brows and shook her head slowly.

Gina opened Emily's car door. "Hi there," she said. "I hear you're acing blind school—just like every other school you've attended. I can't wait to hear all about it."

Emily turned her face to Gina. Her eyes were red-rimmed and her nose ran.

Gina's heart lurched at the sight of her friend's tear-stained face. She didn't need to ask if Emily had listened to Connor's message.

"Gina?"

"Who else?"

Emily swung her feet onto the pavement and hoisted herself out of the car.

Gina pulled her into a hug. "Since Connor couldn't come, I jumped at the chance to have you to myself again. We'll have a sleepover and a girls' weekend."

"How did you know he wasn't coming? He said that his boss just invited him to his bachelor party this morning."

"I had lunch with him."

Emily stepped back and snapped her cane into place. "You and Connor—"

"Yes. I had some things I wanted him to bring to you," Gina said hurriedly. "More audiobooks … and another little surprise."

"Thank you," Emily said, sweeping the cane from side to side in front of her.

"Let's go in."

"Can I … can I help you?" Gina said.

"No. I've got this. I can navigate to Mom's front door now."

"That's great! Lead the way."

Martha stepped around them and unlocked the door.

Emily proceeded confidently up the steps and into the house.

"I'm impressed," Gina said. "You learned all this in just one week?"

"I did, but I've got a lot farther to go," Emily replied. "It feels good, though." She led them to the living room where they piled onto the sofa like they had when they were high schoolers.

"How's your eyesight? Any change?"

"Not really. It's not getting worse, but it's not getting better, either."

"I'm sorry."

"Why don't the two of you catch up while I fix dinner?" Martha asked. "I made a big salad this afternoon and potatoes have been in the oven since before I left to pick up Emily. All I have to do is throw steaks on the grill."

"Mom was making Connor's favorites," Emily said. "We even have a homemade lemon meringue pie for dessert."

"Sounds fabulous," Gina said. "He'll be doubly sorry he missed it."

"Yep. Poor Connor. He has to spend the weekend in Las Vegas."

Gina took a deep breath. She didn't blame her friend for being disappointed. "I know I'm a poor substitute for Connor."

"I'm sorry. It's not that. I'm delighted you came. I'm sure you had to cancel plans, and I appreciate your doing that."

"For what it's worth, I don't think he wanted to go. Since his boss invited him and he hopes to get promoted, he felt like he had no choice."

"That's what he said." Emily tossed her hair behind her shoulders. "If he'd talked to me about it, I would have agreed with him. I shouldn't feel so bad. I'll still be here next weekend. And the weekend after that and the one after that."

Gina leaned over and took her friend's hand. "I don't know what to say."

"It's just that I was so excited to show him what I've learned this week." The color rose in her cheeks. "I know this may sound silly to you, but all of this is very daunting. I'm working so hard."

"I'm sure you are—that's who you are, Em. I meant it when I said that you'll be the star student of this place." Gina squeezed Emily's hand and dropped it. "I'm sure he'll call later, and you can tell him all about it."

"I want him to see me in action, Gina." Emily shrugged. "I can't put my finger on it, but things are changing between Connor and me."

"Honey—that man is devoted to you. He's focused on getting this raise so that he can … provide for you both."

"Provide for his blind wife, you mean. In case she can't work again."

"I didn't say that—and neither did he. I think you're just imagining things."

"Maybe. I hope you're right, but I get the sense that he's pulling away from me. That's why I wanted to be with him. So we could talk these things out."

"I'm telling you right now—you're wrong. Everything's fine."

"We'll see," Emily said. She pulled her legs up to her chest and tucked her knees under her chin. "By the way, I want to thank you for writing those thank-you notes. That was nice of you to take the time."

"No big deal. I just dictated them, and Connor did the rest. It was fun to see all the cool stuff you got. We left everything on the kitchen counter for you to … for when you go back to the condo."

"For me to see? You can say that word to me, Gina. It's fine. Blind people use that word all the time."

"I … I didn't know." Gina coughed dryly.

"Enough about me. Tell me what's up with you. Do you have a new guy?" Emily drew in a quick breath. "Since when did you start wearing perfume?"

Gina laughed. "I can't believe you can still smell it. I put it on this morning after my shower."

"What is it? Seems like I've smelled it before."

"Don't laugh. Chanel No. 5."

Emily punched Gina's arm. "No way! We used to make fun of old ladies and their No. 5."

"Well … as it turns out, I absolutely love Chanel No. 5. Always have—even when we were kids. I just couldn't afford it until now.

And if you can still smell it on me, I guess the extra money I spent on it was worth it."

Emily turned her face to Gina and smiled.

"Are you still going to be friends with me now that I reek of Chanel No. 5?"

"Nothing will ever come between us—not even your crazy affinity for perfume that ..." She paused. "I need to reframe my thinking on this ... for perfume that's as timeless and classic as my best friend."

Gina clapped her hands together. "I love you. You always know the right thing to say. I'm so glad that we get to spend the weekend together."

"We can go for walks. I want to practice," Emily said.

"And can I take us all out to breakfast in the morning?"

"No!" Emily recoiled into the couch. "I'm not ready for that yet."

"But ... wouldn't that let you practice? You'll be with me and your mom. What's the problem with that?"

"You don't get it!" Emily stood abruptly. "None of you do. You think it's all so easy."

"I'm sorry. I didn't mean to upset you." Gina inhaled slowly. "Can you explain why it's a problem to go out with us? You'll be safe—you know that."

"I understand that—intellectually. But being in a crowd makes me unbearably anxious. All the talking and the noise." Emily stepped back to the couch. "People have become obstacles in my path to avoid, not enjoy. My classmates all say the same thing. It's difficult."

"Okay. We'll just do what you're up to doing."

"I'm sorry I snapped." Emily deflated into the couch. "I just need time to adjust."

"It's okay." Gina placed her hand over Emily's. "You'll get there, Em—I'm sure of it. You'll know when you're ready."

Chapter 25

"We're going to the dentist today," Katie said, securing my doggie seat belt. "I'm getting my teeth cleaned." She ran her hand over my back. "You know how I brush your teeth at bedtime?"

Did I know? Was that when she put that tiny pearl of poultry-flavored paste on a brush and ran it over my teeth? I loved that. I wished she'd forget about the brush and give me more of the paste. It was delicious.

"I brush my teeth twice a day," she said.

That explained why she couldn't share more of the paste with me.

"But I still have to go to the dentist to have them thoroughly cleaned and make sure I don't have any decay."

I opened my mouth and my tongue hung out. I could tell that it was important to her and that was good enough for me.

She got behind the wheel of the car, and we were soon at our destination.

We entered a three-story concrete building with lots of windows. The lobby floor was cool marble and the space was scrupulously clean. My nose was assaulted with a myriad of acidic, sharp smells. They weren't the warm and friendly aromas of food.

I stood rigidly next to Katie while we waited for the elevator.

"This is a medical office building, Garth." She scratched between my ears. "Guides take their handlers to visit doctors and dentists in places like this all the time."

My eyebrows twitched as we entered the elevator. If guides had to come to medical offices, then I'd become an expert at navigating them.

One floor up we entered a room lined with chairs where a woman sat reading a magazine and two men were looking at their phones. Another man stood in front of a window that was open to a woman seated at a desk behind it.

Katie approached the window and stopped behind him. I sat at her side. "Good boy," she said.

"You're all set. See you in six months, Dhruv," the woman behind the window said, passing him a small card.

He fumbled in his pocket for his wallet, and a small bright blue bag with bold graphics tumbled to the carpet. The man called Dhruv didn't appear to notice as he placed the card in his wallet and put it back in his pocket.

"Have a nice day," the woman said to Dhruv.

He nodded to her and turned around, almost bumping into Katie.

"Sorry," he mumbled.

"That's okay," Katie said, stepping to one side to let him pass us.

The woman behind the window greeted her and said, "Can you please sign in on the tablet?"

Katie tapped the screen.

I eyed the blue bag on the ground. It didn't smell like the antiseptic aromas that had assaulted my nostrils ever since we'd walked into the building. That bag held food. There could be no doubt about it.

I remembered the trouble I'd gotten into when I'd helped clean up Alex's homework-and-fizz mess. Surely this was a completely different situation.

I glanced at Katie. She was still poking at the screen.

I stuck my snout into the bag and, with one deft sweep of my tongue, channeled its contents into my mouth. I brought my teeth down with one crunch and swallowed.

My first taste of Cool Ranch Doritos did not disappoint—but they still couldn't match the culinary delight of Crunchy Cheetos.

Chapter 26

Emily walked, slowly but steadily, swinging her cane from side to side, around the exterior of the Foundation for the Blind. She forced her shoulders back, her chin up, face toward the sun.

Correct posture was key.

"You're doing great," Spencer called from behind her.

She'd been using the cane for almost three weeks now, and she and Spencer had traveled this route in her daily lesson for at least two of them.

The sounds of heavy traffic to her left told her they were walking along the busiest street bordering the foundation. Being this close to vehicles hurtling down the road was frightening, but she told herself that she knew how to use her cane to stay on the sidewalk and keep herself safe. She had to learn to do this. Her short time at the foundation had brought her into contact with blind people who successfully traveled the world on their own; who climbed mountains and played sports. If they could do it, so could she.

The tip of her cane dipped down and she halted, exploring the space in front of her. The sidewalk had merged into a ramp covered with a grid of concrete cylindrical bumps. She knew this meant she had reached an intersection. Based on the amount of time they'd been walking, she calculated that she was at the southwest corner of the foundation property.

Emily turned to her right, used her cane to locate the edge of the sidewalk on her right side, and proceeded forward. The traffic noises began to fade away. They were now walking along a quiet side street. She smiled. She knew what she was doing.

"Well done," Spencer said. "I think you've got this."

"Thanks," Emily replied. "I think I do, too."

"Perfect. Continue on the route we've been walking, and I'll meet you back in my office."

Emily took two more steps forward and stopped suddenly. "Wait … what?"

"You're ready to do this on your own."

"You mean … without you behind me?"

"Exactly. That's been our goal all along."

Emily felt her cheeks grow warm and knew she must be beet red. "But it's too soon! I can't be out here all on my own."

"I know you can do it. We've already done the leg that runs by the busy street. You're on side streets from here on out."

"I've only been doing this a few weeks."

"And you're picking it up as fast as anyone I've ever seen. You could have done this route on your own a week ago."

Emily began to hunch over, then straightened and took a series of deep breaths, like she'd learned to do when she felt a panic attack coming on.

"I wouldn't allow you to do this if I thought you weren't ready," Spencer said.

"You believe I can do this?" she asked, her voice small.

"I know you can."

Emily began nodding her head. "All right. I'll … try."

"Continue up the rest of this block, then turn right to walk along the north side of our building, then make another right turn as you head south to the front door."

"I know," Emily said.

"See you in about fifteen minutes," Spencer said as he turned and headed in the direction they'd just come from.

Emily used her cane to find the outside edge of the sidewalk. She felt the sun on the left side of her face. She looked back in the direction Spencer had gone, swiveling her head around to try to catch sight of him in the pinhole of vision remaining in her left eye. She wasn't successful and finally gave up.

Emily resumed her path slowly. "I can do this," she said over and over, like a prayer.

About five minutes into the walk, her cane hit a concrete slab at a perpendicular angle to the sidewalk. *I'm at the sidewalk that runs along the north side of the building,* she thought. She confirmed it with her cane and made the first right turn. She could now feel the sun on the back of her neck.

She began to pick up speed as she continued. She was almost to the place where she'd make her last turn when the frayed laces on her old right tennis shoe snapped. Emily stepped out of the shoe, pitching forward and landing on her knee. She dropped her cane and caught herself with both hands, preventing herself from sprawling on the sidewalk.

Hovering above the pavement on all fours, Emily gulped in air to steady herself. Tears formed at the back of her eyes, and she pounded the sidewalk with the side of her fist. If this was what she had to look forward to as a white cane traveler, then she wanted no part of it.

She took a deep breath and rocked back on her heels. She ran her stinging palms over her body. She wasn't bleeding. Her jeans weren't even ripped. She patted the ground for her cane and found it in the grass, along with the offending shoe. She shoved the shoe onto her foot and then stood up.

She'd tripped, nothing more. She would have done the same thing whether she was blind or not. She wasn't going to let a stupid old shoe stop her now.

She squared her shoulders, lifted her face, turned her back to the warmth of the sun, and pressed on.

R

Spencer had been following Emily's progress from the window in his office. When he saw her tumble, he'd been about to go rescue her when some instinct had told him to stop. He smiled as the young woman with the determined posture and tenacious spirit made her way to the entrance.

Emily knocked on his doorframe a few minutes later. "Spencer?"

"I'm here. Behind my desk. Come on in and take a seat."

Emily made her way to the chair that always sat in front of his desk.

"How was it?"

Emily turned her face to his.

His heart surged as it always did when one of his students completed their first solo walk outside. Her countenance bore a new mantle of hard-won self-confidence that could never be stripped away.

She lifted her chin a fraction and drew a deep breath. "Uneventful," she said.

"No issues?"

"Nothing that had anything to do with being blind." A smile transformed her face. "It was so … empowering. I've gone from feeling helpless when I first went blind to being overwhelmed by everything new I've been learning—"

"That's very normal."

"—to now feeling competent and capable."

"That's exactly how you should feel. Walking outside—by yourself—is a huge milestone."

"I know that I've got a lot more to learn, but now I'm sure I'll get there."

"You will. I promise. Stick with it. Keep doing what you're doing."

They smiled at each other. "I will."

"Good."

"And one more thing, Spencer."

"What?"

"Thank you … for giving me my life back. I'm more grateful to you than I can express."

It was Spencer's turn to swallow tears.

Chapter 27

"It's so good to get out of the house," Emily said. She groped across the restaurant tabletop and found Connor's hand. "And wonderful to be with you again."

"Your mom has been a lifesaver, Em. I don't know what we would've done without her."

"She has been," Emily quickly agreed. "I'm grateful to her. But it's hard not to feel like a kid when I'm living in my childhood bedroom. I'm a married woman, you know." She squeezed his hand. "I want to be with my husband."

"I guess I'm just nervous about how you're going to do at my … our … condo in San Francisco. I don't want a repeat of what happened to you at the burger place."

"It won't. I didn't even have a cane when we went there. I've learned a ton of mobility skills since then. I can't wait to show you." She smiled in his direction. "And you can help me if I need anything."

"I'm not sure I know what to do," he said.

"That's why I want you to come to those classes at the foundation for family members. I don't need you to take care of me, but there are things that you'll find helpful for both of us."

"I told you I'd go. It's just that I'm crazy-busy after my promotion. I should be working this weekend as it is."

Emily slipped her hand back into her lap. "You can spend time at the office this weekend if you need to. I'd like to explore the condo on my own." She turned her face in his direction. "I'm excited to be here, again, with you. This is my favorite restaurant."

"I remember," Connor said. "I took you here on our first date because I wanted to impress you."

"And it worked," Emily said.

The waiter brought over an array of Indian dishes and set them on the table in front of them.

"Do you want me to serve you?" Connor asked, reaching for her plate.

"I've got it."

"How will you know what you're getting?"

"I can tell from the smell of the spices." She patted his hand.

She stretched her hand tentatively toward a steaming bowl, found the spoon handle, and carefully scooped a serving onto her plate.

"Okay … what's that?" he asked.

"It's the turkey curry," she said. "Am I right?"

"You most certainly are."

Emily continued serving herself, naming each dish as she came to it. Her plate was full, her mouth watering. She grabbed her fork and as she lifted it toward her plate her wrist knocked over a glass, spilling water onto her plate.

Connor jumped up and began patting at the stream of water making its way off the table and onto Emily's lap.

"Damn it," Emily said, pushing her chair back roughly.

"It's all right. They'll bring us another plate. You can't help these things."

"That's exactly it, Connor. This shouldn't have happened. My water glass never should have been on the left side. Beverages should be at the two o'clock position, not ten o'clock."

Connor released an exasperated sigh and threw his napkin onto the table.

"I didn't know. I'm sorry, Em."

"If you'd attend the family sessions, you'd learn these things," she snapped.

"I can't seem to do anything right, can I? Let's get the rest of this boxed up and head home."

Emily turned away from him.

"Your blouse and pants got wet. You can't be comfortable like that," Connor said.

"You're right. Let's get out of here—before I ruin the rest of our food."

"It wasn't your fault, Em." He signaled to the waiter. "We'll take it home."

The waiter brought them their check and the boxed-up food. Emily extended her cane and rose from the table.

"Do you want me to guide you home?"

"Nope. I can manage on my own." she said curtly.

"All right. I was just asking."

Emily navigated the two blocks to their condo, including an intervening cross street, without incident.

"That was very impressive," Connor said as they approached the elevator bank in their building.

"I'm going to be valedictorian of blind school."

"I have no doubt about it."

They stepped onto the elevator.

"What do you want to do after dinner?" he asked.

Emily shrugged. She knew what she had in mind—and it was the perfect activity to do with eyes closed. "I don't know. Let's see what we feel like."

They got out of the elevator, and Emily turned right and counted with her cane the number of doorways between the elevator and their front door.

"I'm going to put the food on the counter before one of these bags breaks," Connor said, unlocking the door. "Can you find your way to the kitchen on your own?"

She was about to say that dinner could wait; that she thought they should start in the bedroom. Her words froze on her lips. She detected the unmistakable scent of Chanel No. 5.

R

Emily stretched, pushing her toes to the floor and her hands above her head. She inched over to her husband's body next to her.

She opened her eyes and could tell by the amount of light in the room that it must be morning. She was thankful that she could distinguish light and dark and some vivid colors, in addition to the pinhole of clear vision in the center of her left eye.

Connor stirred and rolled toward her. She slipped her arms around him and ran a row of kisses along his neck.

He caught her hands, bringing them to his lips to kiss them. "You're awake," he said. "How did you sleep?"

"Wonderfully," Emily said. "I missed you." She pressed her body to his.

"What would you like for breakfast?" he asked, moving to the side of the bed. "I got those bagels you like."

"I'm not hungry for breakfast." She reached for him. "Come back."

He shot out of bed. "Stay put. I'll bring you a cup of coffee."

"Connor," she called after him. Emily rolled onto her back and slapped the mattress in frustration, and then the unwelcome but familiar thoughts began to rush in.

Her husband didn't want her anymore.

The blind girl wasn't appealing.

She forced herself into a sitting position. No. Connor wasn't that shallow.

Maybe he was afraid of hurting her.

Or maybe there was another reason—a Chanel No. 5 reason—her husband had pushed her away.

She needed to find out right now or she'd drive herself mad.

Emily felt for her cane on her nightstand and made her way to the kitchen. The sound of the whirring upscale coffee maker served as a beacon.

"What's wrong?" Emily asked.

"What do you mean? Nothing's wrong. I'm getting your coffee, is all."

"You don't need to be afraid of me, Connor. I'm not going to break."

"I ... I know that."

"Then what is it? Why did you jump out of bed like you'd been shot from a cannon the minute I touched you?"

"You're being ridiculous. I didn't do that."

"Yes. You did." She drew a deep breath and caught a whiff of perfume again. The blood in her temples began to pound. "Unless maybe you've found someone else? To take your mind off your poor, pathetic blind wife?"

"What?!" Connor exploded. "Now you've completely lost your mind."

"Oh? Then why do I smell Chanel No. 5 in the condo?"

He remained silent.

"I've never worn it!" She practically spat the words.

"That's Gina," he said. "Gina's stopped over from time to time."

"She has? Why haven't either of you mentioned it?"

"Maybe because when we talk to you the only topic of discussion is you and your blindness."

Emily recoiled.

"I'm sorry, Em. I didn't mean it to sound like that." He sighed heavily. "We didn't mention it because it doesn't mean anything. You know she came by to open the wedding presents so I could write thank-you notes. You asked her to do that, remember?"

"Yes—but that was a long time ago."

"She's also stopped by with audiobooks for you and food for me."

"Food? Why?"

"She … she thought I could use a home-cooked meal."

Emily snorted. "Gina's never made a home-cooked meal in her life."

"I don't know what to tell you. She has for me." Connor crossed to her and touched her hand.

She pulled it back from him.

"Nothing's going on between us," he said, "if that's what you think."

Emily extended her cane and walked to the front door. She stuffed her feet into the shoes she'd worn the night before and reached for the handle to open the door.

"Where are you going?" Connor asked. "Do you want to go out to breakfast?" He moved to the door.

Emily put up a hand to stop him. "No. I want to get some air, by myself. I need to think."

"You can't go alone. You're not capable."

Emily felt the anger expand in her chest and radiate to her extremities. "I'm more than capable," she said stiffly as she stepped through the door and slammed it behind her.

She extended her cane and turned to her left, toward the elevator. She would feel the number of doorways between their condo and the elevator, as she'd learned to do in her orientation and mobility class. She retraced her path three times, confident that she'd be able to find her front door again.

That was all she'd learned, so far. She really should go back inside, but weren't they always praising her about what a fast learner she was—how easily she was picking up these new skills? Surely she could ride the elevator and come back.

Emily went back to the elevator and felt the buttons. She pushed the one that was marked with a distinctive "L". The doors shut and the elevator descended, chiming and lurching to a stop.

Emily felt the open doorway but couldn't find any markings that confirmed she was in the Lobby. She held the door open with her left hand. "Hello," she called. "Is this the lobby?"

No one answered.

What else could it be other than the lobby? Wasn't that the button she pushed?

Emily felt her face flush and her pulse began to race. Maybe she'd had enough solo exploring for one day.

She stepped back into the elevator. She brought her hand to the row of buttons and felt for raised numbers that would indicate floor numbers. There were none.

How was this possible? Didn't the Americans with Disabilities Act require such identification? Stupid building. She'd have to call and complain.

She froze, her hand raised above the buttons on the elevator. How would she find her floor?

What were they always talking about at the foundation? Problem-solving when you were lost? But she hadn't been in the program long enough to have acquired those skills.

She reached into her pocket for her phone and cursed. She'd left the condo in a huff and hadn't taken it with her. She couldn't call Connor for help.

Emily swallowed her rising panic. She didn't want to call him, anyway. He already thought of her as incompetent—somehow "less than." She didn't want to reinforce this view of her.

She pushed the button on the far left. She'd get out, find the first door she came to, and feel the unit number posted by the door. In that way, she'd know what floor she was on.

Their condo was on the seventh floor. Based upon what she found, she'd retrace her steps to the elevator and try to figure out the arrangement of the elevator buttons. They had to be in numerical order, either side to side or up and down. There were a finite number of combinations. The building only had nine floors. It might take some time, but she'd find her way home. She didn't need Connor—or anyone—to help her.

Emily was making her way to the first doorway on the seventh floor to feel the unit number posted by the door when she heard Connor call to her.

"Emily." His voice held a note of alarm. "I was getting worried."

She'd found her way home. She straightened and smoothed her hair. "Here I am," she said, holding up her arms. "Just fine. No need to worry."

She only hoped her face wouldn't betray her as she made her way to him and entered the condo. The last thing she wanted was for Connor to find out how frightening the experience had been for her.

Chapter 28

Katie went to the coat rack in the hall and pulled out the green vest that I wore whenever we went on an adventure. She said it told people I was in training to be a guide and to leave me alone so I could learn. I loved that people knew I was going to be a guide, but I didn't like that they had to leave me alone. Back then, all people ever wanted to do was pet me and tell me how cute I was. *What could be wrong with that?* It was clear I still had a lot to learn.

I stood still while she put my vest on me. I always wanted to make a good appearance when we were out.

"We're going to the puppy raiser club meeting today," she said.

My ears twitched. There was a club we were members of? Why hadn't I heard of this before now?

"It's a beautiful afternoon and we're going to a big, fenced field. You'll be with other puppies-in-training. Some will be older and some younger than you."

I looked up at her and wagged my tail.

"The purpose of this outing is to practice not chasing other animals."

I blinked twice. Ever since the incident with Liloh, I'd never chased another animal again. And it wasn't like I hadn't had the chance. The yard was full of squirrels. They came out every day during After School, when I was outside with Abby and Alex. I wasn't anxious for a repeat of the Liloh performance, so I gave them a wide berth. Besides, I knew better.

Katie hooked me into the backseat and rolled down the window the right amount, just like she knew I loved. We began to pick up speed, and I turned my muzzle to the breeze from the window. I could smell dozens of scents. My nose twitched, and my ears blew back. This was bliss.

We finally came to a stop, and Katie opened my door. I have to admit to being a bit disappointed. I'd have been content to ride around all afternoon.

She took my leash and we entered a large, grassy enclosure. I stood at her side and surveyed the situation. There were a dozen other dogs—all wearing green vests like mine—and their owners. They were racing around, exploring the environment and each other.

"Would you like to go say hello?" Katie asked, kneeling down to look me in the eye.

I lifted my head and wagged my tail for yes.

Katie laughed. "All right, you can get acquainted for a few minutes before we get to work." She unclipped my leash, and I raced off to make friends.

The other dogs were all nice and well behaved. One other male—about my size—and I wrestled for a while, like I used to do before I came to my family's house. We opened our mouths and put our teeth on each other, but neither of us meant business.

A big man with a red face clapped his hands and said something to our puppy raisers.

Katie called to me, and I reluctantly left my new friend and went to her. She told me I was a "very good boy" and clipped the leash back on me.

"Here's today's lesson," she whispered in my ear. "Down," she commanded.

I obeyed, resting my muzzle on my outstretched paws.

The other dog-and-human couples did the same.

We were arranged in a circle around a grassy opening.

My eyes shifted back and forth, searching for what was to come next. I didn't have long to wait.

A furry white blur erupted from somewhere on my right and streaked through the center of our circle, yipping its fool head off. I raised my head from my paws. Whatever this creature was, it had clearly lost its mind.

The thing circled behind us, dodging in and out.

I gathered myself on my haunches, and Katie said, "No." I lifted my eyes to hers. *Really?*

"No," she reiterated.

Well then, no it was. I relaxed back onto the soft grass.

A younger puppy on the other side of the circle jumped up and tore after it. Her human called to her sharply but was ignored. The big man who had started the whole thing by releasing the insane white blur—which happened to be a small dog—got involved, then, and much discussion ensued between the noncompliant puppy, its owner, and the man.

I grew bored with the whole thing and closed my eyes. I heard Katie say "good boy" again before I drifted off to sleep.

Chapter 29

Emily sat on the glider on the front porch, rocking back and forth. She'd been there since right after lunch, and it seemed like the perfect way to spend a Saturday afternoon—if only she could let herself enjoy it.

Connor was supposed to be here spending the weekend with her, but after the tension between them last weekend, she was relieved when he'd called yesterday morning to say that he had to work all weekend. His team was making a presentation to a significant prospective client on Tuesday and they had to prepare together, in the office.

She'd expected to be disappointed, but in truth she was glad he wasn't coming. Her classes at the foundation, Monday through Friday, were exhilarating and exhausting. She wanted nothing more than to relax for a couple of days.

She tilted her head into the slight breeze created by the swing and relished the feel of it slipping along her cheeks.

A car rolled onto the paved driveway. Emily stopped the glider and listened as someone got out and walked across the lawn and up the steps of the front porch. The gait was familiar.

"Dhruv?" she called.

"Yes. How did you know?"

Emily smiled. "I'm learning that people have very distinctive characteristics in the way they walk. You, for example, drop your heels."

"I do?"

"Yep." She stood. "What's up? Why are you here?"

"I finished work early today and decided to come see you. I called your mother, and she said you weren't doing anything." He cleared his throat. "That your husband wasn't here this weekend."

"He had to work," Emily replied.

"What have you been doing?"

"Just sitting here, swinging. I was thinking about going for a walk."

"It's a beautiful day. Let's go."

"All right." She reached for his shoulder.

"Did you learn to use your cane?"

"I'm in the process of learning, yes."

"How's it going?"

"I'm pretty good."

"Will you show me? I'd love to see you in action."

"Sure. Actually, I'd like that. Whenever I go anywhere with my mom—or Connor—they want to guide me. They haven't said anything, but I think the cane makes them nervous. I know it's quicker for them to guide me, but it doesn't help me practice."

"Good. You'll practice with me. We'll walk all afternoon."

"I'll go inside and get my shoes and my cane. I'll text Mom to let her know that I'm out with you."

"Do you want me to text her?"

"Nope—I do voice texts on my phone." She patted his elbow as she passed him on the way to the house.

Dhruv was waiting by the door when she came out. She began sweeping her cane back and forth, in shoulder-width arcs, as she made her way to the steps.

"Careful …" Dhruv began.

"It's okay," Emily interrupted. "I've got this."

"What do you want me to do?"

"Don't let me step out into the street, but let me explore with my cane and find my own way. That'll be the most helpful."

"I can do that." He followed her down the steps to the sidewalk. "Lead the way."

Emily turned right, and they began walking down the long, tree-lined residential street. They turned a corner and came out of the shade onto a patch of sidewalk in front of a vacant lot. There were no trees on the lot and the sun beat down on them.

Emily pointed to her left. "That's west, isn't it?"

"Yes. How did you know?"

"I can feel the sun more strongly on my left side. By this time of day, the sun is starting to set in the west. I'm learning to orient myself using the sun."

"That's smart. You're like an olden times tracker."

Emily laughed. "I've still got a lot to learn."

"You're making great progress," Dhruv said. "How is it going with the technology aides?"

Emily turned around, and they began to retrace their steps. "Fabulous. You can't imagine the things they have to assist the visually impaired." She halted and turned to him. "I didn't believe it when I started at the foundation, but I'll be able to do my old job just fine with the new aides. It won't be a problem at all."

"Are you ready to come back to work?"

Emily flushed at the sound of genuine pleasure in Dhruv's voice.

"Not yet, but I'm getting close."

"When?"

"I'm picking up the technology training very fast—faster than I am the other parts of the program. I need to wait until I learn it all."

"What about coming back part-time and working from home?"

"That might be okay." Emily paused. "I'll think about it."

"I want you to think about something else."

"What's that?"

"Getting a guide dog."

"Oh, Dhruv," Emily sighed. "I don't think I want to take on a dog."

"I've done research and talked to people with guides. That's what they're called—guides."

"Who do you know who has a guide?"

"They're all over the place," he said. "Once you start noticing them, they're everywhere."

"So you … what? You went up and talked to their owners?"

"Yes. Their stories are amazing. Every single person—they're called handlers—is happy that they have a guide. The dogs make

148

them safer and more efficient when they travel, and they love the companionship."

"You're a dog softie, Dhruv. How many dogs do you have at the moment?"

"Four. That has nothing …"

"Four? When did you get a new one?"

"A couple of weeks ago."

"Let me guess. You rescued a stray."

Dhruv cleared his throat.

Emily extended her free hand, found his back, and patted it. "You are a kind soul, Dhruv. There's nothing wrong with that. I think it's not the right thing for me. Connor doesn't really like dogs, and our condo is only a two bedroom. I've been around guides and their handlers at the foundation. You have to feed them, exercise them, take them out to relieve themselves, and a bunch of other stuff."

"Having someone to love and take care of is good."

"I've got Connor," Emily said.

"There's a place near here that trains and supplies guide dogs," he continued. "I've done the research. The dogs are free and everything. There's a workshop for people who are considering getting a guide— to see if they'd like it. I think you should go."

"Thank you for thinking of me, Dhruv, but I'm really not interested." Emily picked up her pace, and they made their way home.

R

"Who was that?" Zoe asked. "It's Zoe."

Emily groaned inwardly. After the long walk, she'd been looking forward to resting on her quiet porch, but Emily never had the heart to turn the lonely little bundle of curiosity away.

"Thanks for identifying yourself." She patted the cushion next to herself. "That's Dhruv, a friend from my work. And he's a very nice man."

"Did he want you to do work?"

"No. He came to see how I was doing—and to try to talk me into getting a guide dog."

Emily could feel Zoe sit up straighter. "Like the ones you see out with people? They wear vests that tell you about them?"

"Yes."

"I saw a poodle going around the hospital when Gramma and I went to visit her friend."

"That was probably a therapy dog and not a guide dog."

"What's the difference?"

"Therapy dogs give people comfort."

"Don't guide dogs do that, too?"

"Yes … of course. But they're also mobility aides for people who can't see. Guide dogs navigate as a person directs them. They stop if a car's coming, halt at steps and changes in elevation. They'll even stop if a person is going to bump their head on something."

"Wow. That's so cool."

"There are other kinds of assistance animals, too. Veterans have dogs that help them adjust to life after war. Some dogs let diabetics know when it's time to eat or take medicine."

"Are you getting a dog?"

"There's a lot that goes into having a guide dog. It's a big commitment. I don't think having a dog fits in with the lifestyle that Connor and I have."

"Aren't you going to have a new lifestyle now?"

Emily paused. The impertinent—but insightful—question from this eight-year-old caught her off guard. "Yes … I suppose I will. All the more reason to wait on getting a dog. We'll need to figure out things ourselves, first."

She could feel Zoe shaking her head from side to side. "I wouldn't wait. I'd get a dog."

Emily was grateful when Martha opened the front door and interrupted them.

"Your grandmother just called, Zoe. She needs you to come home for dinner."

Zoe stood. "I'm going to learn about guide dogs when I'm done with my homework." She turned and ran down the steps and across the lawn to her grandmother's house.

R

Martha hovered by her living room window and pretended to fluff the sofa pillows, her eyes trained on the sidewalk that ran north from her driveway. Emily had said that she'd be returning on this side of the street and that she'd be gone twenty minutes.

Martha had wanted to argue, to protest that it was too soon for Emily to navigate their neighborhood on her own. She'd known, however, that she needed to let her daughter do this. She shouldn't allow her own fears, as a mother, to undermine all of Emily's efforts to regain her independence. Emily was working very hard at the foundation. If they thought she was ready, Emily was ready.

Martha glanced at her watch for the hundredth time. Emily had been gone for more than thirty minutes. She should be home by now. An icy knot of fear formed in her stomach.

She was punching Emily's number into her phone when she spotted her daughter on the sidewalk in front of the neighbor's house. Zoe was walking beside her, talking and gesturing wildly with her hands.

Martha smiled. That's why Emily was late. She went to the door in time to hear Emily tell Zoe that she was tired and coming inside to nap.

"You'll think about it, won't you? Promise me?"

"Yes. Getting a guide dog might be a good idea for me— sometime in the distant future."

"I still think you should get one now. I'd get a dog if I could."

Emily tousled the girl's hair. "You just want a pet. Why don't you talk to your grandmother about it?"

"I have been. She says dogs are a lot of work. I'd take really good care of my dog," Zoe said. "I'd feed and walk him every day. I wouldn't forget. Gramma wouldn't have to do anything."

"I'm sure you would," Emily said. "You're a very responsible young lady. I'm going in now. See you tomorrow after school?"

"Yep," Zoe said.

"Okay, then," Emily made her way inside as Zoe turned and skipped down the steps.

"Mom—is that you?"

"Yes."

"Did you wait here—by the door—the whole time I was gone?"

"Ahh …"

"I'm fine, Mom. You don't need to hover."

"You were gone way longer than you said," Martha said, shaking her phone at Emily. "I was getting worried."

"How much longer?"

"Fifteen minutes."

"That's all it took to make you panic?"

Emily reached for her and ran her hand along her mother's arm. "Under the circumstances, I guess that's understandable. I should have called you. I'm sorry. It's just that Zoe came up—with a bee in her bonnet. You've seen how that little girl can talk when she's passionate about something."

"What was on her mind?"

"She saw Dhruv yesterday and wanted to know who he was and what we talked about. He wants me to get a guide dog."

"You mentioned that last night."

"Well, that was the wrong thing to say to Zoe," Emily said, moving to the sofa. She folded her cane and placed it on the end table. "Apparently Zoe is extremely interested in dogs." She sat, tucking her feet under herself.

"Irene says she's always begging to get one."

"She spent all last night researching guides. She watched YouTubes of them in action and—I swear—she must have read every word on every website of every organization on the West Coast that provides guides." Emily shook her head. "She's the only person I've ever met who can out-research Dhruv."

"Good heavens. That's saying something!"

"It sure is. Plus, she's way harder to shut down than he is. I told her that Connor doesn't want a dog and that it wouldn't fit our lifestyle. She wouldn't hear it."

"You know who she reminds me of at that age?"

"Who?"

Martha looked at her daughter and smiled.

"No … really? Me?"

"The very same."

"Did I drive you and Dad crazy?"

"Sometimes. We realized that your … tenacity—let's not call it stubbornness—as a child might be annoying but that it would stand you in good stead as an adult."

Martha sat down next to her daughter.

"And I think it's been a very helpful character trait in your current situation. I'm so proud of how hard you're working and how much progress you've made."

"Thanks, Mom. It's been so nice to be able to live here while I'm in school. Are you sure you're not getting tired of having me underfoot?"

"Not a bit. Truth be told, I'll miss you when you move back in with Connor."

"I think it'll be soon," Emily said. "I'm getting closer to being ready."

Chapter 30

"Emily! Guess what?!"

Emily extended her foot to stop the porch swing. "From the sound of your voice, I'd say it's something good." She patted the seat next to her.

Zoe flopped down, sending the swing on a sideways loop. "I got all A's on my report card!"

Emily heard Zoe crinkle a paper she was holding. "That's wonderful. I'm so proud of you!"

"Know what the best part is?"

Emily shook her head.

"I get straight A's all the time—on everything except P.E. Gramma said that if I got straight A's—even including P.E.—she'd let me get a puppy!" Zoe squirmed with excitement. "I got an A in P.E."

Emily smiled. "That's wonderful news! I know how much you've wanted a dog." It could be good news for Emily, too. Maybe now Zoe would stop pushing for her to get a guide dog.

"We're going to the pet store right now. Gramma says there's a free adoption clinic today. It closes in an hour."

"You're getting a rescue dog?"

"Uh-huh. Gramma says that they make great pets—that they always know you saved them and they're grateful."

"What kind of dog do you want?"

"Gramma says it has to be under twenty pounds. She said no big dogs."

"That's fine, isn't it? Do you care what kind you get?"

Zoe shook her head vigorously. "Oh … sorry. I just want one that's cute and cuddly."

"I'm sure there'll be plenty of those to choose from. You'd better get going so you have lots of time."

Zoe laid her small hand on top of Emily's. "Would you come with us? You could help me pick it out."

"Oh ... no ... you don't need me there. I don't know anything about dogs."

"But ... you're my friend," Zoe said in a small voice. "I want to share this with my best friend."

A lump rose in Emily's throat, and she swallowed hard. Surely this lonely little girl had friends her own age? Even as she thought it, she knew it probably wasn't true. Sometimes being the smartest kid in class wasn't a good thing. "All right," Emily said, squeezing Zoe's hand.

"Yeah!" Zoe leapt off the swing, sending it careening backward.

"I'll tell my mom and we can go. But you have to promise me one thing."

"What?"

"That you won't leave me alone in the store. I'm still not totally comfortable going out in public, so you can't get excited about your puppy and leave me by myself."

"You'll know where I am every minute." Zoe grew solemn. "I promise. I won't let you be afraid."

R

"Remember," Emily said, "you're my sighted guide. I'm bringing my cane with me, but I'm not going to use it. I'll be relying on you."

"I know," Zoe said, unbuckling her seat belt. "I'll come around to your side of the car to get you."

Zoe's grandmother stepped out of the car. "Thank you, Zoe," Irene said. "Being responsible today will show me that you're ready to take care of a dog."

Emily opened her car door and swung her feet to the pavement.

Zoe took Emily's right hand and placed it on her left shoulder. "Ready?" Zoe asked.

Emily inhaled slowly through her nose. She listened to cars passing in front of them. Perspiration formed on her upper lip. She dreaded entering the chaos of a big-box pet store, especially one hosting an adoption event. Why had she agreed to come? She blew out the breath she had been holding and inhaled again. Cleansing breaths were supposed to help when she was feeling anxious. She'd agreed to come because Zoe had asked her to—Zoe wanted her to be there and Zoe had become important to her.

"Yep. Lead on," Emily forced herself to say.

The three women began walking.

"Look both ways," Irene said.

"I am," Zoe said, halting briefly before moving forward again.

The automatic doors of the pet store whooshed open and they stepped inside.

Emily felt a rush of supercooled air envelop them. She was surrounded by the sounds of excited chatter. Barking of every variety—from short yips to deep throaty blasts—punctuated every snippet of overheard conversation. She tightened her grip on Zoe's shoulder.

Zoe brought her right hand to Emily's and squeezed it. "It's okay," she said over her shoulder. "The dogs are over there … to our right."

"Thank you," Emily said. "Giving me cues like right and left is very helpful."

They began walking and the barking grew louder. Zoe slowed her pace.

"Can you describe where we are?"

"We're going around the outside of a large wire enclosure." Zoe leaned into Emily to be heard over the barking.

"Is this where the dogs are?"

"Yes. Most of them are in crates. A couple of them are in an open pen."

"Let's walk around and look at all of them first. Get an idea of what's available." Irene said.

"Great idea." Emily said. "Can you tell me about them?"

"They're all small," Zoe said. "Just like Gramma wanted."

"What breeds? There's probably a sign on each crate that gives the name, age, and breed."

Zoe pulled Emily's hand forward as she leaned in to read each animal's information.

"Lots of chihuahua and terrier mixes," Emily said. "Do you like any of them?"

She felt Zoe shrug.

"You don't have to get a dog today, if you don't find one that you want to," Irene said. "You're making a commitment to an animal for ten or more years when you adopt one. You need to be sure. We can keep looking."

"Your grandmother's right," Emily said. "If you don't feel drawn to one of them, don't get a dog just to go home with one."

A dog in a crate in front of them gave a raspy bark.

"I like this one," Zoe said.

"The one that just barked?" Irene asked. "It sounds like he's got laryngitis. We don't want to adopt a sick dog."

"Surely they wouldn't put a sick animal out here," Emily said.

"It's a girl. Her name's Sabrina," Zoe said, reading the sign on her crate. "She's a miniature Schnauzer. It says she's been debarked."

"I've heard about that," her grandmother said. "Seems inhumane, if you ask me. Looks like someone's done a bad job of trimming her ears, too. Poor little thing."

Sabrina stuck her nose against the wire grid of the crate and wagged her stub of a tail furiously.

"Why don't we see if you can take her out to get to know her? Do they have a get-acquainted area?" Emily asked.

"Good idea," Irene said. "I'll ask one of the attendants to help us."

"What does Sabrina look like?" Emily asked.

"She's mostly white with gray mixed in. Her nose and eyes are black. She's smart—I can tell from her eyes," Zoe said.

Sabrina emitted a short, muffled bark.

"Your grandma said that her ears … don't look right."

157

"They look perfect to me," Zoe said. "She's beautiful."

"I hear you'd like to spend time with our Sabrina, here," a woman's voice grew louder as she approached. "Good choice. She's one of the nicest dogs we've ever had. She's shy and a bit reserved, so not many people have been interested in her. Plus, her cropping was badly botched so that may have interfered with her finding her forever home." She slipped a leash onto the squirming dog. "She certainly doesn't seem to be wary of you."

The woman handed Zoe the leash. "You can take her to the back of the store. It's quiet there. Walk her around. Sit on the floor and allow her to come to you. Just make sure to keep her on the leash."

"Thank you," Zoe said. "Come on, Sabrina," she said as she and the prancing dog led the way to the rear corner of the store. The walls were lined with large cardboard boxes containing dog kennels that were stacked to the ceiling. The area was deserted.

Zoe stopped and Emily felt the leash pull as Sabrina kept going.

"Stop," Zoe said.

Sabrina stopped.

"Sit," Zoe said, followed by "Good girl!"

Emily released her hold on Zoe and reached for the animal. Her first contact was with a cold nose, followed closely by a series of quick licks. Emily walked her hand along Sabrina's muzzle and rubbed the silky fur between her ears.

Zoe plopped on the cold tile floor and threw her arms around Sabrina's neck. Emily pulled her hand back, imagining the scene that must surely be playing out in front of her.

"Would you look at that?" Irene said. "She's not the least bit standoffish with either of you."

Zoe giggled as Sabrina crawled into her lap and covered Zoe's face and neck with doggy kisses.

Irene leaned over and patted Sabrina on the head.

"She's the one," Zoe said.

"Don't you want to take some of the others out to get acquainted with?" her grandmother asked. "This is the first dog we've looked at. We shouldn't make a snap decision."

"I want this one."

"The lady said that nobody's been interested in her. We have time to look at other dogs. She'll still be here."

"No, Gramma. I'm not going to let her go. Sabrina is mine." Zoe turned to Emily. "You think so, too, don't you?"

"She's awfully sweet," Emily said. "But your grandmother has a good point. You've only just begun to look."

"When you get a guide dog, you don't get to pick. They match you up. I've read about it," Zoe said. "It's called the magic of the match. I think that's happening here—with Sabrina and me. We're a magic match."

Sabrina emitted a barely audible woof.

Emily felt a warmth wash over herself. She couldn't see Irene's face, but she would have sworn she could hear the woman smile.

"Call me crazy, but I believe you're right. The two of you look like a match made in heaven to me," Irene said.

"Then I can get Sabrina?" Zoe's voice cracked with emotion. "We can be her forever home?"

"Yes. We most certainly can. Let's go tell the lady that we're taking her home with us and find out what we'll need to buy for her."

"Can I pick out a pretty collar and some toys?"

"Of course," her grandmother said. "Emily—can you go with them while I get the adoption paperwork started?"

"I'd love to," Emily said, surprising herself by meaning it. Sabrina rested her front paws on Emily's knee, and Emily bent and ran her hand along the dog's back. For the first time since her wedding, she felt truly happy.

Chapter 31

"You're sure you want to go back to the burger place?" Connor asked.

"I am. I want to try it again." Emily held up her cane. "I'm so much more confident now that I have this."

"It's a Tuesday night, so it won't be as busy as last time."

"Exactly. I'll still need you to be my sighted guide if I go to the ladies' room, but I won't panic if I come out and you're not where I can immediately find you."

"Don't worry—I'll be there this time! No matter what."

"If you weren't there, I'd ask for help getting back to my table."

"All right, then. I'm starved. Let's go."

"Did you ask Mom if she wanted to come with us?"

"I did but she said that we should go out and enjoy ourselves." He turned his back to her. "Do you want me to guide you to the car?"

"I'm good with my cane," Emily said, stepping from the porch. "I'm amazed that you took a couple of days off in the middle of the week to see me. I wish you'd told me ahead of time—I can't miss my classes."

"I don't want you to skip class." Connor opened the door for her, then grabbed her hand and planted a kiss on her fingertips before helping her into the passenger seat. "In fact, I'd like to come with you, if I can."

"Really? It's so much better than hearing me talk about them. I didn't think you were interested."

"I'm interested," he replied in the tone she'd heard him use with customers when he was trying to close a sale.

The muscles between Emily's shoulder blades tightened, and a frisson of alarm ran down her spine. Something was on Connor's mind.

He put the car in gear, and they were on their way.

"Is there any other reason that you're here?" she asked.

"Do I need another reason?"

"No—I just sense that there's something you're not telling me."

Connor pressed a button on the dashboard and her favorite singer filled the space. They listened in silence until they turned into the parking lot and found a spot close to the door.

Connor came around the car quickly and helped her out. The hostess seated them right away. The dining room was quiet, with the only hubbub coming from the take-out station.

"I want another of their world-famous bison burgers," Emily said.

"Me, too." Connor placed their order.

Emily scooted her chair closer to his, making sure that her cane was still within reach.

"There's something else, isn't there?"

"What do you mean?"

"You didn't come down here just to see me or observe classes at the foundation. You've got something you want to tell me." Her voice cracked. "You're making me nervous, Connor."

He cleared his throat. The waiter arrived at the table and put their drinks in front of them.

"Your Coke is at two-clock," Connor said.

"Thank you," Emily replied.

Silence hung between them like a wall.

"Tell me. Please."

"Do you remember me telling you about my company's expansion into the Japanese market?"

"Sure. They're opening an office in Tokyo."

"That's right."

"Next year sometime?"

"They've accelerated the expansion. They want to send a skeleton crew there next month and be fully operational next year."

"How ... nice," Emily replied. "Sounds like the company is doing well."

"It is," Connor said. "This new territory is going to double our gross margin—maybe triple it. If everything goes as planned, they'll expand all over Asia. That's where the growth for the future will come from." His words picked up speed. "This sort of opportunity only comes along once in a career. The next generation of top executives will come from the Asian teams."

A bead of perspiration formed on Emily's upper lip.

"That'll be nice for … whoever gets those jobs."

"That's what I want to talk to you about."

Emily froze, her soda halfway to her lips. She set it back down on the table.

"What do you mean?"

"I've been chosen to head up the Tokyo office," he said in a rush. "It's the plum position, and they've given it to me."

Emily's head jerked up. "What are you talking about?"

"I'm going to have to go to Tokyo—next week."

Emily recoiled into her seat. "Next week? I can't go to Tokyo next week."

"No. Of course not. I know that."

"So … what about me?"

"You'll stay here, in school. You told me yourself that it'll take you a year or more before you can return to work."

Emily leaned her elbows on the table and cradled her head in her hands. "I told you last week that I've mastered all the assistive technology devices. I'll be able to return to work much sooner."

"And you said that you still need to work on your mobility skills. That you could work part-time from home—from your mom's—while you complete the rest of the program. That's why I wanted to see you in your classes."

"To make sure I'm not ready to return to the condo any time soon—so that you don't have to feel guilty about leaving me?"

"That's not fair, Em."

"Why did you even apply for this job when you knew I wouldn't be able to go with you?"

"I thought that nothing would happen until next year." He blew out a deep breath. "Frankly—it's the chance of a lifetime. I've been hoping for something like this since I started working. If I didn't put my hat in the ring, I'd be pigeon-holed at my current level for years."

"You could have changed companies—gotten a new job. You're always telling me that headhunters are constantly calling you."

"I'm working for one of the most prestigious companies in my industry. I don't want to throw all of my good performance reviews and connections away to start over somewhere else."

"You've got a blind wife!" Emily cried, her voice rising. "I'm just beginning to learn to cope here. I'd be starting all over in Japan— with my career and … everything. What about my Mom, too? Did you think of me at all?"

"Of course, I did," he snapped. "Nobody's thought of anyone but you—and your blindness—since your accident."

"I wouldn't be in this position if you hadn't pushed me into going horseback riding."

"So it's my fault? Is that what you think?"

"You knew I didn't want to go—that I was afraid of something like this happening. I was trying to please you."

They sat in silence, the accusation lying between them.

"I'm sorry, Em," Connor said. "I never in a million years dreamed there'd be a problem. I shouldn't have pushed for that damned photo. If I could turn back time, I would."

Emily inhaled slowly.

"That wasn't fair. I know you didn't intend this." She pushed her plate away. "It was an accident—it wasn't your fault."

"Thank you."

Connor took a long, slow sip from his soda.

"As for the job, I really didn't think anything would happen until next year. You know how these things go—I expected the start date to get delayed, several times. I never thought it would be moved up. I expected your vision to improve, like the doctor said." He sighed. "I thought that all of this training at the blind school would prove unnecessary."

"Even if that had happened, a move to another state—much less another country—is something we should have discussed. Together. We should consider my job and my family, too. I don't want to be so far away from my mom. She's still adjusting to life without my dad."

"The timing sucks, but I can't do anything about it now. The job got offered to me last week and I leave for Tokyo on Sunday morning."

"Just like that?"

"I'll be back at the home office at least one week a month. I'll see you then."

"Your decision is made?"

"I can't turn this down."

"Can't? You mean you won't turn this down," Emily said. Her voice was quiet.

"Try to understand, Em."

"Oh … I think I do." She reached for her cane and snapped it open. "I'm not hungry anymore. Let's get out of here."

"Don't be like this."

Anger flashed through her. "I'm sure you have a lot to do before Sunday. You'll have time to get back to the condo at a decent hour, after you drop me off at Mom's."

"Come on. There's no need to be so dramatic."

"Dramatic? You have the nerve to call me dramatic? You're moving to Tokyo in less than a week!" She stood and made her way to the door. She spoke into her phone and stepped outside.

Connor paid for the burgers they hadn't eaten and followed her outside. He took her elbow, and she pulled it away.

A vehicle turned into the lot and pulled up to them. The driver got out. "Emily?" he asked, coming around the car to open the door for her.

"What are you doing?" Connor asked.

"I called a rideshare. I can get myself home. Just go. I don't want to talk about this anymore." She got into the car, slamming the door behind her.

Chapter 32

"You were such a good boy today!" Katie sat on the floor with me and drew me into her lap. I loved it when she did this.

"You made it from one end of the mall to the other without being distracted by anything. You didn't even turn your head when we walked by the soft pretzel vendor. That place smells irresistible to me—I can't imagine what it must have been like for you."

I thumped my tail. I was particularly proud of that feat, too. Hot, soft pretzel is the most pleasing aroma in all the land.

She picked up my paw and began to massage my toes.

I sighed heavily. This made my sacrifice worthwhile.

"You know what?" Katie stopped rubbing and leapt to her feet. "I've got something even better than this."

What was she talking about? Nothing was better than a toe massage.

She rushed over to the pantry and grabbed the jar she used to make the kids' lunches. Abby and Alex were still at school. Why did she have to make them sandwiches, now?

I followed her to the kitchen island, where she pulled something red from a bag on the counter. "See this?" She held it out to me. It looked like three rubber balls stacked on top of each other in decreasing size. "This is a Kong."

I thumped my tail on the floor. If she was excited about it, so was I.

"Kongs are dog toys," she continued. "They're for you to chew on."

I sniffed and gave it a tentative lick.

"You've been so good that I'm going to make this really special for you." She turned back to the counter. "I know I'm supposed to use kibble, but I'm going to bend the rules just this once." She scooped peanut butter from the open jar and packed it into the middle of that rubber thing she called a "Kong."

It was impossible not to get my hopes up.

She turned to me. "I think this may be your first taste of peanut butter. Here you go, Garth." She set the Kong in my crate, and I dove in after it.

I lapped the peanut butter that oozed out in two easy passes of my tongue. It was creamy and salty and sweet all at once. The peanut butter stuck to my teeth and coated the roof of my mouth. I thrust my tongue in and out of my mouth, trying to sweep it away. I'd never encountered a food that didn't pass quickly over my gums and down my throat.

I lay on my back and tried to place the tip of my tongue against the roof of my mouth. No amount of contortion would allow me to accomplish this. Saliva rolled down the sides of my mouth, and I kept licking. Eventually, the creamy substance dissolved. Katie was right— peanut butter might be better than a toe massage.

The peanut butter deep inside the Kong presented even more of a challenge. Every time my tongue was about to reach the desired substance, the Kong slipped away. Even backing it into a corner of my crate didn't help.

As my trainer Mark later told me, I have "tenacity"—which he said is an excellent quality in a guide dog. It's also a good quality if you want to get every last bit of peanut butter out of a Kong.

I grasped the Kong between my front paws, settled on my stomach, and attacked it with my tongue, turning my head one way or another until I'd licked every molecule of peanut butter out of that toy. I gave the outside of the Kong a few final swipes with my tongue, then turned on my side, rested my head on my crate blanket, and fell asleep. It turns out Kongs can be very tiring.

Chapter 33

"I'm so glad you're here," Connor said, opening the condo door and motioning for Gina to come in.

"No problem," Gina said. "Sorry I didn't get your message until this morning. I was out of town for work and just got back a little while ago. My flight was delayed for over two hours in Denver."

"That's rough," he said, taking a step back and tripping over one of the suitcases lined up at the door.

"Are you all right?" Gina eyed him curiously as she shut the door behind her and put her purse on the kitchen counter. "Is Emily here?"

"No ... no, she's not."

"Are you going somewhere? That's a lot of luggage."

"I leave for Tokyo in the morning."

"Japan?"

"Yes."

"Are you going for business?

"Yep."

"For how long?"

"I'm moving to Japan."

"What? When did this happen?"

"That's why I called. I wanted to tell you about it ... and Emily." He motioned to the sofa.

Gina followed him and sat at one end. Connor plopped himself down next to her.

"Have you been drinking?" She narrowed her eyes as she took in his day-old stubble and uncombed hair.

"I've had a few," he said. "Where are my manners? Would you like a drink?" He picked up a half-empty bottle of bourbon from the floor next to the coffee table. "I'll get you a glass." He began to get up.

"No. I don't want any." She held out her hand and took the bottle from him. "I think you've had enough, too. Now—tell me everything."

Connor sank back into the sofa and the week's events all came tumbling from his mouth in one long, drunken run-on sentence.

"And you haven't spoken to Emily since you left the burger place?"

Connor shook his head.

"She won't pick up her phone."

"Have you tried Martha?"

"She says Emily refuses to come to the phone."

"Em does have a stubborn streak," Gina said.

"I know. That's why I called you. Have you heard from her?"

"No, I've been so busy this week."

"Will you talk to her? Explain my side to her?"

"Connor—you should patch this up before you leave."

"It's too late for that. And—as you noted—I'm in no shape to go to her now, anyway. I haven't had anything to eat since breakfast and this"—he pointed to the bottle with his toe—"has really caught up with me."

"Let's get some coffee into you," Gina said. She rose and went into the kitchen.

Connor followed her. "You understand why I had to take this job, don't you?"

"I understand why you wanted to take the job," Gina said. "I don't think you had to take it. And I completely understand how Emily is feeling about this."

Connor rested his back against the counter and sagged his head in his hands. "I guess I've completely messed this up. With Em, I'm always the bad guy. Every time. Nobody's on my side."

"I didn't say that," Gina said, putting her hands on his forearms and pulling his hands away from his face. She leaned toward him and tilted her head to one side until he was looking into her eyes. "I think you're a very good guy, Connor. A wonderful guy." She felt his hot breath on her cheek. "You know how I feel about you."

Connor slipped an arm around her and pulled her to him.

She stiffened. "What are you doing?"

"It's been a long time since I've felt like I'm wonderful to anyone." He touched his lips to hers.

She pulled her lips away and turned her face. Connor trailed kisses starting at her ear and along her jawline until he returned to her mouth.

She moaned softly and finally gave way to years of pent-up desire.

They stood in the kitchen, arms entwined, kissing hungrily, until they heard the front door click open.

R

The driver dropped Emily at the building's entrance. She extended her cane, found the large glass doors, and made her way to the elevators. This time, she was easily able to read the braille numbers and select the correct floor. She retrieved the house key from her purse while the elevator was ascending.

Emily made her way to their door. She smoothed a hand over her hair, tucking a stray strand behind her ear, before turning the lock and entering the apartment.

She could discern light from the right. Someone was in the kitchen.

"Connor?" she called. "It's me. Are you home?"

"Sweetheart," he called. "Stay there. I'm coming."

Connor crossed the kitchen and took her in his arms. "What are you doing here?"

"I had to see you," Emily said, smelling stale booze on his breath. "I didn't want to leave things … between us … that way."

"I tried to call … over and over."

"I know. I'm sorry I wouldn't talk to you. I wasn't ready—I needed to think."

"Why didn't you call me?"

"I tried ... you didn't pick up. I figured maybe you were mad at me."

"I've been busy ... getting ready to go."

And drinking, Emily thought. She leaned against him and caught a whiff of another scent.

"Did Martha drive you?"

"No. I got a rideshare."

"Ah ... that's good. Let's go into the bedroom so we can talk while I finish packing."

He took her arm and turned with her toward the bedroom. Emily looked back toward the kitchen. It was a sea of light and shadow. Was it her imagination, or was one of the shadows moving?

Connor put his arm around her shoulders and clamped her to him as he began to move them past the kitchen island to their bedroom.

The unmistakable scent of Chanel No. 5 slapped Emily like an open palm. She stopped and whirled around.

"Who's there?" she shouted. "I can smell you!"

"What're you talking about?"

Emily pushed against him hard, setting herself free. She stumbled backward and reached out a hand, grasping the kitchen island.

She heard something slide across the granite countertop, and she lunged toward it. Her nails dug into the soft leather of a purse strap.

Emily and the other woman stood on opposite sides of the kitchen island, faces turned to each other, the purse stretched between them.

Emily let the strap drop from her hands. "It's you, isn't it?"

The room was silent except for the ticking kitchen clock.

"Yes, it's me," Gina finally said. "And it's not what you think."

"Oh no? And what do I think, Gina?"

Emily whirled on Connor. "That Connor was trying to get me into the bedroom so that you could creep out?" Her voice was hard. "Nothing suspicious about that."

"I can explain," Connor reached for her.

Emily slapped his hands away. "Don't you dare touch me."

"Oh, Em." Gina began to cry. "I'm sorry—"

"How dare you!" Emily dropped to her knees and felt her way back to the living room where she found her cane on the coffee table. She extended it and flung the door open, making her way as fast as she could to the elevator.

Connor chased after her. "Where're you going?"

"That's not your concern." She stabbed repeatedly at the elevator button.

"We can't leave it like this."

The elevator arrived and she stepped into it. "We can and we will. Goodbye, Connor." She pressed the button for the first floor.

The doors began to shut. Connor thrust his hand between them, forcing them apart. "You can't just stalk out of here ... at this time of night ...." He hesitated, then finished his thought. "Blind and everything. It's not safe."

"Actually, I'll be perfectly fine. I've got this, Connor. And I don't need any help from you."

The elevator began to buzz.

"Get out of the elevator, Connor. Let me go!"

"If that's what you want," he said in a voice that telegraphed regret.

Emily struggled to keep her voice even. "It is."

Connor pushed the button for the lobby then stepped out of the elevator. "When you come to your senses, call me."

The doors closed. Emily's tears began to flow as the elevator descended. Her husband and her best friend. What a horrible cliché. She rested her forehead against the wall of the elevator. She had to think.

What was she going to do now? It was far too late to ask her mother to drive in to pick her up. She needed to get away from her cheating husband and her faithless best friend.

She retrieved her phone from her pocket and summoned a rideshare. If she had gotten herself there, she could get herself home. At least she could take pride in that.

Chapter 34

Martha rose from her chair and began pacing. She was only able to force herself to sit for a few minutes before she found herself on her feet, again, walking from the living room window to the front door and back again.

She'd been getting ready for bed when the first of three texts, in rapid succession, had pinged on her phone. She'd spit out the toothpaste and quickly rinsed her mouth. This wasn't normal.

The first one had been from Emily. She'd curtly stated that she was on her way home and asked Martha to wait up to let her into the house. Emily had planned to spend the night with Connor—to make up with him after their fight earlier in the week. The fact that Emily was on her way back to Martha's when she couldn't have spent more than a half hour with Connor was not a good sign.

Martha scrolled and read texts from Connor and Gina. They both asked Martha to let them know if Emily came home. Martha stood, clutching her phone, rocking back and forth. Something had gone terribly wrong between Emily and Connor. She was sure of it. The fact that Gina was involved—and wasn't in direct contact with Emily—made her stomach sour.

Martha placed a call to Emily, but it went directly to voicemail. She texted that she would be waiting up for her daughter—that she was there if Emily wanted to talk. She'd pressed send and listened to the whoosh from her phone.

At that time of night, it would take Emily about an hour to get home from the condo; maybe less. Martha put on the coffee pot, turned on a late-night television program, and began pacing.

She was on her third cup of coffee when she looked out the living room window and saw headlights approaching her home. They swung into her driveway, and Emily got out of the car. Her daughter fumbled with her cane and her purse hung haphazardly from her shoulder.

Martha flung open the front door and raced down the steps to meet her.

Emily stopped trying to extend her cane and fell into her mother's arms. The tendrils of hair around her face were wet and her cheeks were damp.

The car pulled back out of the driveway.

Martha and Emily stood, arms entwined, as the mother let her daughter weep.

"Let's get you inside," Martha whispered in Emily's ear when her sobs began to subside.

They walked up the steps and into the house with their arms around each other's waists.

"Do you want—" Martha began but Emily cut her off.

"I don't want anything. I just want to go to bed." Emily allowed her purse to slip to the floor. Her phone tumbled out and began to ring, the voiceover feature announcing that the caller was Gina.

Emily scooped up the phone in one swift motion and hurled it at the wall. It hit with a thud and ricocheted off, landing on the sofa below.

Martha inhaled sharply. Her dark supposition appeared to be true.

"I'm here, when you're ready to talk," she said as Emily trudged past her without another word.

Martha picked up the phone from the sofa. "Do you want your phone?" she said to Emily's back.

Emily shook her head. She entered her room and shut the door firmly behind her.

Martha stepped to the door and raised her hand to knock, then brought it back to her side. Her daughter needed time to process whatever had happened. Emily would reach out to her when she was ready. Martha needed to respect that.

She returned to the living room, locked the front door, and turned out the lights. She picked up her own phone and scrolled to her text messages. She began typing a reply to Connor, then deleted it. If he and Gina had done what she suspected, they didn't deserve a response.

Martha walked to Emily's door once more and pressed her ear to it. She could hear Emily crying. She stepped away from the door quickly as her own tears welled up inside. The last thing her daughter needed was a broken heart. She cursed Connor and Gina and tried to feel sorry that she had done so but couldn't muster any remorse.

Martha climbed into bed, leaving her door open in case Emily should call to her in the night.

R

"It's Zoe, Em," Martha said one afternoon at the end of the next week. "And Sabrina. Zoe's excited to show you what she's taught Sabrina"

Emily rolled over in bed, putting her back to her mother.

"She wants to see you, honey. That little girl adores you."

"I'm … I'm not up to it," Emily said.

"What do you want me to tell her?"

"That I'm sick—like you've been telling the foundation."

"I can't 'call in sick' for you for the rest of your life. I know that you've been hurt …" She stopped abruptly as Emily ripped off the covers and launched herself out of bed.

"Oh … so you know how your poor, pathetic blind daughter feels, do you?" Emily swayed on her feet.

Martha took a step back. "Don't turn on me—I'm on your side."

"If you were on my side you'd go away and leave me alone."

"You can't stay in here forever. At some point you're going to have to go back to your classes at the foundation. You'll need to see people again. And you have to talk to Connor and Gina."

"Connor? Gina?" Emily almost spat the words.

"They've both been calling—multiple times a day."

"They can both go to hell!"

"I'm just talking about Zoe right now. She's stopped by every day this week."

Emily groaned and slumped back onto her bed. "I'm not ready yet, Mom. Don't push me."

"She'll be back tomorrow," Martha said.

Emily pulled the covers up around her ears. "I can't. I just can't."

Chapter 35

Restaurant? Did I want to go to a restaurant? If Katie was going there, I wanted to go, too.

Today started like any other day. We walked the kids to the bus stop and watched it pull away. I was decked out in my green vest with the white stitching that proclaimed I was a Guide Dog in Training. I knew I looked sharp, and even though I was a regular fixture at the bus stop, I still got a lot of admiring glances. Wearing that vest was a status symbol.

It was a beautiful, crisp morning and I was in the mood to stretch my legs. I trotted along next to Katie, willing her to keep going when we came to our house. She must have sensed what I was thinking—as she often did.

"Not yet, Garth," Katie said as she led us up the driveway and into the garage. "I have a big report to finish and submit. If everything goes well, I should be done by eleven. I'll take us out for lunch to celebrate."

I wagged my tail. I had no idea what she was talking about, but I liked it when Katie talked to me—just me and nobody else.

"I need to teach you how to behave in a restaurant. I think you're ready. You're such a good boy."

My tail-wagging speed increased dramatically at these last two words.

Katie opened her laptop on the kitchen island and perched on one of the high stools. I settled at her feet. I tried to keep my head up and remain alert, in case she needed me. Sometime during the morning, I'd rested my head on my paws and closed my eyes—simply conserving energy.

The next thing I knew, Katie was stroking my back and calling my name.

"Wake up, sleepyhead," she said. "I'm finished! What do you say about going to a restaurant? Are you ready for that?"

I got to my feet, stretched in what I've now learned is appropriately called the "downward dog pose," and looked up at her.

She clipped the leash on my harness, and we headed for the car.

"Do you like Mexican food?" She glanced at me in the backseat. "I really shouldn't—it's not on my diet—but I'm celebrating. I can cheat—just this once."

I swept my tail along the car seat and extended my nose toward her. I knew I liked anything with the word "food" in it. She reached a hand back and scratched the skin behind my nose.

Katie rolled the back window down a few inches—just how I liked it. She set out for the restaurant, whatever that was, while I concentrated on the scents pouring in the window.

The lot was almost full, and it took her a while to secure a parking spot. We walked up to the building to find a group of people seated at a bench along one wall. If my nose had been busy on the way out here, it was in overdrive now. Food. I smelled food. Beef and chicken—spicy and fried.

Katie and I approached a woman standing behind a tall counter.

"I don't have a reservation," Katie said to her. "How long is the wait?"

The woman glanced at Katie, then caught sight of me. She smiled broadly. "Give me a minute. I'm sure I can find a place for you." She stepped away and into the dining room

Katie leaned over and patted my back. "See that, Garth? You're my good luck charm."

I opened my mouth and my tongue slid out. The smells from this place were unbelievable—like nothing I'd ever experienced before. I wouldn't mind if we had to spend the rest of the day right where we were.

The woman returned. "Follow me, please."

Katie and I trailed along behind her to a booth along the back wall. She handed Katie a large, plastic-coated rectangle.

Katie sat down and positioned me at her feet, under the table. I immediately began sweeping my muzzle in circles along the carpeted floor, searching for anything edible. Other than one tiny thing that could have been a tortilla chip or landscaping mulch—I couldn't be sure—I found nothing.

"Stay, Garth," Katie said. She reached into the compartment of her purse that I knew was devoted to me and removed a treat. "This will tide you over while I eat my lunch."

I dispatched the treat in two bites.

Katie ordered her lunch and was eating something that sounded deliciously crunchy when the trouble began.

I was lying at her feet, head on my paws, in what Jon had dubbed my "screensaver mode." I still have no idea what that means. I was replaying in my mind all the commands I'd learned so far—or else I was sleeping—I'm not sure which.

A woman entered the dining room at the other end of a leash that was hooked to a large black and brown dog with a pointed snout and small, thick ears. The dog was wearing a red vest with the words Service Dog emblazoned on the side. The dog was straining at its end of the leash and turning its head wildly from side to side.

"Jester," I heard the woman snap at the unruly animal.

Jester paused momentarily, then redoubled his efforts to pull her along.

They were almost even with us when Jester stopped abruptly, recoiled, and bared his teeth at me.

I brought my head up and inched deeper into the booth. The other puppies at the center sometimes showed their teeth when they wanted to play, but it was nothing like this. Jester meant business— the unpleasant kind.

Katie set the soda she'd been bringing to her lips back onto the table. "Hey … have you got him under—" She didn't have time to add "control."

Jester lunged at me, aiming for the area below my collar. The "kill zone," as I later learned, was that area where a dog could puncture another dog's lung, resulting in death.

I pushed myself against Katie's legs, crossed at the ankles under the table. He'd have to go through me to get to her.

Jester missed the mark and swung his open mouth toward my face, growling and snapping.

I let out a yelp—more in fear than in pain. He hadn't sunk a tooth into me. Yet.

Katie dove across the tabletop, sending plates, cups, and silverware flying. She lunged underneath the table from the other side, grabbing a handful of Jester's hide at the neck. She hung on.

I retreated further into the booth until my back was against the wall and the underside of the tabletop was above me. I was pinned in place.

Katie slipped her other hand into Jester's collar and jerked him up, turning his face away from me. His hind paws scratched my stomach and his tail slapped me in the face.

I thrashed and barked.

"What are you doing to him?" yelled the woman, who still held the leash.

Katie planted both feet on the floor and dragged the snarling animal out of the booth.

Jester yipped.

"Come here," commanded the woman.

Jester stopped struggling.

"Get your damned dog out of here!" Katie turned her face to the woman but did not release her hold on Jester.

"I have a right to be—"

"You have no right to be *anywhere* with this vicious creature."

"He's a service dog; he's my therapy animal. The law says I can take him anywhere."

"No way is he a trained service animal," Katie said, her voice rising. "My dog—Garth—is in training to be a guide dog."

The words hung in the air.

"*He's* the real deal, lady. Yours is just a pet wearing a vest that you bought on the internet."

The woman took a step back, tugging on the leash.

"Look at him," Katie cried, releasing Jester and pointing to me, still cowering in the corner. "He's terrified. Traumatized. You may have ruined him for the life of service that he was destined for."

"I … didn't mean …"

"I'm sure you didn't, but the damage has been done."

A man approached, introducing himself as the manager. "Is there a problem?"

"This woman's dog just attacked my guide dog." Katie's voice was loud.

"I'm sorry," the woman began. "He's a service dog—he's never done anything like this before."

"Bullshit," Katie seethed. "That isn't a service dog. What organization? I don't see it identified on his vest."

The woman stared at Katie. "By law, I don't have to reveal that."

"This is your own stupid, surly, untrained pet, isn't he?"

The woman took a step back.

"You don't want to leave him home, do you? You bought this phony vest online and think it's all fine, don't you?"

"I don't have to listen to this," she said, turning to leave.

"You're selfish and thoughtless, and somebody needs to call you on it. If Garth is too traumatized to become a guide dog, someone who needs him is going to have to wait—to cope without his assistance. That's on your head." Katie was yelling now. I'd never seen her like this.

"I'm sure we can work this out," the manager said. "Maybe we can seat you over there?" he asked the woman, pointing to the other side of the restaurant.

"Are you kidding me? Didn't you see what just happened?" Katie spun on the man.

"Let's calm down, all right?" he replied.

"Never mind," the woman said. "I'm not going to stay in the same place as … her," she said, lifting her chin at Katie. "Come on, Jester," she said, tugging on the leash and dragging Jester away.

I remained huddled in the corner. I'd never felt my heart race like that, before or since—not even that time I tried those stairs to nowhere in the puppy center.

Katie knelt at the end of the booth, beckoning me to come to her.

I stayed where I was, unable to command my limbs to move.

Katie crawled under the booth until she was next to me. She petted and stroked me, putting her lips against my ear and whispering that I was okay; I was safe now; everything would be all right; the bad dog was gone.

My saliva pooled on the floor.

Katie remained where she was, kneading the fur on my back.

I eventually closed my mouth and took a tentative step toward the end of the booth.

"Good boy," she said softly. "Come on."

She eased out from under the booth, and I stuck to her. I didn't want to be out of her reach.

The manager stood to one side, swaying nervously. "Is he hurt?" he asked, pointing to me.

Katie squatted beside me and ran her hands over my side and neck. "It looks like that monster got his teeth into Garth's vest," she said, indicating a tear in the green fabric, "but it didn't go through to his skin."

"That's a relief," the manager said. "I'm glad he's okay."

"He's not okay. Can't you see him trembling?" Katie jerked her head around to look at the man. "Didn't you hear what I said? This may ruin him from becoming a guide dog. This never should have happened."

"I'm sorry, ma'am, but we can't deny access to someone who tells us they have a service dog."

Katie's face grew redder. "You can deny access to any animal that isn't under control—service or not. You are not required to accommodate a dangerous animal."

The manager looked at Katie with wide eyes.

"Can we …" he paused, searching for something to suggest. "Can we get you another entrée?"

"No," she said in a steely voice. "We're not staying." She stood and told me to heel.

I tried to follow her command, but my legs shook and wouldn't move.

Katie stood next to me, breathing deeply.

"You … you can't just stand here in the aisle," the manager stammered.

"I can and I will—as long as it takes for both of us to recover." She glanced up at him. "I'm trying to act calm, for Garth's sake, but I'm very shook up. That damned dog could have bitten me, too."

"Did he … get you?"

Katie turned her hands over, inspecting them. "No. Will you get my purse, please? It's on the bench."

The man did as she asked.

Katie fished out her phone. "I'm calling my husband. I'm in no shape to drive." She patted the top of my head while she placed her call to Jon.

"I'm sorry, ma'am," the manager muttered. "I really am."

"Sorry doesn't change a thing," Katie said.

I looked around the restaurant while we waited. We were the center of attention. Katie ignored the curious glances of the other customers, but I was aware of them. She continued to stroke me with her gentle hands.

I heard the familiar tread before he came into view. Jon headed straight for us. He dropped to one knee.

"What's happened to you?" he asked. He looked at Katie. "To you both. Are you okay, honey?"

"I'm fine," Katie said. "I got a few scratches, but nothing to worry about."

"Are you ready to go home, boy?" Jon addressed me.

I moved my tail in a shallow arc.

Jon took the leash from Katie and patted his left thigh. I fell into position on unsteady paws, and we made our way to his car.

Katie patted the backseat, then tossed a biscuit toward it.

I sprang into the car after it. And Katie followed me in.

Jon rolled down the window, but I wasn't interested in sticking my nose out into the wind rushing by. I settled against Katie's thigh and closed my eyes.

That night, when bedtime came, Katie turned back the covers and Jon reached for the light switch. Their eyes met, and then they looked over at me. Jon whistled as Katie patted a spot on the bed between the two of them.

I picked my head up and stared at Katie.

She smiled and patted the spot again. "It's okay, Garth. Just this one time."

I rose and went to the bed, hopping up in one fluid motion. I stretched out between them.

As Jon rubbed my ears, Katie rested her hand on my back and pressed her mouth softly against my ear. "It's going to be all right, sweet boy. We're going to help you get over this."

I closed my eyes, surrounded by the warmth of their touch and the assurance of the last magical words she spoke: "You'll see. You're going to be a guide, after all."

Chapter 36

Martha opened her front door and stepped out onto the porch. "I was wondering when I'd find you here," she said.

Connor raised the enormous bouquet of lilacs that he held in his hands. "I brought these for Em."

"They're lovely," Martha said.

"I know she can't see them, but the lady in the shop said that they're the most fragrant flowers you can find." He looked at his hands. "I thought she could enjoy the smell."

"Is she expecting you?"

He shook his head. "She won't answer my calls. I'm back in town for the week, so I figured I'd come out here. We have to talk. We can't leave things like …" He stopped short. "Can I come in?"

Martha hesitated, pursing her lips.

"Can't you convince her to see me?"

Martha held up a hand to stop him. "This is between the two of you. I'm not going to play mediator. I'm her mother, and I'm on her side. Completely." She took the flowers from him. "Let me give these to her. I'll ask if she wants to see you." She opened the door. "You can wait in the living room."

He followed her inside.

Martha made her way to Emily's bedroom, knocked, then entered the untidy space. The curtains were drawn, the only light coming from the screen of Emily's phone lying on the bed next to her still form.

"Connor's here," Martha said. "He's brought you these flowers."

"I don't want his damned flowers," came a muffled response from the bed.

"Their fragrance is heavenly. He thought you'd enjoy them."

"Give them back to him, throw them in the trash—I don't care. I don't want them anywhere near me."

"He's back from Japan for a week. He wants to talk to you."

184

"NO!"

"You're going to have to work out whatever this is with him at some time, honey. He's still your husband."

Emily threw the covers off and sat up in bed. "Tell him to get the hell away from me and go back to Japan. I don't want to see him."

Martha sighed heavily.

"Go! Tell him!"

Martha backed out of the room and shut the door. She returned to the living room. "You heard?" By the look on Connor's face, she could tell he had.

His shoulders sagged. "I don't know how to get through to her."

"I don't, either," Martha said.

"What do you suggest I do?"

"I don't have any idea. You're going to have to figure that out on your own."

"I worry about her, Martha."

"She's a strong, resilient person—always has been—but losing her eyesight was a crushing blow. And now … whatever's happened between the two of you." Martha shook her head. "I keep praying that something will bring her out of her depression and back to us. That's all I know to do."

R

"I'm fine, Mom. I don't need anything," Emily said in response to the persistent knocking on her door.

Martha opened her daughter's bedroom door halfway and stepped into the darkened room. "Zoe's had a seizure and the paramedics are on the way," Martha said.

Emily sat bolt upright in her bed. "What? When?"

"She's had a cold, and it's gotten increasingly worse. She stayed home from school today. Irene just called. She'll go in the ambulance with Zoe and wants me to follow them to the hospital."

"Oh my God!"

"I wanted you to know. I'm not sure how long I'll be gone. I'll stay at the hospital with Irene until she hears from the doctors."

"Of course."

"Will you be okay here … on your own?"

"Yes. Don't worry about me."

The sound of sirens approaching interrupted them.

"That must be the paramedics," Emily said. "Go, now." She grabbed her cane from the nightstand and walked to where her mother stood in the doorway. "Will you call me when you have any news?"

"It may be very late."

"I don't care how late it is," Emily said, reaching for her mother's arm. "Keep me updated as soon as you know anything."

Martha put her hand over Emily's. "You care for this girl, don't you?"

Emily fought back tears. "I do. I can't stand the thought of something happening to her. I'd like to go with you but … I haven't showered in days. I'm … I'm a complete mess."

"There's nothing we can do right now," Martha said. "I'll call when I have news."

"Give her and Irene my love," Emily said.

"Will do. And call me if you need me, okay? Do you have your phone?"

Emily pointed behind her. "It's on my bed. I'll be fine."

"You're sure?"

"I'm positive." Emily squeezed her mother's hand and released it. "Now go!"

Martha rushed to the garage as Emily made her way to the bathroom. It was time to get herself showered and rejoin the human race.

R

Emily answered the call on the first ring. The last time she'd checked, it was two fifty-three in the morning. It wouldn't be much later than that now.

"Mom?" Emily said.

"They think she has Reye's syndrome," Martha said. "A very serious case of Reye's syndrome."

"How is she?"

"She's in the ICU and unconscious. They've called in a neurologist and have run a CT scan to rule out ... worse diagnoses."

"Can they treat it?"

"Reye's syndrome is treatable, if that's what she has, but it may take some time. They're going to run additional tests to see if she's had brain or liver damage."

"That sounds scary. How in the world did she get Reye's syndrome?"

"We have no idea. They asked if she'd taken aspirin—that can lead to it in children—but Irene says that she doesn't even have any in the house. So it's a mystery."

"But she's going to be fine, isn't she?"

"That's what they're hoping. They aren't saying too much at this point."

"What can we do?"

"Irene's going to stay with Zoe at the hospital. I'm coming home, now, and I'll bring Sabrina to our house. We'll take care of their dog. Is that all right with you?"

"That's a great idea. We can't let anything happen to Sabrina. It would break Zoe's heart."

"I'll wait up for you. I'll put a soup bowl with water on the floor for Sabrina."

"Good idea. I'm exhausted. Have you slept since I left?"

"No. I've been too worried."

"Let's get Sabrina settled when I get home and get some sleep."

"See you soon," Emily said. Her mother might be able to sleep, but she knew she wouldn't. She'd been consumed by self-pity and grief—isolating herself in her bedroom—long enough.

Chapter 37

Emily stood in the before-dawn darkness on the front lawn, clutching her cane with one hand and her phone in the other. Was she really going to do this alone? Her heart thudded against her chest, and she was starting to feel light-headed. She began to backpedal toward the porch, when her foot caught a low spot in the grass and she stumbled, shuffling her feet to regain her balance. She straightened and, for a moment, her head cleared.

She wasn't going to let another panic attack derail her.

What had she learned about stopping one? She took a deep breath, held it for a count of five, and then released it. Perspiration trickled down her neck and into her collar.

She repeated the breathing exercise four more times.

Emily heard the hum of an approaching engine and moved back to the edge of the driveway as the sound grew louder. Her phone announced the arrival of her rideshare.

"You're headed to the hospital?" the driver asked, helping her into the backseat.

"Yes."

"We'll be there in ten minutes," he said. "This time of night, traffic's light. You need the ER?"

Emily shook her head. "No—I'm fine. I'm going to visit a"— what was Zoe? —"a very dear friend."

"I'm sorry to hear that, miss," he said. "Must be serious."

"They're not too sure. She just went in yesterday afternoon." Her voice grew small. "She's only eight."

"I'm doubly sorry to hear that. What's her name?"

"Zoe."

"Do you mind if I say a prayer for your friend Zoe?"

Tears stung the back of Emily's eyes. "That'd … that'd be nice." She bowed her head as the driver offered a simple supplication for Zoe's healing.

The car made a sharp right-hand turn and proceeded slowly until it came to a stop.

"We're at the main entrance, miss," the driver said. "Do you want me to go in with you? Help you find your way to Zoe?"

"That's very kind of you," Emily said. "But I'm sure someone will help me once I get inside."

The driver walked with Emily as she swept the walkway with her cane. The automatic doors whooshed open and Emily turned to him. "Thank you for being so kind. I can take it from here."

"I'll keep Zoe in my prayers, miss," he said. "And you, too. I hope that everything turns out well."

Emily stepped into the hospital and instantly regretted refusing the driver's help. Could she really handle this? She swallowed her rising panic and forced herself to move forward.

She'd proceeded no more than ten steps when a woman's voice in front of her asked if she could help. "You've almost reached the reception desk," the woman said. "Only three more steps."

"Thank you," Emily said, approaching the desk. "I'm here to see Zoe Klein. She was brought in yesterday afternoon."

Emily heard fingers tapping on a keyboard. "Ah ... yes ... she's in the Pediatric ICU. Visitation is for families only. Are you family?"

Emily inhaled slowly. "Yes ... I'm family."

"She's in the next building, on the second floor. It's quite a hike. Can I call someone to take you over there?"

Emily hesitated. Shouldn't she be able to navigate to the Pediatric ICU on her own? "Yes, please," she heard herself respond. Maybe the fact that she'd left the house and gotten herself here was enough of a victory for one day.

"I'll call a volunteer to take you. It'll be a few minutes."

Emily turned her back to the woman and waited. Was she insane for coming here? She wasn't really family. What if they found out she'd lied? She shook her head. She was here now; she was going to see this through.

A pair of rubber-soled shoes squeaked on the marble floor of the lobby. "Do you need help getting to the Pediatric ICU?" came a male voice attached to the shoes.

"Yes. Thank you."

"You can take my shoulder, here," he said, lifting her hand and putting it in place.

"You know how to be a sighted guide?"

"It's part of our training to be a hospital volunteer." He began to lead them. "People don't realize how much goes into being a volunteer." He launched into a detailed description of his duties, and Emily offered encouraging oh's and mm-hmm's at appropriate intervals—but she wasn't really listening. Her mind was on what she would say to Zoe.

"Here we are," the man said as he came to a stop. "This woman would like to visit someone in the Pediatric ICU."

"Thank you. I'll help her from here."

"Good luck," the man said as he stepped away from Emily.

"Thank you," she called after him.

"Who are you here to see?"

Emily gave Zoe's name.

"And you are?"

"I'm ... a neighbor ... a close family friend."

"We can't allow that without authorization from the family. I'm afraid ..."

"Emily!" Zoe's grandmother called her name, and Emily turned toward her voice. "What in the world are you doing here?"

"I ... I had to come. I want to see her."

"Where's your mom?"

"She's at home—asleep. With Sabrina. Mom brought her to our house. They were both crashed out in Mom's room when I left."

"Who's with you?"

"No one. I came on my own."

Emily heard the older woman's short intake of breath. "I can't believe you came all this way on your own, in the middle of the night, just to see Zoe."

Emily straightened her shoulders and nodded. "I couldn't stay away."

Irene took Emily's hands in hers. "She's stable—resting comfortably—but she's not awake. I know she'd love to see you, later, but right now I'm not sure she'd even know that you're there."

Emily sniffled, forcing back tears.

"You need to see her for yourself, don't you?"

Emily nodded and lowered her face to the floor. "I'm so sorry I haven't been around. It's just that things have been …"

"Hard. Don't worry, dear." Irene squeezed Emily's hands gently. "You're mother's told me that you've been going through a rough patch. I'm just glad that I stepped out of her room when I did. I was on my way to the bathroom. Why don't you go to Zoe's room, and I'll meet you in there?"

"Will you tell her?" Emily asked, gesturing to the woman who sat at the desk behind them.

"I most certainly will." She leaned in and kissed Emily on the cheek. "You're a wonderful girl, and I love you for doing this."

R

Emily heard the whirring monitors and could see blurry pinpricks of red and green lights when they entered the room.

"This is where Zoe's grandmother was sitting," the nurse said, guiding Emily to a chair. "You're right next to Zoe at the head of the bed."

"Can I touch her hand? I don't want to interfere with any of her tubes."

The nurse placed Emily's hand on the bed and moved Zoe's hand into it.

"It's warm," Emily said softly.

"Her vital signs look good," the nurse said.

"Do they have any idea what's caused this?"

"The doctors will talk to her grandmother tomorrow." The nurse rested a hand on Emily's shoulder. "Try not to worry. She's in good hands here."

"Is she still unconscious?"

"She is."

"Do you think she can hear me if I talk to her?"

"The doctors will tell you that they don't know the answer to that."

"What do you think?"

"I've worked in the ICU for almost thirty years. I'm convinced that people in comas hear what's being said to them, and I'm sure they feel the presence and love of the people who visit them." She stepped to the door. "I'll give you two a few minutes. If you have something you want to say to this child, say it."

Emily held Zoe's hand lightly and turned her head until her pinhole of vision was trained on Zoe. She looked across the familiar face, now in complete repose.

Emily carefully leaned closer to the small form in the bed.

"Hi, Zoe. It's Emily. I had to see you. I came here by myself— with my cane. Thought you'd like to know that."

Emily drew a deep breath. "You're going to be fine. They'll find out what's wrong, and they'll fix it. You'll be home before you know it. Sabrina's staying with my mom and me while you're here. We're going to take real good care of her."

The small hand twitched in hers.

"I'm sorry that I haven't come out to the porch to see you. I was upset about … well … never mind. It doesn't matter. I'll be on the porch when you come home from school from now on. In fact, why don't we do something special when you get out of here? Something really fun? You pick it, and I'll find a way to make it happen."

A tear rolled down Emily's cheek and onto their cradled hands. "If you can hear me, start thinking about what we're going to do, okay? I can't wait to see what you come up with. We'll have the time of our lives. I promise."

The door to the room opened, and Irene came to stand next to Emily. "I'm going to try to sleep in the recliner in the corner. You can stay if you want."

Emily gently placed Zoe's hand on the bed and stood. "I'm going home. I have classes tomorrow. Will you let us know the minute you learn anything?"

"Of course. Will you be all right getting back?"

"I got myself here and I can get myself home." The tone of self-confidence in her own voice surprised her. "Don't worry about me."

"Thank you for coming, dear." She drew Emily into a hug. "You're a brave young woman, and I'm so glad that Zoe has you to look up to."

Chapter 38 .

Katie was talking on the phone in a soft and serious voice. She kept glancing at me and then turning away—like she did when she didn't want the kids to hear what she was talking about. Which was crazy because I could hear her talking even when she was in the next room.

I also knew it was about me because she'd say "Garth" and "guide" every so often. I usually loved when those two words were used together, but something about her tone made my mouth taste sour.

When she finally put the phone down, Katie got down on the floor with me under the kitchen island. She took my muzzle in her hands and lifted it until our eyes met.

"You were doing so well, boy. The best puppy in our club. You were supposed to go to advanced guide-dog training at the end of the month." She ran her hand over my back, and I felt a current of happy excitement flow from the top of my ears to the tip of my tail. "But you've changed since that horrible fake service dog attacked you. You're afraid now, aren't you?"

I gazed into her eyes and didn't blink.

"I can tell that your self-confidence is shaken. And you need to be confident to be a guide."

I wasn't sure what she was getting at. I'd been shaken—no doubt about it. But I'd get over it.

"I just got off the phone with the Guide Dog Center. They're going to send someone out to visit us. I think it may be time for you to have a career change." Her voice sounded funny on the last two words, like something was stuck in her throat.

Whatever career it was, I knew instinctively I didn't want it. I turned my head and fixed her with one eye.

"You'll get to work with people who need other kinds of help, like veterans who have PTSD or diabetics. Or you may become a family pet. Would you like that? If that's what they decide, you could live with us and we'd be your forever family."

If all of this was such a good thing, why was she so sad?

"I'm so sorry, Garth," Katie said. "If I hadn't taken you to that stupid restaurant, this wouldn't have happened." She slipped her arms around my neck, but this wasn't a happy hug.

I lowered myself to the floor.

The doorbell rang, and Katie released me.

I stayed where I was, my stomach in a knot, waiting for her to come back.

She returned to the room at a run. Her energy was entirely different. She snatched my Guide Dog in Training vest and my leash from their hook on the wall.

My tail began to wag.

"We've got a plan!" she cried as she secured the vest into place.

I liked the sound of this.

"That's one of the other puppies and puppy raisers from the club. She heard what happened to you. Everyone in our club's heard about it. They decided that you should have individual play dates with the dogs from the club—to help you feel comfortable with other dogs again. She stopped to see if we want to go for a walk with them. What do you think about that?"

"Yes" was always the answer to any question that had the word "walk" in it.

She clipped on my leash. "Let's see how you do, boy. You may become a guide dog yet!"

There was that word again, directed at me with hope. I stood and shook. I'd had enough of serious talk—it was time to move.

We headed out the door and down the driveway to a golden/lab mix that I thought I recognized. She was a bit younger than me. She was also wearing a vest.

We looked at each other. She wagged her tail and I wagged mine.

The other puppy raiser spoke to Katie. "That's good. He didn't back away."

I could hear the smile in Katie's voice. "I think so, too."

"We're all behind you, Garth," the other puppy raiser said, leaning over to scratch between my ears. "You're a good boy, and we're not going to let that other dog take you out. Not if we can help it."

Katie began walking, and I fell in beside her with a spring in my step that I hadn't had since the day we'd left the restaurant.

Chapter 39

Connor stood and held out a chair for Gina. He motioned for the waiter. "What'll you have?"

"Nothing. I'm not staying," Gina said.

"Don't let me drink alone."

"Seems like you've been doing a lot of that lately."

"Can you blame me? My wife is blind, and now she won't talk to me."

The waiter approached their table in the dimly lit bar. Connor raised his glass. The waiter nodded and looked at Gina. She shook her head.

"Getting drunk isn't going to solve your problems."

"I know that. That's why I asked you here. We need to talk to Emily."

"How do you propose we do that? She won't answer my calls or texts, either."

"This is ridiculous," Connor said. "We have to convince her nothing happened."

"Was that kiss nothing?"

"We don't have feelings for each other. I was lonely and frustrated. The whole thing was completely my fault. I was drunk." He swirled his bourbon, the ice cubes tinkling in the glass. "You wouldn't have let anything else happen, even if I had tried."

Gina turned her head and stared at a couple at the end of the room, holding hands across a table.

"You and Em have been friends your whole lives. She'll listen to you."

"What are you asking me to do?"

"Go to Martha's. Stand outside Em's bedroom door if you have to. Tell her nothing happened, and we mean nothing to each other."

"You're an idiot." Gina swung back to him sharply. "I'm in love with you, Connor. Have been for years." She began to cry, tears coursing down her cheeks. "God help me. I know it's wrong."

Connor set his drink on the table and stared at her.

"I let you kiss me, and if Emily hadn't interrupted us ..." Her voice broke. "I'm just glad that she did. I'm consumed with guilt over how I feel about you and what almost happened. I don't know how I could have lived with myself if she hadn't interrupted us."

"I ... I had no idea."

"Really, Connor? All those remarks about what a great catch I'd be for some lucky guy. You weren't coming on to me—even a little bit?"

"No! I was ..."

"What? Just being polite?"

Connor took a generous swallow of his drink.

"The thing is—I love Emily." Gina lowered her gaze to the table. "I'm devastated that she's lost her sight and ... now ... she's been betrayed by her husband and her best friend. Me!"

"What're we going to do to fix this?"

"I don't know." She rubbed her hands over her eyes. "The one thing I'm sure of is that I can't see you anymore. I need to stay away and somehow come to terms with what I've done. I've been praying that Em will forgive me, in time."

"I'm sorry, Gina."

"Me, too. I hope that you and Emily patch things up, but I can't be part of your attempted reconciliation."

"Surely there's something that the two of us can do to change her mind. I don't know how I'll convince her by myself."

"You'll have to figure this out on your own." She stood and took a step back. "Goodbye, Connor. Good luck."

Chapter 40

Martha padded across the dark kitchen to the coffeepot. She ejected the pod and replaced it with a new one and pushed the button, moving to the window over the kitchen sink while she waited for her coffee to brew. Outside the first rays of sun were washing the landscape with streaks of pink and gold.

"Good morning."

Martha whirled around, clutching her bathrobe. "Emily! You scared the life out of me!"

"I'm sorry. Didn't you see me sitting here at the table?"

"No. I usually don't turn the light on until I've got my coffee. I like to watch the sunrise through the kitchen window."

"I remember you doing that when I was in high school."

"I've started my day this way for almost thirty years," Martha said, her heart rate returning to normal. She flipped on the overhead light. "What are you doing up so early?"

Emily opened her laptop. "I wanted to send out some emails before school."

Martha's coffee stopped brewing and she took her cup to the table, pulling out a chair to sit with Emily.

"You're going back to the foundation?"

"I am. I'll be completing the program in the next couple of weeks."

"That's wonderful!" Martha said, regarding her daughter carefully. "Have you put makeup on?"

"Yes. They taught us at the foundation. There are blind bloggers who give hair and makeup tips, too."

Martha rocked back in her chair, speechless.

"How does it look? Did I do it okay?"

"It looks fine. You've done a wonderful job."

"You're not just saying that? You wouldn't let me go out of the house looking like a clown?"

"Not unless you were dressed as a clown." Martha patted Emily's hand. "Of course, I wouldn't."

"I got up extra early to get some things done before I go," Emily said. "I want to be available after school today in case Zoe wants to see me."

"I'm sure she will," Martha said. "Irene says that she talks about you all the time. Something about an adventure with you when she's better."

Emily's head snapped up. "She said that?"

"That's what Irene said. What does Zoe mean by that?"

"I promised her that we'd do something fun together when she got out of the hospital; that she could pick it. She was unconscious at the time, so I didn't know if she heard me or not."

"She heard you, all right," Martha said.

"Oh, boy. I guess I'm going to have to make good on my promise. I wonder what she'll want to do."

"Knowing Zoe, it'll be very interesting—and not the least what you'd expect from a third grader."

"What have I gotten myself into?"

"You'll find out soon enough. She's scheduled to come home today."

"They got it under control fast, didn't they?"

"Yes, thank goodness. IV fluids and diuretics did the trick. And she's had no damage to her brain or liver."

"I'm so relieved."

"You've become very close to her, haven't you?"

Emily nodded. "I guess I needed a new friend."

Martha sipped her coffee as Emily tapped out another email on her laptop.

"Going to the hospital in the middle of the night—all on your own—was courageous. I'm proud of you."

"It's what I've learned to do for myself, Mom. I have to be able to get around on my own." Emily turned to her mother. "I know this sounds stupid—and I'm so sorry that Zoe had to go through this horrible experience—but it jarred me out of my depression."

"That's how it seems to me, too."

"I need to get on with my life. I'm so lucky to have a job that I can do with all of the assistive technology—and an employer and team of employees who will be happy to have me back." She reached for her coffee cup.

"Would you like a refill?" Martha asked.

Emily rose from her seat. "I've got it." She felt her way to the coffee pot. "I want to return to work as soon as I'm done at the foundation. I just sent an email to my boss and my team."

"That's wonderful! I can't tell you how happy this makes me. Will you go back to the condo? It's too far to commute from here."

"I've asked to work remotely," Emily said. "I'd like to live with you for a while longer. Would that be all right?"

"You know it would be. You're welcome here as long as you like."

They sat in silence, sipping their coffee.

"Will you ever go back to the condo?"

"You mean will I ever get back with Connor?"

"I haven't wanted to pry …"

"I'm not sure what I want to do about all of that. I'm still furious and unbearably hurt, but I don't have the time or energy to focus on it right now. I need to concentrate on completing my program at the foundation so I can resume my life. I'm craving a new normal—whatever that will be. Can you understand that?"

"I most certainly can. I think you've got your priorities straight."

"He's in Japan, so that gives us a breather. I thought about moving into the condo while he's over there—it's closer to my office—but I never really lived there so it's not familiar to me, and it's full of …" her tone grew harsh, "horrible memories. It's too much to think about while I'm trying to learn to live as a blind person."

"Have you told Connor that?"

"Yes. I asked him to leave me alone—to quit contacting me—so I can rebuild my life. I asked for some privacy and said I would contact him in three months."

"What about Gina?"

"I asked for the same from her."

"Good for you. Give yourself time to reflect on everything."

"That's what I thought. Finishing my classes and returning to work will be enough for now."

"Don't forget about Zoe's adventure."

Emily smiled. "No—I won't forget about that. I'm anxious to hear what we'll be doing."

"My guess is that you'll find out this afternoon when you get home from the foundation."

"Speaking of which, I'd better be on my way."

"I'll get my keys."

"No." Emily held up her hand. "I've got this. I've already scheduled my ride—it should be here any minute."

"You don't have to …"

"I know I don't have to, but I want to. This is part of the new, independent Emily."

Martha walked her daughter to the door and hugged her hard. "I'm so proud of you, honey. You're my hero—always have been and always will be."

R

"Hi, Zoe," Emily said as she used her cane to enter Zoe's bedroom. "I'll bet you're glad to be home."

"I sure am. They were really nice to me at the hospital, but I missed Sabrina." Zoe rustled under the covers. "Turn a smidge to your left and six feet forward."

"Listen to you!" Emily said, approaching Zoe's bedside. "You've become very good at this."

"I asked a bunch of questions about blind people when I was at the hospital."

Emily smiled. That sounded exactly like something her young friend would do.

"Sabrina's curled up on the other side of my bed. You can sit here," she said, patting the mattress, "if that's okay with you."

"Well, duh. Where else do girlfriends sit?" She lowered herself onto Zoe's bed. "Sorry I wasn't here when you got home."

"That's okay. Sabrina and I took a nap. I'm still pretty tired." She leaned forward. "Gramma said you went to the foundation; that you're almost done."

"That's right. I'll be done at the end of next week."

"What will you do then?"

"I'll go back to work. My employer kept my job open. Do you remember the man you saw leaving my mom's house that time?"

"He has a name with a 'D'?"

"Good memory! Dhruv. I'm going to work with him again."

Zoe's voice grew small when she asked, "Will you come back to your mom's to visit me?"

"I'm going to work from home, at my mom's house. We can see each other, but maybe not until after I'm done working."

"That's great!" Zoe's voice expanded. "And we've also got that special outing you promised we would go on."

"I'm surprised you remembered that."

"Are you kidding? I did a ton of research in the hospital to pick it."

"Research, huh? I can't wait to hear—what are we going to do?"

Zoe shifted herself onto her knees and bounced up and down. "We're going to the GDC!"

Emily took a sharp breath. "What are you talking about?"

"The Guide Dog Center—they train guide dogs! I found out a ton about them. They give guide dogs to handlers—that's what they'd call you—for free, and they give lifetime medical care for the dogs. People called puppy raisers work with the dogs until they're fifteen months' old, and then they go to GDC—that's what they call the

Guide Dog Center—for eight weeks of intensive training, and GDC matches you with your dog ...”

Emily held up a hand to stop her. “Whoa. Slow down there, sweetheart. I’m not in the market for a guide dog. You know that. And I’m sure you can’t just march in there and get a dog, anyway. It’s not like the pet adoption clinic where you got Sabrina.”

At the sound of her name, Sabrina lifted up her head and wagged her tail against the covers.

“I remember,” Zoe said. “We’d go to an all-day seminar that GDC holds for people who *might* want a guide dog. So you can learn about it to see if you’d want one.”

Emily paused.

Sabrina stepped around Zoe and pushed her head into Emily’s hand.

Emily began to stroke Sabrina. “That sounds ... reasonable.”

“There’s one a week from Saturday. Right after you’re done with school! And Gramma said that she’ll drive us there and pick us up. It’s an hour and a half away.”

“Well ...” Emily said, trying to think up a way to get out of it.

“You don’t have to get a dog if you don’t want one,” Zoe said. “It takes years, anyway. They have a long waiting list. This is just to learn about it.”

“Wouldn’t you rather go to an amusement park? Or a movie or museum? How about shopping?”

“Nope. You told me I could pick, and I pick GDC.”

Emily cleared her throat.

“You promised.”

“So I did.” Emily reached her arms out to the persistent girl.

Zoe pressed herself into Emily and hugged her hard.

“Then that’s what we’ll do. Do we need to make reservations?”

“I already have.”

Emily smoothed Zoe’s bedhead. “You’re a very special girl, you know that?”

Zoe snuggled deeper into Emily’s embrace.

Chapter 41

Something is very different this morning. Alex slipped me an entire piece of bacon, under the table. Jon saw but didn't say anything. I should have refused—I know the rule about people food and table scraps—but it was *bacon*, after all.

Abby clung to me, rubbing her tear-stained face against my neck until Jon spoke to her in a gentle voice, telling her they were going to be late for school. They were late a lot and he never used that tone of voice with her when they were.

Jon, Alex, and Abby rushed out of the house in a flurry of backpacks, lunch sacks, and gym bags. I headed toward my crate for my first morning nap when Katie intercepted me. She dropped to her knees and drew me to her, holding me tightly to her chest. I felt her breathing go from deep to ragged.

I turned my nose to her face and licked, surprised to taste salty tears.

"Today's the day, boy," she said in a halting voice. "You've made it, and I'm so proud of you."

If she was so proud, why was she crying?

"You got over that horrid attack by the fake service dog, and you get to continue your training. They'll be here in an hour to pick you up."

I stood quietly in her embrace and let her continue. Frankly, I didn't know what she was talking about.

"You're going back to the Guide Dog Center today for advanced training," she said. "You're going to become a guide."

My ears twitched. There was that wonderful word. I thumped my tail against the kitchen floor.

Katie shifted and took my head into her hands, looking me directly in the eyes. "You are going to be one of the greatest guides in the history of guides, Garth. I can feel it right here," she laid her hand on her heart. "You'll become someone's hero, right hand, other half. You'll change a life in a way that a human cannot."

Tears coursed down her cheeks. "I'm so thankful that we got to raise you and help you on your way. We'll always—*always*—love you, and you'll forever be welcome here. Don't forget that. But you've got a bigger destiny, and you're ready for it."

She rested her chin on the top of my head, and I felt my fur getting moist. She took a deep, shuddering breath.

"I'll pray for you every day, Garth—that you'll be matched with a person who will care for you and love you like we do."

I shook and pressed my nose into her neck.

"And that they'll find this exact spot where you love to be scratched." She laughed as she worked the spot.

I leaned against her, willing her to continue.

"This is your destiny, sweetest boy. You're ready for it and it's time."

I heard a vehicle turn into the driveway. I pulled away from her and sat up straight. Katie pulled me back to her and held me tight.

The doorbell rang.

I swiveled my eyes to hers.

She pressed a kiss into the top of my head and brushed tears from her cheeks. "That'll be the van from the Guide Dog Center," she said. "Don't ever forget what I told you." She released me and went to answer the door.

Chapter 42

"This place is so cool!" Zoe said. "Look at all the buildings—and all the neat vans with pictures of puppies on the sides."

"It's very impressive," Martha said. "I had no idea."

"Thank you for driving us out here," Emily said. "I hate that you had to cancel your plans—again—for me."

"Nonsense. It's not a big deal. Irene can't help that their water heater went out." Martha turned in place. "Besides, it's a beautiful day, and I enjoyed the drive out here."

"What will you do while we're in the seminar? It's too far to drive back home."

"I'm going to explore the area. The town looks quaint. We passed some antique shops. I thought I'd poke around."

"Good," Emily said. "Just don't get so carried away that you forget to pick us up."

Martha laughed. "That could happen. You never know."

"Really?" Zoe sounded worried.

"No," Emily and her mother said in unison.

"I'm just kidding," Martha said. "It's time for the two of you to find where you need to go for your seminar."

Zoe pulled a rumpled piece of paper out of her jacket pocket. "It says it's in the administration building." Zoe pointed to the sign on the structure in front of them bearing the word "Administration."

"That would be it," Martha said, pulling over. "Do you want me to go in with you? To make sure?"

"We can do it," Zoe said.

"Don't worry," Emily said, opening the passenger door and resting her cane on the sidewalk. "I'm in good hands."

Martha ruffled Zoe's hair gently and leaned in to kiss Emily on the cheek. "You most certainly are. I'll be back here at three. Have a good time."

"It's not over until three-thirty," Zoe said.

"I'll still be here by three." Martha moved away as Zoe took Emily's hand and placed it on her shoulder.

"If you had a dog, you wouldn't need me," Zoe said.

"I have my cane—I can get along fine with it."

"You said …" Zoe began to protest.

"I know. I said that I'd keep an open mind about getting a dog and I will. I'm curious about all of this."

They stepped through an autonomic door.

Zoe consulted her paper. "It says to sign in here and go to a conference room at the end of the hall on the right."

"Can you do that?"

"Yep." Zoe stepped away to sign them in and returned quickly. "Let's go. I can't wait. I hope we meet some guide dogs."

Zoe's wish was granted when they stepped into the conference room. They were greeted by two instructors who were accompanied by their guides.

"You must be Emily," said a young woman. "We're happy that you came today."

"I can thank my friend here—Zoe—for this," Emily said. "She did all the research to find you and made the arrangements."

"That's wonderful, Zoe! A lot of people find out about guide dogs because a friend or family member brings them to us. Will you stay with Emily?"

"Yes. I think it'd be neat to have a guide dog."

"It's helpful for many people, but not everyone is suited to working with a guide. We'll talk about that in the seminar," the woman said. "We're about ready to get started. Why don't you and Emily find a seat?"

Zoe took Emily's hand and guided them to chairs at one of the tables arranged in a large "U."

R

The male instructor gave an overview of the day's program. "As I said, you'll find out what a dog can—and cannot—do. These dogs love to work and get bored if they don't go out, so the handlers need to be active and to reinforce the training that the dogs receive here."

"How do we know how to do that?" asked an older man to their right. "I've never had a dog before."

"If you're selected to receive a dog, you'll come back here to live in our residential facility for two weeks of intensive training with the dog that we've matched you with."

"I don't get to pick my dog?" asked another attendee.

"No. We assess you first. You have to be proficient in mobility with your white cane. We also look at your home and your work environment. From there, we can pick the best dog for you. It isn't one size fits all," he said. "Around here, we call it the 'magic of the match.'"

"How much does it cost?"

"Guide dogs and their medical care are provided free of charge—and so is the two-week residential training course. All the handler has to pay for is food and incidentals."

"Where do the dogs come from?" asked a young woman on their left.

"We have our own breeding program here. We train labs, golden retrievers, and crosses between the two breeds."

Zoe cupped her hand over Emily's ear and whispered. Emily nodded.

Zoe shot her hand into the air.

"You have a question, young lady?"

"I have a miniature Schnauzer, and she's awesome. Could she become Emily's guide?"

The instructor smiled. "I'm sure she's a wonderful dog, but a guide dog requires very special traits in addition to those that make a great pet. We only match people with dogs from our program."

Zoe wriggled back into her chair.

"Let's get into our presentation. We'll have time after lunch for all attendees to test out the guide-dog lifestyle. First, you'll walk holding a harness that's led by a person. After that, we'll put one of our senior, trained dogs into the harness for you to work with an actual dog."

Zoe squirmed in excitement. "This is so cool," she whispered to Emily.

Emily put her hand on Zoe's back and rubbed in a circle. "It sure is," she whispered back.

They listened attentively to the program, Zoe scribbling copious notes into a spiral-bound notebook she removed from her backpack.

R

Zoe sat on a bench in the inner courtyard while Emily completed her Juno training, holding a harness while a human on the other end mimicked the actions of a guide dog. Zoe crossed her ankles and swung her feet as she gazed out across the lawn to a long, low building at the far end of the courtyard.

A van, wrapped with photos of puppies in green vests, parked in a spot and the driver got out. He opened the rear door and a large black Lab in a green vest hopped to the pavement. He sat, surveying the scene in front of him, while the driver put him into his harness.

As the driver took hold of the harness, the dog spotted Zoe. They stared at each other, and Zoe raised her hand in a quick wave.

Garth wagged his tail before setting off to the low building, the driver at his side.

R

"That was very interesting," Emily said to the Juno instructor. "Is that really what it feels like to work with a guide dog?"

"You'll be able to see for yourself. Would you like to travel the same path with an actual guide?"

"I definitely would," Emily said.

"We've got one for you now. Her name is Sugar." The instructor handed Sugar's harness to Emily. "You'll have to direct her. The command to use—when you're ready to move—is 'Forward.'"

211

"Hello, Sugar," Emily said, leaning over to pat the top of her head. "Are you ready to show me how it's done?"

Emily straightened.

Sugar stood at her side, waiting patiently.

"Forward," Emily said.

Sugar began to move.

Emily hesitated.

"I'm right behind you," the instructor said.

Emily forced herself to move, and she and Sugar took off on the sidewalk that wove through the Guide Dog Center's campus.

Sugar was sure and swift.

Emily relaxed, and she and Sugar were soon sailing along in perfect harmony.

They made four laps around the courtyard before the instructor directed them to stop.

Emily brushed the hair off her face and addressed the instructor. "That was wonderful," she said. "I haven't walked that fast and that freely since ... since before I lost my sight. I'm even a bit out of breath."

"These dogs are athletic, and they like to move. It always surprises everyone how fast they walk. When we match guides and handlers, that's one of the things we look at: Can the person keep up with the dog?"

Emily brought her hand to her chest and her voice was thick with emotion when she continued. "I'd forgotten how nice it is to move. I've been told that I'm good with my cane, but it's nothing like this."

"So—what do you think? Are you ready for the guide-dog lifestyle?"

Emily rested her hand on Sugar's head. "Yes. I am." She pursed her lips. "I came here today to keep a promise I made to Zoe. I never thought I'd want a guide dog, but now that I've felt the freedom a guide can give me, I'm convinced. What's the next step?"

"We'll sign you up and start the process. Someone will interview you and assess your cane mobility skills. As we've said, you have to be mobile with a cane before you can get a dog. I've watched you with your cane this morning, and you're not going to have any problems with that. We also do home visits to make sure that you've got an appropriate place for a dog."

"How long does that take?"

"A couple of months."

"Then I'll be matched with a dog and come here for two weeks of training? I'm going back to work next week and want to know what to tell them."

"We'll also do a site visit to your office," the instructor said. "When all that's done, you'll go on our waiting list. It usually takes two years to get a guide."

Emily sighed heavily. "That long? Now that I've gotten a taste of what this will be like, I'm anxious to get going."

"I understand," he said. "Once in a while someone who's been matched with a dog has to cancel, and we fill their spot from our waiting list."

"Doesn't that guide go to the next person on the list?"

"Not necessarily. Remember—we match the dog and handler based upon a whole host of factors. We want to make sure that the match works for both parties. It's not just the next person on the list."

"Well … I guess I'll have to wait my turn," Emily said. "The person who'll be really disappointed is Zoe."

"She's quite a young lady, isn't she? I'm very impressed with her. Shall we go give her the good news? She's been sitting on a bench, watching you this whole time."

"Can Sugar lead us to her?"

"That's a great idea," he said. "Let's go."

Chapter 43

Emily thanked the rideshare driver and stepped out onto the sidewalk, extending her cane in front of her. She made her way to the entrance of the building, found the keypad to the right of the door, and swiped her badge in front of it. The lock made a soft *click*. She felt for the door handle, pulling it toward her, and stepped into the building where she'd worked for almost a decade.

At the elevator bank, her hand found the button for the ninth floor easily, having pressed it so many times in the past.

Her team had no idea she'd be attending the scrum meeting in person. For the past five weeks, she'd been participating from her computer at home, and even she didn't know if she'd go through with this in-person meeting, until she stepped into the rideshare.

Her team had been ecstatic to have her back. She'd been nervous about resuming her position—would she be able to handle the same workload?—but the new assistive technologies at her disposal answered that question in the affirmative. She'd still found it difficult, however, to insert herself into the team's projects. Everyone was overly solicitous of her and continued to shoulder the brunt of the work.

The elevator doors pinged, and she stepped out, turned left, and traversed the short distance to the daily meeting room.

She knew it wasn't a conscious effort to exclude her. Even Dhruv was reticent to discuss technical issues with her. They didn't know what to expect from her.

Emily had to take charge of the situation. The only way to rectify it was to show them—in person—that she was just as capable of performing her job as she had been before she lost her sight.

Her phone announced that it was ten minutes before nine. Emily felt her way to the area where the scrum master usually stood and waited for her team to assemble.

"Emily?" Michael was the first to arrive.

214

Emily turned to him and smiled.

"You're … you're here," he said, stepping to her and hugging her.

"I'm going to lead the meetings, again, now that I'm back."

"Oh … okay."

"You've done an outstanding job, Michael, covering for me for all of these months. I appreciate it, but it's time I resumed my role—in full."

"None of us know how much you can do now."

"I understand," Emily said. "I'm going to address that when everyone gets here."

"Is that the real Emily Main?" came Rhonda's voice as she approached.

"In the flesh," Emily said.

"It's so good to see you," Rhonda said, putting an arm around Emily's shoulder and squeezing.

"It's you," Dhruv said at her elbow.

Emily reached over and patted his arm. "Let's get started. We're not going to tarnish our record of limiting these meetings to fifteen minutes. I wanted you all to know that I'm back and—with the help of all of this new technology—I can perform every task that I used to before I lost my eyesight. We're going to go on as we did before." She turned to Rhonda. "Please tell us about the coding issue that we're committed to solving today."

Rhonda launched into her explanation, and the group responded.

"Our fifteen minutes are up," Emily said, "and I think we all know what we need to do."

The group was silent as people nodded their heads.

Emily cleared her throat. "One tip—I can't see you nod, which I'm assuming you're doing now, so please verbalize your responses."

A chorus of yeses sounded through the group.

"I know that this breaks our fifteen-minute rule, but I want you all to know that I am more grateful than I can express for your support and encouragement since I lost my sight. The fact that you held my job for me—came out to my house and ripped up my resignation—

was exactly what I needed. Your kindness was the catalyst that got me to the foundation to take the training that gave me back my life." Her voice cracked and she lowered her face to the floor, breathing in and out to steady herself. "You saved me."

Michael began to clap, and the other members of her team followed suit. "We're so glad you're here, Emily."

"We'd do it all again," Rhonda said. "Does this mean you'll be back in the office?"

Emily had only intended to appear this once, to clear the air. She was surprised to hear herself say, "Yes. That's my plan. There are logistics to work out"—*like where I'm going to live*, she thought—"so I'll work from home a while longer. But I'll continue to pop in from time to time. If you need me to be at a meeting, you can schedule me. And with that," she said in a steady voice, "I think we'd better tackle that list we've come up with for today."

"One more thing before we get started," Rhonda said. "How about we all meet back here at noon? Let's go out to that Thai place on the corner to celebrate Emily's return."

"Great idea!" said a team member.

"I'll pick up the tab," Emily said. "It'll be a team meeting."

"Even better," said another member of the group.

She heard the others move off. "Dhruv? Did you have something else?"

"Where are you going to live when you come back to work?"

"My husband and I have a condo in the city," Emily said. "You know that—you've been there."

"It's a long commute from that condo to the office," he said. "My uncle owns an apartment building near here. I live on the second floor. He sometimes has vacancies."

"That's good to know, Dhruv, but I haven't really thought about all of that yet."

"Just in case. You should know."

"Thank you. Now—do you have time to answer some questions for me on today's project?" She turned. "Let's go to my office."

Chapter 44

We walked past the door, then doubled back. My nose twitched, with dozens of scents fighting for my attention. Some were familiar—I could pick out chicken and fish—and some were new to me and made the insides of my nostrils sting.

My trainer Mark opened the door and instructed me to go inside. I knew where we were, now: a restaurant. I hesitated, one paw raised over the threshold.

He bent over and placed his mouth close to my ear. "I know, boy. I know. But if you want to be a guide, you'll have to go into restaurants. You're safe with me, and you'll be safe with your handler." He stroked my back. "I trust you and, now, you'll have to trust me."

Mark stood up and gave the command.

I brought my paw down and stepped inside.

The room was full of round tables surrounded by chairs, but no one was sitting in them. The only people inside had aprons tied around their waists and were leaning against a far wall.

"Are you open for business, yet?" Mark asked.

"At eleven." A man wearing an apron pushed himself away from the wall and came toward us. "You're early, but I'm happy to seat you."

"Thank you."

"Anyone else joining you?"

"Nope. Just me and Garth."

The man led us to a table at the front of the room, by the window. "Is this all right? Maybe Garth would like to look out the window?"

"Perfect." Mark sat, and I lay down at his feet, under the table.

"You doing okay down there, boy?" He patted my head. "Nothing to be afraid of."

I knew what he was referring to—that vicious attack from the fake service dog that had almost ended my career as a guide before it had even begun. I thumped my tail once on the floor to let him know I wasn't going to let one unfortunate incident derail me. I'm made of sterner stuff than that.

The waiter came back with a menu for Mark. He had a bowl of water with him, too. "Can I give this to …"

"Garth."

"Garth?"

"Sure. That's very nice of you. He'll like that."

The waiter put the water down near my head. I leaned over and took a long, noisy drink. Restaurants weren't that bad, after all.

Mark placed his order, and we sat back to wait. I rested my head on my paws but kept my eyes fixed on the door. A stream of people crowded into the restaurant and the noise level rose.

I remained focused on the door.

The waiter set Mark's food on the table, and he began to eat. I lifted my nose in the air. I knew I was forbidden from begging for food from the table, but there's no law against enjoying the smells.

A group of six people approached the hostess and asked for a table. I was distracted by the scent from a plate delivered to the table next to us that I would later learn is called curry. I almost missed that the group included a young woman with a white cane.

I knew what that meant. But where was her guide dog? Weren't people with white canes supposed to have someone like me with them?

I stretched into the aisle between our table and the next to get a better look at her. She was tall and thin, with a mass of hair the same red color as some of the golden retrievers at the center. I was no expert on such things, but I thought she was pretty.

I was staring at her, still incredulous that she didn't have a guide at her side, when she swung her face to me. Her eyes may not have seen me, but they broadcasted intelligence, kindness, and wit. In that moment, I knew—there was something between us.

The man standing next to her pointed to me, leaned in, and spoke to her. I saw her shrug her shoulders, pat his arm, and smile. That smile could light up the entire West Coast.

She turned back to the crowd of people she was with as they were escorted to a table at the back of the restaurant.

I tried to follow her with my eyes, but the restaurant was too crowded by then and I lost sight of her.

Mark picked up my harness. "Find restroom," he said.

I stood, sniffed the air, and led us to the back of the restaurant.

"Good boy," Mark said, pushing the door open.

"Find the door," he said when we came out a few minutes later.

I spotted her as I started toward the entrance. She was sitting, with her back to me, in the next row of tables.

A waiter stepped in front of us.

I used the interruption as my excuse. I guided us to the next row and walked directly to her.

The man who had been standing next to her spotted me and waved to Mark. Mark stepped to the table, and the man spoke to him.

I positioned myself next to her and raised my eyes to Mark. He was smiling and talking to the man. He relaxed his grip on my harness. I put my nose under her hand and raised it up slightly.

The woman patted my head and bent toward me. "Aren't you a good boy?" she whispered. "I hear you're almost done with your training and are going to meet your person next week."

"That could be you," the man at the table said.

"I'm on the waiting list for a guide dog, Dhruv."

"That's wonderful!" Dhruv said. "Why didn't you tell me?"

"I only just signed up," she said. "It takes a couple of years to get a dog."

"I thought I recognized you," Mark said. "Were you on the GDC campus for the last seminar?"

"Yes," she said. "That's when I signed up to get a dog. Did we meet?"

"No," he said, "but I was working with Garth that day and thought I saw you at the center. I'm glad that you signed up."

"Me, too."

"I'm just sorry that the wait to get a guide is so long."

"That's all right. I'll manage." She kneaded my ears with both hands. "I'm just sorry that this guy—Garth, is it? —will already be helping someone else."

"Don't worry," Mark said. "You'll be matched with the perfect guide for you. I don't know how it happens, but it always works out that way." He tightened his grip on my harness. "We'd better get going. Nice to meet all of you." He turned to the woman. "I hope we see you on campus soon."

"Find the door, Garth," Mark said again.

The woman removed her hand from my ears, and I gave it a surreptitious lick before guiding Mark to the exit. I gave her one last look before we stepped outside and onto the sidewalk. If I had any power over my destiny, I wanted my match to be her.

Chapter 45

Emily closed her laptop and slid it away from her. It was time to resume working in the office. Her team's workload was increasing and she'd be more productive there. She stood and laced her fingers, extending her hands over her head and stretching to one side and then the other. She picked up her phone and headed to the kitchen. Her mother might need help with dinner.

Emily stopped in the doorway, inhaling the aroma of roasting chicken. "Smells wonderful," she said.

Her phone began to ring, announcing that the call was from the Guide Dog Center.

Martha looked up from the pot she was stirring on the stove. "Better answer it," she said as Emily double-tapped the phone screen.

"Emily Main," she said into the phone. She was silent for a long while.

"Yes. I'm still interested."

Martha set the spoon onto the counter and came to stand next to Emily.

"I can come next week," Emily said. "I'll make arrangements at work."

Martha watched her daughter's face.

"Yes. Put me down as a definite yes. If you email me the paperwork tonight, I'll fill it out and send it right back."

Martha clasped her hands to her chest.

"I'm sorry that someone had to drop out, but I'm thrilled that their dog is right for me." Emily's voice became thick with tears. "I'll see you Sunday afternoon. And"—she gulped a steadying breath—"thank you so, so much!"

Emily disconnected the call and turned to her mother. "You heard?"

"Enough to know that you're getting a guide dog!" Martha reached for her daughter and pulled her into a hug.

They stood in the kitchen, arms around each other, swaying slightly. Martha leaned back and took Emily's face in her hands. "I'm thrilled for you, honey. I think this will be a very good thing."

"Thanks, Mom. I almost can't believe it's true. I had reconciled myself to the idea that it would be years before I got my guide. I was going to go back to living in the city and working in the office—and waiting for the call from the Guide Dog Center."

"Will you move back into the condo?"

"I'm not sure about that—I need to think about it." She drew a deep breath, and her voice was somber. "I need to talk to Connor."

"It's probably time," Martha said. "But wherever you live, I'll feel better if you have a guide dog with you."

Emily brushed the hair back from her forehead. "Right now, I've got to get ready for two weeks of intensive training"—the corners of her mouth curved into a wide grin—"with my new guide dog."

"Leave dinner to me," Martha said. "I can finish it up and set the table."

"Thank you," Emily said. "I need to email my boss. And Dhruv—I need to send him a separate message. He's been so supportive."

"He'll be thrilled," Martha said. "So will Zoe. You have to tell her."

"Of course!"

"Why don't you go over after dinner? While I clean up. When you get home, I can help you with any of the paperwork from the center—if you want," Martha quickly added.

"Thanks, Mom. That would be super. I've got to get myself packed for two weeks away, too."

"Let's get cracking," Martha said. "These are happy problems to have."

R

"We're almost there," Zoe said to Emily as they sat together in the backseat of Martha's car.

"How do you know?" Emily asked.

"I recognized the big stone wall that we passed when we came to the seminar."

"Only another few minutes," Martha said from the front seat. "We've made good time. We're here early."

Zoe was squirming in her seat. "I can't wait to see your room."

"Thank you for coming with us," Emily said. "This is a long drive for you. You could have been outside, playing with Sabrina."

"I talked to her about it," Zoe replied seriously. "We both thought I should come."

"You won't be able to meet my dog, you know," Emily said.

"I know," Zoe said. "Not until graduation."

Martha slowed the car and put her turn signal on. "We're here."

Martha made the left-hand turn and followed the signs directing them to the drop-off spot for the new class of handlers. They parked and got out of the car.

A volunteer with a clipboard approached them as Emily extended her cane. Emily spoke to him as Martha and Zoe got her suitcases out of the trunk.

"Follow me," he said, "You're in room five."

The three women followed him to Emily's room.

He produced a key and opened the door to a sunny room with a single bed made up in crisp white linens and topped with a thick down duvet. A desk, television, and overstuffed chair completed the furnishings. A marble bath stocked with plush towels opened off of the room. The only clue that they weren't in a luxury hotel was the dog bed in one corner of the room and the large basket filled with dog toys. Water and food bowls sat on the floor by the desk.

He handed the key to Emily. "You've got an hour and a half to explore the room and settle in. I think you'll find everything you need, but don't hesitate to ask if there's anything we've missed." He led her to the set of light switches on the wall. "There's a buzzer here." He guided her hand to the button above the switch. "If you need anything."

"Thank you," Emily said.

"I'll leave you to it," the man said. "We'll bring your guide to you between two thirty and three. You'll have an hour to get acquainted, and then you'll need to come to the orientation at four."

Emily swallowed hard.

"Don't worry. You've gone over the basic instructions we sent?"

"Yes," Emily replied.

"You'll be fine. You've got your cane and your guide knows the room where we'll meet." He put his hand on Emily's arm. "Everyone feels nervous at this point. Try to relax and enjoy these next two weeks. It's going to be fun—and life-changing." He stepped out of the room.

"This is neat!" Zoe said. "Can I … go to the bathroom?"

"Of course," Emily said. "Be my guest."

"It's lovely," Martha said. "You'll be very comfortable here." She rolled one of the suitcases over to the bed. "Would you like me to unpack for you?" She began to lift the suitcase onto the bed.

Emily reached out her hand and stopped her mother. "No. Thank you, Mom, but I think I'd like to settle in on my own. Sort of decompress and center myself."

"OK," Martha said.

"I've got to do things on my own," Emily said. "I might as well start now."

"I understand."

"It's not that I'm not grateful," Emily said. "I really appreciate you spending your Sunday driving me here." She lowered her voice. "And making the entire drive home with Zoe talking your ear off."

Martha chuckled. "Don't worry about that. I've had practice with very talkative little girls, you know."

"Are you referring to me?"

"If the shoe fits …"

"What about fitting shoes?" Zoe asked, coming out of the bathroom.

"Nothing," Martha said, laughing. "And now, we've got to be on our way."

"Can't we stay a while longer?"

"I need to get home," Martha said. "We've got just enough time to stop at the gift shop before we head back. I thought I'd get each of us a T-shirt. Maybe they'll have stuffed animal guide dogs or something else that you might like, too. My treat."

"Cool!" Zoe said.

Emily held out her arms to them. "Thank you both for bringing me here."

They stood in the center of the room, in a group hug.

"Will you send us pictures?" Zoe asked. "I want one of you and your dog."

"Of course," Emily said. "You'll have one tonight before you go to bed. I'll keep you both posted on my progress. And while I'm here, working hard in my school, I expect you to be working hard in yours, Zoe."

The little girl nodded. "I promise." She squeezed Emily around the waist and stepped back.

Martha pressed her lips to her daughter's cheek.

"I'm proud of you, sweetheart. So proud."

Martha released Emily and turned to Zoe. "Let's head to that gift shop. They're bound to be busy and we don't want them to sell out of our sizes."

Emily opened the door to her room. "Safe trip back."

"Don't worry," Martha said.

"Love you!" Zoe said as she raced to the door.

Emily closed the door behind them and sank against it. Her pulse raced and she felt lightheaded. She was here—she was really going to get a guide dog.

What was *her* guide doing right now? Was her dog as nervous as she was?

Emily took a deep breath, counted to ten, then exhaled to a count of ten.

More importantly, would her dog like her?

R

Mark knocked on the door.

I listened to the response— "Come in"—from the other side of the door. A faint scrap of memory hung, just out of reach.

Mark opened the door. "Emily, meet Garth." He signaled for me to enter.

There she was—on the other side of the room—her golden-retriever-colored hair shining in the sunlight and falling around her shoulders.

I stepped across the threshold. It was her—the woman from the restaurant! Emily Main. My destiny.

R

"Are you thirsty, boy?" Emily asked, extending her arm as we walked to the desk. "There's water, right here," she said, touching a bowl with her toe.

I took a big drink.

"And we've got toys for you, too," she said as we walked toward a basket on the floor. She pulled out something that looked like three red rubber balls stacked on top of each other.

"This is called a Kong," she said, holding it out to me. "You want to chew on it? I can fill it with kibble when we go home."

Of course, I know about Kongs. They're high on my list of favorite things. I wagged my tail and clutched the Kong firmly between my teeth.

Emily sat on the floor and crossed her legs, patting the space between them.

I curled myself into her lap, with most of my hindquarters hanging out, mouthing the Kong.

226

"We've got ten minutes until we need to go to orientation," she said, stroking my back. "Are you ready for this?"

I stopped chewing and looked at her.

"Do you think we'll make a good pair?"

I extended my ears forward.

She ran her hands to them and felt their outline. "You've got very expressive ears, don't you? You're telling me 'yes' aren't you?"

I extracted my tail from where I'd tucked it beneath my body and wagged it swiftly.

Emily laughed, and the sound sent ripples of happiness through me.

"We're going to do just fine, you and me, Garth." She brought her face to mine and kissed my snout. Emily tasted salty again.

"I promise to love you and take good care of you, for the rest of your days. We're going to build a happy life—together."

The rest of the day passed in a blur. Orientation was easy for me—I curled up and napped at Emily's feet. I could tell from the stiffness of her body in the chair that she was paying strict attention to every word being said.

We joined the other new guides and handlers—nine other couples—for dinner. Emily talked to everyone there. I got to observe them from my spot at her feet. No doubt about it—my handler was the best. Emily was the pick of the litter.

When we finally returned to our room, Emily slipped my harness over my head and opened a bag with the most incredible aroma. She poured some of the contents into my dish. That familiar pinging sound was one of my favorite things.

"When you're done with your supper," she said, "we need to take a selfie to send my mom and Zoe."

I concentrated on my kibble.

"After that, I'll take you out and then we'll go to bed. I'm beat and we've got a big day tomorrow."

I licked my bowl clean. It clanged against the floor.

"Okay, Garth," Emily said, kneeling next to me on the floor. She put one arm around my neck, extended her other arm in front of us, and said "Say cheese!"

I had no idea what she was talking about, but I opened my mouth and stared at her hand.

She pushed a button and I heard a click, then another and another.

"One of these should be good," she said. She stabbed at the thing she held in her hand, then held it close to her left eye. She moved it around slowly. "There you are," she said. "I can see you in the photo through the pinhole of vision I have left."

She poked at the thing again, and I heard a swooshing sound. She set it on the counter. "You're beautiful, Garth." She ran her hand over my back. "Your coat feels smooth and silky and now I can picture you. You're shiny like a black seal."

She put me back into my harness. "Come on, handsome. Let's take you out and then get some sleep."

Chapter 46

"So this is the building where your condo is located," Mark asked. "And we've got the address of your office?"

"Yes," Emily said.

Garth, wearing his harness and vest, sat patiently at her feet.

"Did you take the bus to work before you lost your sight?"

"That was my plan," Emily replied. "I moved here right after I got married. I lost my sight on my honeymoon."

"That's right—now I remember. So you've never taken this route before?"

"No. But I know I don't have to change buses. It's a straight shot."

"That'll make it easier," he said. "It'll be a long commute. Maybe an hour during rush hour."

"Will that be all right? For Garth?"

"No problem whatsoever. In fact, he'll probably enjoy it. Most guides like adventures. They want to work every single day or they get bored."

"I promise I'm not a couch potato. We'll go out every single day."

"I'm not worried about that. You two are doing great."

"So you think we can do this?"

"Of course, you can."

Emily paused and placed her hand on top of Garth's head. "I think we're going to be fine out there."

"I do, too," Mark said. "Now—your bus comes on the other side of the street. Show me how you cross."

Emily cocked one ear to the street, listening. "The traffic is coming from my right, at a forty-five-degree angle." She turned her body until she was perpendicular to the sound and commanded Garth to move forward.

Emily and Garth walked until Garth stopped abruptly. Emily felt the raised cylindrical bumps in the sidewalk that told her they were at an intersection. Emily listened again. She heard the staccato beeps from the crosswalk button coming from her left.

"Left," she commanded.

Garth turned and they proceeded as the beeping became louder. Garth stopped again.

"Find button."

Garth touched his nose to the crosswalk button, and Emily pushed it. They stood and waited patiently until the traffic in front of them had come to a stop and the mechanical voice from the traffic signal told them to walk.

"Forward," Emily said, and she and Garth crossed the street, Mark walking behind them.

"Find the bus stop," Emily said when they reached the other side.

Garth turned slightly to his right and took off at a brisk pace. He stopped and Emily reached out her hand, locating the steel poles and panels that formed the bus stop.

"Well done," Mark said.

"I remember that all of the buses along this road run the same route," Emily said.

"That's right," Mark said. "The bus route is set up on a grid. Once you learn how it works, it's easy to get around."

"We just wait until we hear the bus pull up and the doors open?"

"Yes. Step to the door of the bus. Garth is trained to wait until anyone getting off at the stop leaves the bus."

"I'll then command him to 'step up'?"

"That's all there is to it. The drivers are trained to hold the door open until you and your guide are safely on board. They try to keep the seat directly behind them open for riders who need assistance."

"All I have to do is pay attention for when my stop is called."

"That's it," Mark said. "You've got a long commute, so the tricky part is to not let yourself daydream. You'll quickly become aware of how long it should take you and how many stops you'll make along the way."

"And if I miss my stop?"

"We've gone over what to do if you get lost; how to problem solve that issue."

"I'll tell the driver that I've missed my stop and ask the driver to let me off at the nearest stop that also has an assisted street crossing to the other side of the street and a bus stop. I then travel back the other direction to my stop."

"That's it," Mark said. "Bus drivers are trained to help the blind."

"And if all else fails, I can get off and call a rideshare."

"Exactly."

The rumbling sound of a large motor and the hiss of air from pneumatic breaks signaled the arrival of their bus.

"You ready?" Mark asked.

"Ready as I'll ever be," Emily replied. She gripped Garth's harness and they approached the bus. "Step up."

Garth paused and Emily heard footsteps on the stairs of the bus as passengers disembarked.

Garth moved forward and lifted his front paws onto the bottom step.

Emily and Mark followed him up and in.

"Good morning, you two," the bus driver said in a booming baritone. "Have a seat right here behind me. Where you going?"

Emily gave him the address of her office.

"That'll take us about fifty minutes in this traffic," he said. "Sit back and enjoy the ride."

Emily and Mark settled into the bench seat, and Garth tucked himself into the space at their feet.

"Well done," Mark said. "You're ready, Emily. You and Garth are more than ready to graduate on Sunday."

R

"Emily? Is that really you?" Connor answered his cell phone on the second ring and rose to shut his office door.

"Yes. It's me."

He checked his watch. "It must be almost midnight there. Is everything all right? God … it's been so long. How are you?"

"Everything's fine, Connor. And it is late here. The time difference is brutal, but I didn't want to wake you. I need to get to bed but I wanted to check something with you; to make sure it's okay."

"Sure—what's on your mind?"

"I've been working at home since I finished my courses at the Foundation for the Blind, and now I want to start working in my office again. The commute from my mom's is too long, so I'd like to move back to the city."

"That makes sense."

"To our condo, if that works for you."

The line was silent.

"Connor? Are you there? Do you mind if I move back in?"

"Mind? Of course not! I'd love it."

"Thank you."

"When do you plan to be there?"

"This Sunday afternoon. Late."

"How will you get to work?"

"I'll take the bus—just like I was planning to do before."

"Will you be okay doing that?"

"I'll be fine, Connor."

"Does this mean that we are …?" He paused, searching for the right words.

"This doesn't mean anything about us, one way or the other. And I don't want to get into all of that right now. As you said, it's late here, and I need to get to bed."

"We need to talk, Em."

"I agree, but we need to do it in person. We can't have that discussion over the phone."

"Understood."

"When do you think you'll be back here?"

232

"I'm not sure." She could hear his deep intake of breath. "I love you, Em. I love you and miss you. And I'm so sorry."

"I just wanted to let you know that I'll be at the condo starting on Sunday. Goodbye, Connor," Emily said and hung up.

She rolled over in bed and draped her arm over the side to where Garth lay, curled into a ball on the dog bed that she'd drug next to hers on their first night together. She stroked his ears.

"You're tense, boy, I can feel it in your ears." She moderated her voice into calm tones. "You heard that, didn't you? Don't worry about Connor. He's a long way away. We're fine—you and me—just as we are."

Chapter 47

I knew the minute Emily threw back the covers and swung her legs over the side of the bed that today was no ordinary day.

"Come on, boy," she said, dropping to her knees and rubbing me briskly, "time to get up and at 'em! We graduate today!"

I'd heard that word—graduate—all week long. It sent a delightful and familiar tingling along my body, just like the word "guide" did.

Whatever graduate was, I knew it was special and important—and that my Emily and I would be the center of attention.

She dressed quickly and slipped my harness over my neck. We went to our usual spot, and I was quick about my business. I sensed that we had things to do—special things.

We hurried back to our room, and Emily poured kibble into my bowl. I ate while she showered and got ready.

She held something that smelled hot against her hair, making it fall against her shoulders in loops.

Then it was my turn. Emily picked up my brush and went over every inch of my coat. I loved the feel of the stiff wire bristles against my skin in all but one spot. When she hit that spot, my right hind leg contracted and scratched at my belly—I was powerless to stop it. The only good thing about it is that it makes her laugh. There is almost nothing better than my Emily's laugh.

I watched her eat a sandwich at the desk. When she was done, she called me to her and took my face in her hands.

"We graduate today, Garth. You and me. We've learned to be a couple, and now we get to go out into the world together and live our life." She leaned her forehead against mine and breathed deeply. I licked her face.

"Your puppy-raiser family will be there, too. Katie and Jon and the kids. You'll get to see them again."

I swept my tail behind me. I remembered Katie and the rest of them. I'll never forget what they did for me and how much love they poured into my heart.

"Let's go," she said. "It's our time."

R

I heard the swell of excited voices long before Emily and I entered the room. Mark was waiting inside the door and led us to seats in the front row.

Emily sat, and I settled at her feet but kept my ears up. I looked behind us but couldn't see anything except a sea of pant legs. I was certain that I heard a familiar voice call my name when we entered the room. Katie. I knew it was Katie. She was in the room. My beloved Katie was nearby.

A woman I recognized from the front office stepped to a microphone and tapped it with her finger. A loud, unpleasant thump reverberated around the room, and the crowd grew quiet.

Beside us in the front row were the other guides and handlers in our class. Emily and I had made friends with all of them. I caught the eye of a yellow Lab who was matched with a young teacher. We nodded to each other.

The woman at the microphone began to speak and each guide and handler in our row took their turn going to the microphone. Other people joined them there, and there was a great deal of talking, followed by cheers and clapping.

I yawned and lay down to wait our turn.

"Emily and Garth!" I heard the woman announce.

Emily stood and grasped my harness. We moved to the microphone. I sat, searching the crowd.

The woman extended her hand to her right and said, "With special thanks to Garth's extraordinary puppy-raising family who overcame a horrific obstacle …" The remainder of her words were drowned out by the rapid swishing of my tail.

Alex and Abby emerged from the crowd and rushed down the center aisle. Katie and Jon followed. They were coming toward me.

My entire body quivered, but I stayed where I was. I knew what was expected of me, and I wanted them to be proud.

Jon took the microphone and addressed the crowd. I locked my eyes on Katie, and she kept hers on me.

The crowd erupted in applause. Emily turned toward Katie as she came to us. The two women I loved most in the world threw their arms around each other.

I wagged my tail so hard that I almost fell over.

Before I knew it, Katie was on her knees, her arms around my neck. "I'm so proud of you, Garth. You're remarkable, and I'm so blessed that we got to have you as our special puppy to love."

I licked her face and tasted salty tears.

The kids were on the ground, hugging me and crying. Jon patted between my ears, and I saw him swipe his hand across his eyes.

"I'm so grateful to you," I heard Emily choke out. "He's the most special dog in the world. We'll keep in touch, and I'll send you photos."

"We'd love to know how you're getting along," Katie said. "Both of you." Her voice wavered. "I feel like we're family now."

"I do, too," Emily said. "We are."

The women hugged again.

Somewhere in all this pandemonium, the woman at the microphone thanked everyone for coming and invited the crowd to come to the courtyard for refreshments.

Alex was draped around my neck when I heard another woman call Emily's name.

"Mom? Over here," Emily said. "I want you to meet Garth and his puppy raisers."

"I've got Zoe with me," the woman called Mom said. "And Dhruv's here, too."

Emily opened her arms and a little girl rushed to them.

"Can I pet him? Garth?" the little girl called Zoe asked.

"Yes, you can," Emily said. She released the harness, and I knew it was all right for me to say hello to this new girl.

"We raised him," I heard Abby tell Zoe.

Emily lifted her chin. "Dhruv?" she called. "I didn't know you were coming. How in the world did you find out? Mom didn't tell me you were coming."

"She didn't know. I went online and read about the graduation. They're open to the public, so I came."

Emily reached for him, and he took her arm. "That's so nice of you! You'll see Garth on Monday at the office. He'll be going everywhere with me ... including work. Would you like to meet him now?"

"Of course!"

Emily introduced me to Dhruv. "He's a dog softie," she said to me, "so you're going to have to help me make sure that Dhruv doesn't spoil you with too many treats."

He bent down to pet me with kind, gentle hands. He was definitely a dog person. There was something vaguely familiar about him, like we'd met once before, but I couldn't place him.

Martha stepped to Emily and began to talk with Katie.

I looked around me—at all the happy, excited people and dogs. Our hard work had been leading up to this moment. The trauma and sacrifices had been worth it. There was nothing that I'd rather do than be a guide. And not just any guide—Emily's guide. I was ready to live my life at her side.

Chapter 48

Emily inserted her key into the lock on the condo's door, pushed it open, and Zoe hurried inside.

"I'm gonna drop this," Zoe said in a rush.

Emily reached for the light switch inside the door and flipped it on.

"Set the bag on the kitchen counter. Can you make it?"

"Yes," Zoe replied.

Emily heard the clink of tin cans on the countertop.

"Nothing broke," Zoe called.

"They should have double-bagged the canned goods at the grocery," Martha said. She joined Zoe in the kitchen, and Emily heard her mother deposit another bag on the counter.

"Zoe," Martha said, "can you put the perishables in the refrigerator while I go get Emily's suitcases?"

"Sure," Zoe said.

"Thanks, you two," Emily said as she and Garth entered the condo.

Martha made her exit, and Emily shut the door behind her.

"I'm going to let Garth look around," Emily said, removing his harness. She heard Zoe opening and closing the refrigerator door.

"Where do these cans of soup belong?" Zoe asked.

"Just leave them on the counter for now," Emily said. "I'll figure out where I want to keep them later."

Garth made his way around the perimeter of the room, his nose down, twitching at all the new smells.

Someone knocked on the door.

Garth stopped his inspection and raised his head, ears alert. He walked over to Emily.

"That'll be Mom with our stuff." Emily patted his head and opened the door.

"Are you sure this is all you'll need for the week?" Martha asked, wrangling Emily's two suitcases and the two large bags that contained Garth's bowls, food, toys, vest, and other items provided by the Guide Dog Center.

"Positive," Emily said. "I've got enough clothes for work right here in the condo, and since you were nice enough to stop at the grocery for me, we're all set."

"What if we forgot something?"

"There's a market around the corner, and you can order almost anything online and have it delivered."

"We'll help you unpack," Martha said.

Emily reached for her mother's arm. "I'll do that later," she said. "It's been a big day for all of us. Right now, Garth and I need to chill out. And it's getting late. You and Zoe should head home. It'll be dark soon. Tomorrow is a school day for her."

Emily heard Martha's heavy sigh.

"I appreciate everything you've done for me. I really do. But I need to keep doing things for myself. These last two weeks have taught me that. I'll be fine, Mom."

"I know you will," Martha said. "In my mind I know that." She sighed. "But in my heart, I feel exactly like I did the first day I dropped you off at kindergarten."

Emily drew her mother into an embrace. "I survived kindergarten and I'll survive this. I'm ready, Mom."

"You're sure you can get back and forth to work? It's quite a commute."

"We've practiced the bus ride both ways. More than once. Garth and I have got this." She stepped back and held out her hand to him. He came to her side. "Haven't we, boy?"

Garth thumped his tail.

"Will you text me that you've gotten to work? And when you get home?"

"Sure. Will that make you feel better?"

"It will." Martha drew a deep breath. "Zoe, we'd better be on our way."

Zoe joined them. "Will I still get to talk to you?" she asked in a small voice.

"I'll be at work when you get home from school, so why don't you call me after dinner when you've finished your homework?"

"Every day?"

"Of course, every day! We're going to have a lot to talk about."

"When can you come to my house again?"

"I was thinking I'd like to come to Mom's the weekend after next." She angled her face to Martha. "Would that be all right?"

"I'd love that," Martha said. "Why don't I pick you up Saturday morning. You can spend the night, and I'll take you home after lunch on Sunday."

"That'd be great. Thanks, Mom."

"Will Garth come?" Zoe asked.

"Of course, Garth will come," Emily said. "He'll go everywhere with me from now on."

"Then he can meet Sabrina," Zoe said. "They can have a play date! Is he allowed to be with other dogs?"

"He certainly is. I'm sure that he and Sabrina will become best friends." Emily extended her arm to the young girl.

Zoe sank against Emily and put her arm around Emily's waist. "Just like we are," Zoe said softly.

Emily tightened her arm around her young friend. "Just like us."

R

"Find condo door," Emily said as she and Garth stepped off the elevator on their floor.

Garth set out in the right direction without hesitation.

"Only one more day to go this week," Emily said. "Tomorrow is Friday. You'll probably hear people say 'TGIF,' which stands for 'Thank God, it's Friday.'" Emily positioned her key in her hand.

"That's because they don't like their jobs and are glad they won't have to go to work over the weekend."

She inserted her key in the lock. "That doesn't apply to us. I've always loved my job, and I think you love going to the office, too. You certainly were the talk of the place this week. You're like a celebrity." Emily turned the key. "People who never knew who I was before know me now—I'm 'Garth's mom.'"

The door swung open.

Garth remained in the hallway, body rigid and ears alert.

"Forward in," Emily said.

Garth and Emily stepped inside. Emily looped the handle of her purse on a hook inside the door, and her foot collided with an object on the floor.

"What the heck?" she muttered, bending to feel what was in her way. She was running her hand over a leather knapsack when the bedroom door opened.

"Em," came Connor's voice. He hurried to her side. "I'm sorry—I thought I'd left this out of the way." He pushed his rucksack against the wall with his toe.

"What ... what are you doing here? When did you get home?"

"About an hour ago. I thought I'd surprise you."

"Well ... you've done that," Emily said.

They stood, awkwardly close.

"Looks like you've got some surprises of your own," Connor said. "When were you going to tell me that you got a guide dog?"

"It came about very suddenly," she said. "I was on a two-year waiting list when someone dropped out and I got matched—with Garth."

Emily placed her hand on the top of Garth's head. He remained still, shoulders tense, ears back.

"I'm just getting home from work," Emily said.

"Would you like to get something to eat?" Connor asked.

"Aren't you tired from the long flight? Why don't we order in?"

"I'm bushed," Connor said. "That's a great idea. I've got a big meeting tomorrow at the main office."

"So that's why you came home? For work?"

"That's not the only reason. I wanted to see you, too, Em." He moved to her and put his arms loosely around her. "I've missed my wife." He nuzzled her ear. "I've got the most amazing view from the bedroom in my apartment in Tokyo," he whispered. "I keep thinking about going to bed, next to you, and looking out at the lights of the city. Very romantic." He kissed her neck. "I've missed you, Em."

Emily sighed heavily and leaned into the sensation of being in his arms. She turned to him and their lips met. They kissed, long and deep. Connor clasped her to him and led her toward the bedroom.

Her right hand grazed the kitchen counter and the memory of their last encounter in this room—with Gina concealing her presence—flooded her mind. She stiffened and drew back, placing her palms on his chest and pushing him away.

"I can't, Connor," she said, harshness filling her voice. "It's not that simple. We can't just forget that night—with you and Gina."

He reached for her again. "I've told you, nothing happened."

"Then why was she here—and why did you try to hide it from me? If nothing happened, it's only because I walked in on the two of you." Her voice sounded harsh to her own ears.

"Then can't we start again? I miss you, Em. I can't wait to take you to Tokyo with me. You'd love it there; the food and the culture. The people are amazing. This is the kind of opportunity to live and work internationally that we always dreamed of before we got married."

"What the hell is wrong with you?" Emily shrilled at him. "Look at me. Things have changed since then. I'M BLIND!" She let her words sink in. "I'm just now learning to cope with my blindness in an area I'm familiar with, at a job I love. I'm surrounded by family and coworkers who care about me. I can't leave this support network behind."

"I'll be with you," he said.

"When you're not working eighty hours a week," Emily said. "And what about Garth?"

"Would you take him with you?" Connor asked.

"Would I take him?" She was yelling now. "Of course, I'd take him. He's by my side every second of every day. Garth's helped me live independently again. Garth and I will navigate life together—from now on."

"I don't know how that would work in Tokyo. I'm sure they have guide dogs there, but my apartment is only five hundred square feet, and it's on the eighteenth floor. It'd be hard for …"

"Garth," Emily supplied.

"And the apartment's already way over my budget. I can't afford anything bigger without moving farther from my office."

"I'm not willing to give up Garth. He's helping me get my life back."

"Sounds like he's more important to you than I am."

Emily took a deep breath and leaned against the wall. "I guess he is," she said quietly. "Look, Connor, things have changed for us. Drastically. It's no one's fault and neither of us wanted"—she ran a hand along her body—"this … diagnosis. But we're stuck with it."

Connor put his head in his hands. "I've failed you, Em. I've really failed you."

"There's no point in recriminations, Connor. You still want the things you've always wanted. And worked hard for." She touched his elbow. "You deserve this new job of yours. And if all of this hadn't happened, I'd have been thrilled to go to Tokyo with you."

He put a hand over hers.

"But we can't undo what's transpired. I need to stay here and regain my life," she said.

"I don't know what to say." His voice was raw with emotion.

"I've changed in other ways, too," Emily said. "You know how we always said that we wouldn't have children?"

He nodded.

"Well ... I've become good friends with the eight-year-old girl who lives across the street from Mom's. And you know what, Connor? I'd like to have children of my own one day."

"Won't that be extremely difficult ... under the circumstances?"

"Lots of blind people are parents. It's doable if you believe it is. I want a partner who believes—and one who is committed to the process. I don't think that's you."

"That's not fair, Em. I haven't had time to think about any of this."

"You've had plenty of time to think about this, and so have I. I know I'm right, Connor. It's tragic that our marriage never got the chance to succeed—but you should go back to Tokyo, and I need to stay here and rebuild my life."

She moved her hand to his face and traced his cheek.

He pressed a kiss into her palm.

"We don't have to decide all of this now."

"I'm going to move out of the condo," Emily said.

"You don't have to do that. You can live here as long as you want."

"It's too far from work, and it's too full of ... you. I need a place for Garth and me that's our own."

"Don't rush into anything," he said. "Maybe you'll feel better about this place in time."

"I already know where I'll go," Emily said. "Dhruv's uncle owns an apartment building by my office, and there's a studio for rent. I can afford it, and it'll be convenient for us." She stroked Garth.

"I don't want you to go."

"It's the best thing for me." She straightened. "This place must be worth a pretty penny. Real estate values are at an all-time high. Why don't you sell it? You can use the money to rent a bigger place in Tokyo."

"I don't need a bigger place. I don't want to sell it. You helped me pick it out when we first started dating. I hoped then that we'd live here together one day. Who knows, maybe one day we still will." He sucked in a breath. "If you really don't want to stay here, I'll rent it out."

"That's your decision," Emily said. "But I don't think we've got a future together."

"I'm not willing to give up on us," Connor said, "but I'll accept what you're saying—for now."

"Thank you," Emily said quietly. "We're both exhausted, and you said you have a big meeting tomorrow?"

"I do."

"Let's order food and get some sleep."

"All right. I'll sleep in the spare room."

"I think that'll be best."

"I'm sorry, Em. I'm sorry about everything."

Later that night, Emily sank to the floor where Garth's bed lay in her bedroom. "You don't like him, do you? You don't like Connor one little bit." She leaned over Garth and picked up one of his paws. She massaged it gently, splaying the toes in rhythmic fashion.

"I can tell by your ears whether you like someone or not; your ears were back when Connor and I were talking." She switched to another paw. "There you go," she said. "I can feel the tension leave your body. That's better."

They continued like that for some time. "He's not a bad guy. Not really. But he's not going to be part of our future. Don't you worry about that."

Garth dug his nose further into his pillow.

Emily bent and kissed his cheek.

"Sweet dreams, sweet boy. We've got a big day tomorrow. We're going to work, and then we'll find a new place to live."

Chapter 49

I trotted along the hallway, next to Emily. We followed that nice man Dhruv, whose clothes always smell deliciously of other dogs and sweetly spicy foods. He also carries a pocketful of treats. He asks permission from Emily before giving me one, and she almost always says yes. I like this Dhruv.

At the end of the hallway, Dhruv unlocked a door and then handed the key to Emily.

We entered the room together. A large, arched window took up the entire opposite wall. Emily's bed was pushed against the window, outlined by the pinks and purples of a beautiful sunset in a cloud-filled sky.

A refrigerator hummed quietly at the end of a short expanse of counter space. A sofa stood in the middle of the space with a low, round leather thing in front of it. The only other furniture was a small round table flanked by two wooden chairs.

The floors were covered with a thick, plush carpet. It was like a wall-to-wall blanket in there.

I spotted my dog bed in the far corner, next to Emily's big bed. My tail began to wag.

"What do you think, boy? Do you like it?"

My tail wagged harder.

"It's got everything you need," Dhruv said. "Your mom and I got your stuff from the condo. It's all here."

"I can't thank you enough, Dhruv." Her voice grew hoarse. "You've been so kind and helpful to me—through all of this."

"That's good," he said, moving to the door. "If anything breaks, my uncle will fix it. And if you need something, I live on the floor below."

"You've helped me recover from the worst thing in my life. You need to know that."

Dhruv shifted his weight from foot to foot.

Emily dabbed at her eyes. I knew this signaled that the people around me were upset. I sat and looked from Emily to Dhruv.

"Can I give Garth," he fumbled in the pocket of his jacket, "a treat?"

I thumped my tail against the floor.

Emily laughed. "I think that's a perfect idea, Dhruv."

I thought so, too.

His hand emerged with a cellophane bag. "I don't have any dog treats today. I have Crunchy Cheetos. I know he's not supposed to have people food, but could he have just one?"

Emily hesitated.

I held my breath.

"Oh … why not. We're celebrating our new home. Sure—just this once."

I shifted my gaze to Dhruv.

The bag crinkled in the most pleasing way as he tugged on the sides, pulling it open. He reached in and took out the orange object I was hoping for. Dhruv brought his hand up in a swift motion and sent the object sailing toward me.

I lasered in on its trajectory. I took a step back and opened my mouth as it cleared the top of its arc and started its downward path.

Thank you for reading!

If you enjoyed GUIDING EMILY, I'd be
grateful if you wrote a review.

Just a few lines would be great. Reviews on Goodreads and Amazon are the best gift an author can receive. They encourage us when they're good, help us improve our next book when they're not, and help other readers make informed choices when purchasing books. Reviews keep the Amazon algorithms humming and are the most helpful aide in selling books! Thank you.

To post a review on Amazon or for Kindle:

1. Go to the product detail page for Guiding Emily on Amazon.com.
2. Click "Write a customer review" in the Customer Reviews section.
3. Write your review and click Submit.

In gratitude,
Barbara Hinske

Book Club Questions

1. Do you personally know anyone who is blind?
2. If so, what is your observation of their ability to live a normal life?
3. What is your personal reaction when you encounter a visually impaired person? Do you offer to help or stay out of their way?
4. The newly blind find going out terrifying and self-isolate. Can you relate to this?
5. Have you had to cope with a life-altering disability for yourself or a family member?
6. How did you feel about Connor's reaction to Emily's blindness?
7. Would you have handled a child's blindness in the way that Martha did?
8. How did you feel about Gina? Do you think she and Emily can-or should-patch things up?
9. What did you think about the portrayal of Garth?
10. Do you know any service dogs?
11. Are you aware of the serious threats posed to real service dogs by fake ones? Have you seen any encounters like the one Garth has in the restaurant?
12. Can you understand how service dogs bring the blind out of self-imposed isolation and provide the comfort and love that all pets do?

Acknowledgements

I'm blessed with the wisdom and support of many kind and generous people. I want to thank the most supportive and delightful group of champions an author could hope for:

All of the faculty, staff, and students at the Foundation for Blind Children for their wisdom, input, and support, and most especially Marc Ashton, Steve Pawlowski, Julie Rock, Spencer Churchill, Mary Wilson, Dr. Lisa Chiles, and Julie Oliver—with extra special thanks to Gnocchi (you have my heart!). This book wouldn't have been possible without you.

Kristy Siefkin for connecting me with the people at Guide Dogs for the Blind in San Rafael, California.

The staff of Guide Dogs for the Blind for your generous input and support, with special thanks to Ribah Dow, Melanie Harris, Theresa Stern, and Jane Flower. You are doing remarkable things in this world.

Puppy raiser extraordinaire Kim Delmot, for your review and feedback.

My insightful and supportive assistant Lisa Coleman who keeps all the plates spinning;

My life coach Mat Boggs for your wisdom and guidance;

My kind and generous legal team, Kenneth Kleinberg, Esq., and Michael McCarthy—thank you for believing in my vision;

The professional "dream team" of my editors Linden Gross, Jesika St. Clair, and proofreader Dana Lee; and

Keri Knutson and Elizabeth Mackey for a beautiful, poignant cover.

About the Author

BARBARA HINSKE recently left the practice of law to pursue her writing career full time. Her novella *The Christmas Club* has been made into The Hallmark Channel Christmas movie of the same name (2019), and she feels like she's living the dream. Barb is extremely grateful to her readers! She inherited the writing gene from her father who wrote mysteries when he retired and told her a story every night of her childhood. She and her husband are slaves to their two adorable and spoiled dogs. They live in a historic home that keeps her husband busy with repair projects and her happily decorating, entertaining, and gardening. She also spends a lot of time baking and—as a result—dieting. Together they have four grown children.

Please enjoy this excerpt from *The Unexpected Path*,
the second installment in the Emily Series:

Chapter One

Emily Main pushed a thick plait of her long auburn hair off her face
and groped around on her nightstand for her phone. "Mom? What
time is it?"

"It's six fifteen. Did I wake you?"

"It's fine. I get up at six thirty to take Garth out to do his
business." Emily sat up and threw her legs over the side of the bed.
"What's up? Are we still on for today?"

"That's just it. We'll have to change our plans."

Emily's heart sank. She'd been so busy with work these past
months that most of her things in the studio apartment were still
in boxes. Martha was supposed to come into the city to help her
organize—they'd planned to make a weekend of it. More than
Martha's organizing prowess, Emily craved the comfort of her
mother's presence.

Unwanted tears stung her eyes. The months she'd spent in her
new studio apartment hadn't been an unmitigated success. She hadn't
slept well, waking to every new floorboard squeak or rattling pipe in
the old building. She'd bashed her shins countless times on unopened
boxes and fumbled to find items that hadn't, as of yet, been assigned
to their permanent homes.

Emily knew, in her mind, that all of these things would get sorted
out in time. In her heart, however, she just wanted her mother.

Garth picked up his head and looked at Emily. "What's ..." Emily
took a deep breath to steady her voice. "Why?"

"Do you remember me telling you that Irene's been having pain in
her hips?"

"She's been complaining of that for as long as she's lived next
door to you." Emily didn't intend her words to sound as sharp as
they did.

1

"I've been telling her she needed to see her doctor about it. Anyway, she fell last night when she was getting ready for bed. Zoe heard her and came over to get me."

"That's awful." Emily pictured how scared nine-year-old Zoe must have been. "What did you do?"

"I tried to help her up, but we couldn't budge her—she was in too much pain. I called the paramedics, and they took her to the hospital."

"I'm so sorry for Irene—and Zoe. Have you heard any more?"

Garth got out of bed and came to Emily's side, resting his muzzle on her knee. She brought her hand to the top of his head and rubbed behind his ears.

"Irene just called. She's broken her hip, and they're going to do surgery tomorrow to replace it."

"I'm sorry she has to go through this, but I'll bet she'll feel much better with a new hip."

"That's what I think. Anyway, I've got Zoe and her miniature schnauzer—you remember Sabrina—staying with me while Irene's in the hospital."

"I figured as much."

"That's why I can't come down to San Francisco. I'm sorry, Em. I was looking forward to spending the whole weekend together."

"I was looking forward to spending time with you, too, Mom." Emily controlled the quiver in her voice. "We'll do it as soon as Zoe can go back home to Irene. I'm perfectly capable of organizing my apartment on my own," she said, not feeling the conviction she spoke with.

"You know how much I love doing that."

"It's one of your core strengths, that's for sure. You can help me fine-tune things when you do come." Emily searched with her toes for her slippers and slid her feet into them. "How's Zoe doing with all of this? After losing her parents in that car accident several years ago, I know she's extremely attached to her grandmother."

"She was petrified last night, but the emergency room doctor that updated us on Irene's condition did a fantastic job of explaining

2

things to Zoe over the phone and reassuring her that Irene should make a full recovery."

"That's a relief. I hate to think of Zoe suffering any more loss."

"Thank goodness she has that miniature schnauzer. She took Sabrina out as soon as she got off the phone, and then they both went to bed. They're still asleep."

"What do you have planned today? Will you go to the hospital?"

"Irene thinks it'll be better if Zoe doesn't see her until Monday after she's had her surgery. I thought we could go to the store to buy craft supplies and make a nice card for Irene. Maybe go to a movie." Martha sighed. "Any suggestions?"

"Well … why don't the two of you come into the city today? Are you too tired to drive in?"

"No. Not at all."

"You could both help me get settled. I'm not trying to inconvenience you—I can handle it all myself—but Zoe is endlessly interested in the adaptations I have to make. I think she'll have fun, and it'll take her mind off of her grandmother."

"You know what? You're exactly right. That's a great idea."

"You'll have to leave Sabrina at home. This apartment is small, and I don't know how she and Garth would do, being cooped up together."

"Of course. She'll be fine." Martha was silent for a beat. "Em—what would you think about Zoe spending the weekend with you? She'd jump at the chance. Is that too much of an imposition?"

"Genius idea! I'd love it!"

Martha could hear the smile in Emily's voice. "I'm going to let Zoe sleep in. I'll text you when we're on our way."

"Perfect. I've got to take Garth out and feed him. Then I'll pull myself together. No rush. I'm happy that I'll get to spend time with my two favorite gals."

"We'll probably be there by mid-morning. I'll stay until after lunch; then I'll come back here to take care of Sabrina. I'll drive in on Sunday afternoon to collect Zoe."

"We'll do Sunday night supper, the three of us."

"You're positive you don't mind? It's not too much trouble?"

Emily leaped to her feet and snatched her robe from the foot of the bed. "Positive." She grasped the guide dog harness from its place on the chair next to the bed and slipped it effortlessly over Garth's head. "See you soon. I need to take care of my best guy here."

Martha chuckled. "Give him a belly rub for me."

Available at Amazon in Print, Audio, and for Kindle

The Rosemont Series
Coming to Rosemont
Weaving the Strands
Uncovering Secrets
Drawing Close
Bringing Them Home
Shelving Doubts
Recovering What Was Lost
No Matter How Far: A Rosemont Christmas Novella

The Emily Series
Guiding Emily
The Unexpected Path

"Who's There?!" Collection
DEADLY PARCEL
FINAL CIRCUIT

Novellas
The Night Train
The Christmas Club (adapted for The
Hallmark Channel, 2019)
Paws & Pastries

I'd love to hear from you! Connect with me online:

Sign up for my newsletter at
BarbaraHinske.com to receive your Free Gift,
plus Inside Scoops and Bedtime Stories.

Search for Barbara Hinske on YouTube
for tours inside my own historic home plus tips
and tricks for busy women!

Find photos of fictional Rosemont and Westbury,
adorable dogs, and things related to her books at
Pinterest.com/BarbaraHinske.

Email me at bhinske@gmail.com or find me at
Instagram.com/barbarahinskeauthor
Facebook.com/BHinske
Twitter.com/BarbaraHinske